RESOLUTION
DEUCES WILD™ BOOK FIVE

ELL LEIGH CLARKE
MICHAEL ANDERLE

LMBPN

DISRUPTIVE IMAGINATION

LMBPN Publishing
PMB 196, 2540 South Maryland Pkwy
Las Vegas, NV 89109

First US edition, June 2019
Print ISBN:

RESOLUTION TEAM

Thank you to our Beta Readers

James Caplan, Mary Morris , Kelly O'Donnell, Daniel
Weigert, Larry Omans, John Ashmore

Thanks to our JIT Readers

Micky Cocker
Dave Hicks
Peter Manis
Diane L. Smith
Jeff Eaton
Misty Roa
Shari Regan
Jeff Goode
Dorothy Lloyd

If I've missed anyone, please let me know!

Editor
Skyhunter Editing Team

Devon, In Orbit, QSD *Baba Yaga*

Tabitha had that sinking feeling in the pit of her stomach.

She knew exactly why Bethany Anne had summoned her to the floating fortress. Even if she hadn't been a smart enough cookie to work it out, the presence of Lillian in the small meeting room when she arrived confirmed for Tabitha that it was time to face the music.

Lillian shuffled nervously in her seat when the impatient cadence of heels on metal announced Bethany Anne's arrival. "Why is she walking here instead of just..." She flourished her hands. "You know? This is killing me."

"It's killing *you?*" Tabitha retorted. "*You're* going to get off lightly."

Bethany Anne spoke into Tabitha's ear. "*None* of you are going to get off lightly."

Dios. Tabitha whirled, finding Bethany Anne standing directly behind her. She took one look at Bethany Anne and scooted her chair back to give herself some room. "Hey."

Bethany Anne's face gave nothing away, which told Tabitha everything. She walked around the table and took a seat across from Tabitha and Lillian. "That's all you have to say? 'Hey?'" However fixed Bethany Anne's expression was, her tone made her hurt perfectly clear. "How about, 'I'm sorry for lying to you for the last seven years?' Hmm?"

Tabitha did her best not to snap and make it worse. She folded her arms, resigned to whatever punishment Bethany Anne decided on. "You should already know I'm sorry for hiding it from you. But I couldn't see Nickie staying out there alone."

Bethany Anne snorted. "*Alone*? She hasn't been alone since she reactivated Meredith. Who do you think gave King Harold the location of the plant he needed to recover from his sickness? Who informed my father that the Six were having issues? I spent many nights awake coming up with a solution to her energy limitations once she had used up her power packs."

Tabitha sucked in a breath through her teeth. "I had no idea."

"Me either," Lillian admitted.

Bethany Anne narrowed her eyes. "You were so focused on getting Nickie home, you missed that I was molding her into someone who could handle being here."

Lillian gave a brittle laugh. "This is ridiculous. What was the point of sending my Nickie away when neither of you let her be the whole time she's been gone? It looks like Barnabas stepped in at the right time." She held up a hand to Bethany Anne in apology. "I'm sorry, I can't get around your logic. I had no idea about any of this."

Tabitha wanted to know the same. "I'm with Lillian. Why exile Nickie if you were going to keep pulling her strings the whole time? And why keep it such a secret?"

Bethany Anne pointed at Tabitha. "It was a secret because *you* decided to make it into one. Besides, would she have listened if she had heard it from me? From any of us? Nickie's exile was a kindness to us all. Beating some damn sense into her wasn't going to work. She would have continued on the path she was on until it was too late." She sighed, grateful that she didn't have any of these issues with Alexis and Gabriel. "I wanted better for Nickie, just like you. But she had to find it for herself. That child has entirely too much 'fuck you' in her to be told a thing. It's a Grimes trait."

Lillian looked like she was going to argue with that for a moment. "I can't disagree that her time alone hasn't straightened her out," she conceded. "I just... I wish I could have done more to keep her on the straight and narrow in the first place. I can't help think that if I'd put more effort into finding time for her instead of letting my dad put his foot down so hard she couldn't breathe..." Her voice trailed off, regret stealing her train of thought.

Bethany Anne shrugged, thinking of her recent reaction to how her own children were straining for more autonomy. "You did what you thought was best. What more can you do as a parent?"

Lillian shrugged. "Maybe I should have married after she was born. Given her a father figure to make up for the time I had to spend at work. Dad was always so tough with

ELL LEIGH CLARKE & MICHAEL ANDERLE

her, and Mom was too soft. I don't know. I don't think any of us got it right with her."

Both Bethany Anne and Tabitha reached out to comfort Lillian.

"I was at fault, too," Tabitha admitted. "I undermined you all way too much. I wasn't 'Fun Aunt Tabitha,' I was just immature and reckless."

"What's done is done," Bethany Anne told them gently. " The important thing is looking forward.

"It's like she's become the woman I always knew she could be."

Tabitha banged her hand on the table. "I *told* you. What did I say? She just needed time to work out who she is."

Bethany Anne raised an eyebrow. "She's not completely back in the fold yet."

Lillian bristled. "Just because *you* have two perfect kids who never put a foot wrong. My Nickie was never going to fit inside the lines. All I ever wanted was for her to find her place and be happy."

Bethany Anne held up a finger. "Nickie is where she needs to be right now. I'm happy she looks to be finding her way at last, but don't try to compare your experiences of parenthood to what you imagine mine are. It's not realistic. Alexis and Gabriel come with a whole list of challenges of their own, regardless of their mostly appropriate behavior."

Tabitha held her hands up between them. "Can we just agree that Nickie has seen the light and we're all happy?"

Bethany Anne arched an eyebrow. "I suppose your interference with her EI had nothing to do with her epiphany?"

Tabitha shrugged. "I did what I thought was necessary. That EI was stuffy enough to drive anyone over the edge."

Lillian bristled. "What's wrong with the personality I chose for Nickie's EI?"

Tabitha shook her head, folding her arms on the table defensively. "Nothing. I just added a few extras to help Nickie along the way. Like the ability to take a joke."

Bethany Anne raised an eyebrow. "That's not all you've done. Is it? Truth time, Tabitha."

Tabitha dropped her head onto her arms. "Okay, okay. I hacked Meredith and rewrote her personality, and I've been helping Nickie as much as I could the whole time." She hid her smirk. "It hasn't been easy. You know how many people I sent before she accepted Grim?"

Bethany Anne's mouth twitched in amusement. "Something tells me we're about to find out."

"She won't be happy when she finds out," Lillian warned.

Tabitha snorted. "You don't think I know that? I'm pretty sure she's close to the truth. She'll get over it as soon as she figures out I did it to protect her." She sat up, scrutinizing Bethany Anne for any sign she was still angry and finding none. "Until then, I'm saying nothing. I can't even believe I got any of this past you. I'm sorry for lying."

Bethany Anne waved a finger in a circle. "We'll get to how you can make it up to me later. I want to hear your story."

"You want a good laugh at my expense, is what," Tabitha bitched, her smirk returning. "Fine. Laugh away."

Bethany Anne pressed her lips together. "I'm laughing at us all for being such dumbasses. We'll just do better in the future, okay?" She sat up straight. "Hold that thought. There's something missing." She vanished, reappearing less than a minute later in the chair next to Lillian with a massive bowl of popcorn. "*Now* we're ready."

Lillian grinned. "Good call."

Bethany Anne plucked a handful and pushed the bowl toward Lillian. "I know, right? Go ahead, Tabitha. We're listening."

Lillian helped herself and put the bowl back on the table. "This takes me back to being a child. I used to beg Dad for the story about you walking off a building."

Bethany Anne snickered, crossing one high-heeled boot over the other. "I don't know, I kind of like the *other* one where she walked off a building better."

Tabitha narrowed her eyes at them and reached for the bowl. "I hate you both. Okay, so around the time Pete and I moved into the guardhouse, I got tired of waiting for her to reactivate Meredith. I decided she needed a push in the right direction."

"You're lucky your push didn't backfire," Lillian cut in.

Tabitha inclined her head. "You haven't heard the story yet. It almost did. *Twice.*" She placed a piece of popcorn in her mouth and chewed thoughtfully. "First person I sent, she made straight away. Which was what I got for listening to Pete and sending one of his Guardians."

Lillian snorted. "Did she at least send your Guardian back intact?"

Tabitha made a face. "Physically, sure. It can't do much for male pride to get a beatdown from a tiny unenhanced woman. Joe took it fine, and it wasn't the worst fuckup I made. Remember that girl she hung with for a while? Alicia?"

Lillian put a hand over her eyes. "The girl she got into a fight with over a boy?"

Bethany Anne's eyes widened. "You *didn't* send her old love rival after her."

Tabitha winced, remembering the scathing note from Nickie that the woman had attached when she returned Tabitha's finder's fee—most likely under duress. "Mmhmm. Not my finest moment, I'll admit."

Bethany Anne snickered. "I'll say. And Grim'zee? Who appears, by the way, to have lost a century or so in age since we left him on Yoll."

Tabitha hesitated. "I can't see you liking it."

Bethany Anne waved a hand. "Just tell me. I'll try not to lose my shit."

Tabitha shrugged. "Okay, then. A century and a half, and that part was easy. I gave him some of my blood and snuck him into one of the Vid-docs to bake."

"Without my permission?" Bethany Anne caught herself. She held up a hand. "Go on."

Lillian's head went back and forth as she followed the conversation.

"Grim came out of the 'doc feeling like a kid," Tabitha continued, falling into the memory. "Sofia dug out his old exosuit and gave it a few tweaks, and off he shot to the outer edges of the Federation to pick up her trail. He found her in some skeezy bar playing poker with a bunch of lowlifes."

"This was near the Torcellan quadrant, right?" Bethany

Anne asked. "That was when ADAM got a lock on her location."

Tabitha nodded. "Yeah, that was the fight where she ran out of options and reactivated her enhancements. Complete coincidence. Grim just about shit himself when everyone started shooting the place up." She snorted. "He dove under a table. You'll like this bit: her first thought after she got to her feet was for her shoes."

Bethany Anne almost choked on her popcorn. "You're kidding?"

Lillian snickered. "That's my Nickie, all right."

Tabitha nodded. "Oh, hell no. What is it with skinny women and shoes? You only care about what you look like from the ankles down?"

Lillian rolled her eyes. "And the waist up. It's okay for you, with all those curves. It's all I can do to fill a bra, thanks to my nanocytes being less than helpful in that department. Don't mock my love of fine footwear."

Bethany Anne glanced at the five-and-a-half-inch stiletto heel on her armored boots with love. "I remember Nickie trying to walk in my heels when she was a child." She smiled at the recollection of eight-year-old Nickie wobbling around like a newborn gazelle. "Maybe the way to tempt her in is with shopping?"

Lillian laughed brightly. "Sure! We'll whisk her off to Larkratia and drop the price of a planet on a single item." She paused, realizing everyone in the room could actually do that if the fancy struck. She waved her daydreaming off. "The story. What happened when Grim found Nickie?"

Tabitha waved her hands, falling into the narrative. "The craziest thing I ever did. So, Grim was there hiding under the table, totally out of his depth and frozen up. Nickie had just gone down, although he missed."

"Didn't he spend time in the Guardian Marines?" Bethany Anne asked. "I remember John taking a shine to him after the business on Yoll way back."

Tabitha grinned, remembering the out-of-shape, overweight, ungracefully-aging Yollin who had turned up on their doorstep. "He'd been working as a cook since the Federation was formed. He hadn't thrown so much as a punch in over a decade. I kinda yelled at him and made him get up. This was while Nickie was out on the floor."

She paused to clamp down on her rising laughter. "I swear, I didn't expect what happened next. I was yelling, right? All of a sudden, Nickie gets up, and Grim just clicked into gear. Begged me to tell him what to say to make the scary Grimes not kill him."

Lillian spilled her popcorn. "Fuck my *life*. Did it work? Well, obviously, it did."

Tabitha nodded, straight-faced. "Uh-huh. She told him her friends call her 'Nickie,' and I told him to say he'd have to earn that. It worked just fine; she took him with her. They beat the crap out of a company of Skaine mercenaries like a good pair of Rangers-in-training and stole that ship she has."

Lillian gaped. "Damn, she's resourceful, that girl of mine. What did she do next?"

Bethany Anne continued for Tabitha. "That was just before she came across the colony," she told Lillian. "Did she tell you she saved hundreds of lives there? Or that she spent months there helping them rebuild after the Skaines attacked?"

Lillian shook her head. "She said she worked for her keep at a colony for a while. She didn't tell me she'd saved it."

Tabitha smiled. "I didn't teach her modesty. That's got to have come from somewhere else."

Bethany Anne shifted in her seat and began tapping her nails on the table. "We need to get serious. Hiding things, even to protect each other, hasn't gotten us anywhere. From here on out, there are no more secrets. We work together." She turned to Lillian. "If Nickie can be mature enough to put aside her emotions for the good of everyone, so can you. Make it up with your mom, or don't. But find a way to work with her. You're going to QT2."

Lillian nodded. "Whatever you need. It will give me the opportunity to see Nickie face to face."

Tabitha pouted. "Everyone gets to see her except for me."

Bethany Anne lifted a shoulder. "All good things, and all that. You are going to be far too busy working your ass off to make it up to me for lying."

Lillian paused in getting to her feet. "This sounds like something I should stay to hear."

"You have a trip to pack for," Bethany Anne reminded her, smiling to soften her words. "And it's classified information."

Lillian wrinkled her nose. "Nice to know I'm not wanted." She sniffed and flounced out, muttering under her breath.

Tabitha watched her go, then turned to face Bethany Anne. "I guess this is to do with the Bakas?"

Bethany Anne nodded solemnly. "You guessed right.

We're facing a split of the Bakas on Devon if one of Mahi'-Takar's brothers tries to pull a coup before we've secured our alliance." She resumed her tapping. "I can't pause to take care of this. My focus has to be on working out what the Kurtherians' next move will be, preferably before they have time to work it out for themselves and send the Ooken to enact it. I need the Bakas, Tabitha. I need their numbers."

Tabitha was well aware of the potential for civil war among the Bakas, and how that would impact their ability to hold the Ooken at bay. "We've already done a hell of a lot to stop that from happening. You fostered Mahi'Takar's son to protect him from his asshole uncles, and my classes are taking root with the Bakas who have been with us from the start. I think they've gotten past thinking small, and if they don't? They will get left behind."

"I have no doubt that the majority of the people will side with Mahi' once we reveal our intention to fight for their home." Bethany Anne frowned. "It's her family I'm concerned about. What I'm planning is going to require the certainty they won't stab her in the back at the first opportunity. Until we can be assured that they will remain loyal to Mahi' and Trey, I want you to make sure the message sinks in."

"No problem." Tabitha hesitated a beat. "What about Nickie?"

Bethany Anne got to her feet. "Nickie will be just fine. Barnabas managed to keep *you* on the straight and narrow, didn't he?"

Tabitha growled at the empty space Bethany Anne had occupied the moment before and left to find Mahi'Takar.

CHAPTER 2 NICKIE

High Tortuga, Space Fleet Base, Barnabas' Office

Onscreen, General Lance Reynolds dropped his unlit cigar into the ashtray on his desk and shrugged. "What do you suggest we do? Bethany Anne's demands for more ships aren't slowing down any. The Admiral needs more materials than I'm currently able to supply to keep up."

Barnabas sighed, wishing they had spent less of their previous planning meeting kicking back to enjoy the scenery and good food of Biorilluim and more getting the details of the logistics network in place. "We have all these unaffiliated independents running up and down the supply routes, and it's an administrative nightmare. I just don't know how effective it will be to continue sneaking these smaller consignments through the Interdiction."

"I would say not at all," Lance replied. "The last increase in Jean's order was difficult enough to keep quiet."

Barnabas leaned forward and steepled his hands on the desk in front of him as he considered Lance's concerns. His thoughtful look passed quickly as he came to the conclusion that moving his plans for Nickie ahead was the only solution. "I understand the position you're in. Are you able to complete this shipment, at least?"

Lance lifted his hands. "I don't know. It's too bad we can't just do this out in the open." He chuckled softly. "I can't see a trade agreement with Devon as being likely, especially when the other Federation leaders learn they'd be negotiating with Baba Yaga."

"It's a thought I have already considered," Barnabas agreed. "You are, however, aware of the potential threat of discovery by the Ooken. If we begin sending resources openly through Devon, it will take them exactly two minutes to trace the shipments back to the Federation." He raised an eyebrow. "Do *you* want to be the one to tell Bethany Anne that happened after she's gone to so much effort to prevent it?"

Lance shook his head, his eyes widening fractionally. "Not in a million years. So we can't send larger shipments to High Tortuga. Not unless you want to do it out in the open where everyone can see."

Barnabas spread his hands. "Actually, that is exactly what I intend to do."

Lance touched his fingers to his tired eyes and sighed. "Didn't we just agree that being seen out in the open was a bad idea?"

Barnabas lifted a shoulder. "I said it would be a bad idea to run them through the Interdiction. With a touch of subtlety, we can circumvent the need to include Devon in the supply chain altogether."

Lance looked out from his hands. "You want me to send the consignment straight to High Tortuga?"

Barnabas shook his head, a wry smile touching his lips. "Not even Federation ships can pass this end of the Interdiction. Which, to quote your charming daughter, is a complete pain in the ass—but necessary to keep High Tortuga protected while she's away."

Lance's confusion deepened. "Barnabas, you're making zero sense. Where *do* you want me to send this consignment? Help me out here. I get enough obfuscation when I'm in sessions at the Federation."

"I don't want you to send it anywhere." Barnabas held up a hand to halt Lance's interruption. "A fleet of Federation freighters turning up at High Tortuga? I can't allow that. Same issues with discovery. Bethany Anne has lifted interplanetary trade restrictions for certain companies planetside. I had the Silver Line Co. transferred to Nickie's name, and we're going to make her Fleet Captain and bring them all in under her command."

Lance almost choked. "And how did Nickie take that? She's not exactly Little Ms. Team Player."

Barnabas smiled serenely. "I haven't told her yet. All in good time."

Lance's face fell. "Do you really think it's a good idea to upset Lillian that way? That woman has had enough heartbreak to last her two extended lifetimes."

Barnabas smiled. "You would be surprised at how much softer Nickie has become over the past year. I do not think Lillian will suffer the heartbreak you are expecting her daughter to cause. Besides, the pickup should be done at a location with as few prying eyes as possible. I had Nickie's crew investigate the Voidrux issue, and the universe decided to smile upon us. We now own all the infrastructure of Voidrux industries, as well as retaining the full roster of employees. They were almost too happy to hear we'd stepped in."

"I can't argue she didn't get the job done there." Lance poked around the ashtray with the end of the cigar as he considered. He looked up a few moments later. "Has Nickie really made that much progress? Can we trust her not to fuck this up?"

Barnabas nodded, pride evident on his face. "Indeed. Nickie isn't the same pampered brat you knew, Lance. She isn't even the same woman who turned up here a year ago. She is nearing balance, and she's done a great deal of the work to get there herself. She is working well with the assignments I give her, and she takes good care of her crew. *I* know she's ready. I just have to convince her of the same."

Lance's eyebrows went up. "I have to say, I don't know if I can believe it. I thought we'd lost Nickie forever."

Barnabas dismissed the General's disbelief with a wave. "I had no such doubts. It's that Grimes streak—she's got it a mile wide."

High Tortuga, Southern Continent, Capitol

"*Why*," Nickie punched the Shrillexian in the face in time to her bitching, "can't you *assholes* just fucking *learn* that if you *pull* this shit, I'm going to come *looking* for you and I'm going to make you fucking *hurt*?"

Grim, who was hovering around the edge of the altercation, grimaced. "This wasn't exactly what I meant by opening up communications with the criminal under-world, Boss."

She paused to catch her breath, still gripping the limp Shrillexian. "I'm communicating just fine," she refuted. "It's this asshole who isn't playing nice."

Grim stood to the side with his arms folded, wincing with every punch she landed. "My good man, I would just tell her what she wants to know. She's not going to stop hitting you until you do."

Grim leaned over to Nickie. "You've got to stop at some point, right?"

Nickie laughed and drew her fist back again. "I dunno, I can keep this up all fucking day if this scumbag doesn't start entertaining me with the information I asked him so nicely for. I've got shit to get on with, you know?"

The Shrillexian groaned as his head bounced off the permacrete wall again. "*Gnuuugh! Haaannnnt!* STOP!"

Nickie obliged, dropping the Shrillexian to the floor to give him a moment to gather his breath—and his missing teeth. She stepped back, her hand near her hip, tapping her foot while she waited for him to spill the beans. "Well?"

The Shrillexian gently probed his bleeding face, which was rapidly forming contusions around the cuts. "Okay, okay. I'll *tell* you. Just stop hitting me!"

Nickie turned and flashed a grin at Grim. "See, I *told* you my way would work better."

Grim rolled his eyes and shrugged. "You know how I feel about violence, although in this case, I approve."

Nickie snorted. "I'm so glad you're on board. I wouldn't want to smash this drug-smuggling ring without your approval of my methods." She punched the Shrillexian one more time just to make extra sure he was cooperative.

Meredith spoke up in Nickie's mind. *Well, your Aunt Bethany Anne always did say that the application of pain was the best motivator.*

Really? Nickie asked. *I always thought that was my grand-dad's line.*

Meredith snickered. *Where do you think he learned it?*

She dragged the Shrillexian to his feet and hoisted him back into the chair she'd kicked him off upon entering the room five minutes before. "Go ahead, then." She waved a hand, leaning in. "Speak, shit stain. My patience is thinner than your chances of surviving this if you don't start running your mouth. *Right. Fucking. Now.* Where and when is the exchange?"

The Shrillexian babbled incoherently for another moment before gathering his wits in a last-minute act of self-preservation. "The docks...over on the south side by the bridge. One hour. It's going down while the guards are changing shift. That's all I know, I swear!"

Nickie flexed her fingers and reached for the shaking Shrillexian. "If that's all you know, then you're of no use to me anymore."

The Shrillexian scrabbled backward, falling out of the chair once again. "D-don't kill me."

Nickie looked at the Shrillexian like he had lost his mind, then at Grim with an offended expression. "Do I *look* like a murderous fucking bitch?"

Grim shrugged. "Um... Kinda?"

Nickie considered herself for a moment. She was dressed head to toe in black leather, and had various weaponry strapped around her body and two Jean Duke Specials glinting malevolently on her hips. She snickered and flicked her long coat back. "Okay, you've got me there. But no. Asshole criminals go through the Justice system, where they can be put into their natural environment with all the other asshole criminals."

The Shrillexian had rather handily backed up against the heat convection unit, ready to be tied up. Nickie fished a few cable ties out of a pouch on her belt and walked over with a no-nonsense grin.

Mere, call the cops to pick this trash up.

It would be my pleasure, her EI replied.

Nickie secured the Shrillexian to the heater and strode out of the warehouse purposefully. "Come on, Grim. We've got a smuggling operation to crash."

Grim hurried to keep up with her. "The south side of the docks is a large area. How will we know where the meet-up will be?"

Nickie shrugged. "That's Addie's job."

And Addie has it all under control, the woman in question answered. *I've directed a transport to your present location.*

Nickie's lip curled when the beat-up hovercar arrived. *A cab? Really?*

It was the fastest option, Adelaide told her. *Remember, you're not supposed to be here.*

Vigilantism sucks. I want a battleship. Nickie rolled her eyes and climbed into the hovercar after Grim.

The driver, an android wearing a flat cap and vest, turned in its seat when Nickie sat huffily in the back. "Where to?"

"Docks, south entrance," Nickie told it. "Just get us there as fast as you can."

The android looked her up and down, making a soft whirring noise. "Docks, south entrance," it repeated. "Gotcha."

The hovercar bobbed a couple of times and set off. The android looked back in the mirror, meeting Nickie's eyes after another glance at her weapons. "Long day of maiming?"

Nickie met the android's eyes in the mirror and flashed a wicked grin. "Like you wouldn't *believe*."

The android turned back to the road. "Rough justice," it muttered, shaking its head. "Rough justice."

"Just drive fast," Nickie growled.

Nickie and Grim ducked under a deactivated section of the electrified fence at the boundary of the docks with a few minutes to go before the scheduled meet.

They moved quickly and quietly toward the coordinates Adelaide had given them on the ride over, switching to the Etheric comm to talk in the well of silence.

The meet was just getting underway when they arrived at the bridge. The two groups of criminals stood facing each other, each trying to out-intimidate the other.

Nickie thought their efforts to conduct an illicit deal in the middle of the night in a dark place fell a little short since both groups of Noel-nis were displaying the kind of nervousness that only came with the fear of discovery.

Their body language practically screamed, "I don't

belong here." Nevertheless, Noel-nis were naturally excellent fighters. Nickie knew all too damn well not to get cocky with a whole mob of them.

Grim glanced at Nickie in alarm when he saw how many they had to contend with. *Are we going to be able to do this?*

Nickie snorted softly. *Duh, yeah. Have you seen those amateurs? They all look like they wish their mommies were here to hold their precious hands.* She shrugged. *I wasn't planning on arresting any of these wastes of good oxygen. You can go back to the ship if you want.*

Grim shook his head. *No, I'm not leaving you. We've got this.*

Nickie counted the dead criminals walking as she drew her Jean Dukes Specials. *We can do this,* she told Grim confidently. *None of them have weapons anywhere near as good as ours. It's going to be just fine. Now, let's go fuck shit up for some people who couldn't deserve it more.*

Adelaide spoke up over the comm before they could make a move. *Nickie, are you okay with this?*

Nickie frowned. *What do you mean? Why wouldn't I be okay?*

Adelaide made a small, indecipherable sound. *You know.* Her mental voice dropped to a whisper. *There are* drugs *there. You like drugs... Um, liked them... Oh, you* know *what I mean.* Her voice trailed off for a moment, then filled with concern. *Just tell us if you're tempted and we'll talk you out of it.*

Nickie almost laughed aloud and gave away their location. *Oh, Addie, never, ever stop being so innocent. And on the drugs, I'm more than done with all that self-destructive shit.*

Meredith spoke to Nickie privately. *I'm very glad to hear that.*

Want me to get all mushy and say it's all because I have a family now? Nickie snarked.

You wouldn't be lying, Meredith put in quietly.

Nickie kept her thoughts to herself. This wasn't the time for introspection. She dialed her Jean Dukes Specials up to seven and stepped out from cover. *Shush, Meredith. I know.*

High Tortuga, Space Fleet Base, Underground Access Elevator

Nickie cursed her stubbornness in refusing an antigrav cart for her post-op purchases. She shifted the weight of her heavy-ass load and exited the elevator, listing sideways as the doors began to close. "Fuck you, CEREBRO," she bitched, spotting Barnabas approaching from the corridor leading to his office. *Ugh. I just took care of that gang problem, and before that, he had me investigating that company for fraud.* She shuddered at the memory of the slimy company CEO. *What does he want me to do now?*

I have no idea, Meredith replied, similarly curious. *Perhaps it has something to do with his recent return from Devon?*

Nickie narrowed her eyes. *He's up to something. He left me alone for two whole weeks without a peep, then it's been random assignments one after the other since. If he thinks I'm going to put up with it for much longer, he's not gonna like it when I decide it's time to move on. I'm bored as all hell.* She lifted a heavily-laden arm to give him the finger, then thought better of it when her bags slid jerkily toward her elbow. *Ah, fuck it.* "Hey, Uncle B. I got your message. I need to put all this in my office right now, and we can talk there."

Barnabas nodded. "Very well. I will be interested to see how you treat your own belongings."

Nickie threw him a sour look and pushed the door open with her shoulder. She went in ahead of him, not bothering to repress her poor mood. "You're gonna have to keep waiting. I haven't had the renovators in yet."

Barnabas followed Nickie into her office, which was exactly as Tabitha had left it, save for the Ranger badge nailed to the wall. "Nice to see you didn't hesitate to put your stamp on the space."

Nickie snorted. "You wound me. Wherever I lay my ass is fine by me. I'm not fancy." She dumped her bags in the corner and dropped into her chair with a sigh, putting her feet up on her desk. "So what's my assignment? I assume you have one for me."

Barnabas nodded infuriatingly. "Something like that." He ignored Nickie's impatient glare, taking the guest chair opposite her desk. "It's time for you to decide."

Nickie raised an eyebrow, unprepared for Barnabas' solemnity. "Time for me to decide what, exactly?" She wasn't sure she liked where this was going.

When do you ever? Meredith asked gently. *At least hear him out before you reject what he has to offer. You might be surprised.*

What do you know? Nickie grumped.

CEREBRO isn't mad at me, Meredith replied airily.

Barnabas folded his hands in his lap, drawing Nickie

back to the room. "Your sabbatical is over, and you've seen the kind of work I'm offering. Are you ready to come home?"

Nickie reacted despite her resolution of a second ago. "I don't have to answer that." *Shit, Mere. Have you and he been practicing lines together? Why don't you two write a book? You can call it "How to talk to Nickie without her blowing her top." For fuck's sake. None of you can let me be for a damned minute.*

Meredith wisely remained silent.

Barnabas nodded. "You don't *want* to answer. There is a difference, you know."

Nickie glared at Barnabas, done with the subject. "When I start giving a fuck about that, you'll be the first to know. Do you have an assignment for me or not? I've got a crew to pay and a ship to run. Sitting around talking about feelings like a bunch of old women doesn't pay well enough to waste time on."

Barnabas sighed. "There *is* an assignment if you want to take it. Your cover from the Vietania operation is still viable, which suits my needs right now."

"You want me to run cargo?" Nickie affected a yawn, relishing the slight twitch under Barnabas' right eye as she did so. "Boring. If you think trapping me in a nice little routine is going to make me settle down, you've got another think coming. I don't care what the pay is. I'd rather die fighting on some nameless world than waste away doing *nothing*."

"I am aware of your proclivity for chasing adrenaline," Barnabas assured her. "However, as I said, it is time to acknowledge your decision to return to your family. We are at war, Meredith Nicole. It's time to step up or go your own way."

Nickie decided nonchalance was the way to go, not wanting Barnabas to know how badly she'd been itching to get involved in the war she'd trained for half her life. She put her feet up and waved a hand to dismiss Barnabas' stuffiness. "When is Aunt Bethany Anne *not* at war? She'll wipe out whatever alien menace there is this time and go back to micromanaging everyone's lives, and I'll be chained down again. You honestly think I'm going to agree to that?"

Barnabas frowned. "Grow up, child. Do you believe Bethany Anne fights because she wants to?"

Nickie didn't have a clue what motivated her aunt. It was pretty cathartic, taking out her frustration on the assholes she came across. Maybe when you were an Empress, the stupidity occurred on a universal scale. She could see that for Bethany Anne. "Dunno. Hadn't thought about it much beyond her always being pissed about something when I was a kid."

Barnabas sat back. "There has to come a point in your life where you stop seeing your family as all-powerful beings who deliberately failed you and accept responsibility for your choices." He smiled gently, diffusing the argument on Nickie's lips. "Bethany Anne fights because she sees no other way to protect those she loves."

"She must love the whole fucking universe, then," Nickie retorted. Maybe she and her scary-as-shit aunt weren't so different after all.

You and Bethany Anne share the same habit of going off the rails when you lose someone you love, Meredith revealed. *She's just had an extra couple of centuries to come to terms with it.*

Nickie didn't know how to reply to that.

Barnabas hadn't finished his speech. "The Ooken invasion is no joke, Nickie. It puts the Kurtherians two steps away from the Federation. The fleet is the only thing holding them back, and without a supply line to support it, well..."

Nickie held herself in check, mostly. There was no need to give her uncle the satisfaction of knowing how she felt about being welcomed back. "Yeah, yeah, I get it. I guess now you're going to tell me playing delivery girl is vital to Bethany Anne succeeding. Just skip the pep talk and get to what you want."

Barnabas smiled somewhat smugly for someone who wasn't supposed to be looking at Nickie's thoughts. "As you wish. The Silver Line Company has been transferred to your name and is now registered here on High Tortuga. The company has been granted permits to transport cargo between the Federation and High Tortuga, and as far as the Federation is aware, this is a simple trade agreement."

Nickie narrowed her eyes at the mention of subterfuge. "What's the real deal?"

Barnabas shifted in his chair. "You are aware that the Federation treaty exists on the condition Bethany Anne remains in exile. Our brief is to obtain the materials for building without endangering the stability of everything we have all worked toward for almost two centuries."

Nickie dropped the attitude for a second, but just one. "Wait..." She jumped to her feet and leaned over the desk, fury washing her vision red as she worked out the reason for Barnabas' smugness. "You've been steering me toward this the whole fucking time, haven't you?" she demanded.

Barnabas got to his feet as well, looking as though butter wouldn't melt in his mouth. "I have no idea where you get these ideas, Nickie."

Nickie knew if she had to look at his serene smile for one more second, she was going to try and tear it off his face. "Get out of my office, you manipulative sonofabitch," she barked, reaching for the paperweight on her desk. "I'll take the fucking assignment, but you can send my orders to Meredith. I don't want to see your face for a *long* fucking time."

Barnabas backed out of her office without breaking eye contact. "If that's what you need. I'm proud of you for doing your duty, Nickie."

"Fuck you!" Nickie retorted. She threw the paperweight at Barnabas as he closed the door, giving fewer than zero fucks as it smashed through the glass.

She dropped into her chair when the adrenaline dump hit her as suddenly as her rage had.

The tears came before she could stop them. *Mere... Meredith.*

I know, Nickie, Meredith soothed. *It's okay, I'm here.*

27

Devon, First City, The Hexagon, Network Command, Security Center

The last time Tabitha had been here, it had been far too early in the morning for her to appreciate the setup. Since she mostly worked out of the APAs in the arenas, she'd had little time or reason to be up here in Mark's domain.

Her time wasn't as flexible these days, and she'd missed the feel of a physical keyboard under her fingertips like she missed Pete's touch when he was away. Today she had all the reason she needed to indulge herself...and maybe, just maybe, she was feeling a little of the rebel in her bubbling to the surface.

Tabitha placed the box of equipment she'd brought on the break table at the side of the room and sat down at the console. She glanced at the holoscreen, the temptation too much to resist, and checked the time on High Tortuga before opening the space fleet base directory.

Her throat constricted when she saw that Nickie's location marker on the base map had her niece as being in her old office. She exited the directory and got up from the console, her courage gone for the moment.

Sabine and Mark arrived a little while into Tabitha's efforts to assemble the device she'd been working on.

Sabine came straight over to peer at the partially assembled EI cradle next to the device Tabitha was squinting at as she wired it. "How is it we need a separate EI for this?" she asked. "Winstanley couldn't take care of it?"

Tabitha jerked her chin toward a spherical container the size of a baseball, not moving her eyes from the device. "There are half a billion camera- and audio-capable drones in there, and I have more being printed. That amount of data needs to be processed through an exchange."

Sabine picked up the container, opened it carefully, and glanced at the shimmering, pale blue powder inside. She closed it again quickly "This looks like dust. Sparkly dust, but still."

Tabitha grinned as the fiddly connection went into place. "Mmhmm. Fresh from Jean's imagination. I helped with the programming, but she's the one who figured out that the new nanocyte technology could be used this way."

Mark wandered over, drawn by the lure of new tech. "How does the system work?"

Tabitha waved her hands as she explained. "The 'dust' is released over the city, programmed to attach itself to any unnaturally flat surface it finds. Think of it as a security blanket. The individual drones record everything around them in a five-meter radius."

Sabine frowned. "Doesn't that mean lost data from the ones that get destroyed?"

"Not if there's enough overlap for the processor to build the holoprojection," Mark ventured, glancing at Tabitha for confirmation. "Am I right?"

Tabitha winked, patting the cradle before she picked it up to fit it to the processor. "Gold star for the smart kid. Everything they record is dumped straight into this EI's processor to be amalgamated and passed along to whatever system I connect it to. That way, we don't lose a thing."

Mark's face reddened slightly. He dropped his bag on the empty chair and started unloading the contents. "This is pretty heavy for surveillance measures. We're going to get everything that happens in the city on camera."

Tabitha chuckled. "Another reason to run it through the EI first. Do you want to sort through the most private moments of people's lives?" She gagged as a thought hit her. "I sure as hell don't want to see Da'Mahin soaping himself in the shower."

High Tortuga, Space Fleet Base, Barnabas' Office

Nickie stomped into Barnabas' office and dumped herself in the antique wingback visitor's chair. "I didn't get an assignment."

Barnabas looked up from the letter he was handwriting and raised an eyebrow. "Yes, well. You needed some time to cool down." His eyes became distant a moment. "We will discuss your assignment in due time."

Nickie felt like Barnabas was holding her at arm's length. Whatever; let him play the intrigue game. She sighed, allowing her head to fall back against the dark, cracked leather. "As long as you're finally sending us off-world. There's a war going on, and here *we* are stuck clearing up petty crime on the planet Bethany Anne made everyone forget."

Barnabas smiled that infuriatingly calm smile of his. "You and your crew did a stellar job. I would hardly describe the prevention of all those drugs and weapons from being distributed on High Tortuga as 'clearing up petty crime.'"

Nickie pouted, her frustration spilling over. "Yeah, well, *I* would. I want to go *fight*! C'mon, I'm doing everything right, right? I've been toeing the fucking line like it's a sobriety test. Not a single stumble."

"And you have received your reward." Barnabas smiled. "You're getting the opportunity to do more."

Nickie had to acknowledge the truth. The logistics gig wasn't actually that repugnant to her. Still, there was the question of what making that commitment would mean for her freedom. She licked her lips, wondering why her mouth was suddenly drier than the Outback. "I'm... I'm ready."

Barnabas smiled. "I'm glad to hear you say that. As for the role I have to offer, I believe you have earned it." He leaned back in his chair, folding his hands lightly on the table in front of him. "I will remind you that accepting the role is entirely optional, and you will be given time to transition into it."

Nickie brushed off his assurances. "What if I decide not to take it?"

Barnabas lifted his hands. "Your choice, Merry. May I remind you that you are free to leave whenever you wish?

However, it will be to continue your personal journey toward wholeness alone."

Nickie opened her mouth to argue, but what could she say in the face of her uncle's all-knowing and serene expression? "Wholeness, my enhanced left ass-cheek," she muttered, scowling. "Sounds like the biggest load of bistok-shit I've ever heard. And will you *please* quit calling me 'Merry?' I'm a grown-ass woman, not a four-year-old. Just tell me what you want me to do, for fuck's sake. You might have practically everlasting life, but I'm aging, here."

Barnabas' mouth twitched as his sometime tactic of reminding Nickie who she was struck the intended nerve. "I cannot see a few minutes as making so much of a difference. Now, your assignment. That is, if you are quite done with this," he waved a hand to encompass Nickie's uncooperative slouch in his antique chair, "performance?"

He has a point, Meredith interjected.

Nickie narrowed her eyes. *I know when it's time to shut the fuck up.* "I'm listening."

Barnabas' eyes flickered for a moment, and Meredith informed Nickie that she had just received the assignment brief.

His expression was deadly serious. "Listen to me, Nickie. This is how you get to contribute to the war effort. You may not be out there on the front, but this assignment is just as vital to our success as is fighting the Ooken."

Nickie's face dropped as she scanned through the assignment brief. "You're joking, right? You want *me* to go into the Federation? Are you fucking crazy? My mother is there!"

Barnabas gave her a stern look. "Your mother is

currently based on the QBBS *Helena*, where she has had to come to terms with repairing her relationship with Jean. Maybe, if you are ready, this would be a good time to begin repairing your relationship with them both."

Nickie jumped to her feet, her lips drawing back in a snarl. "Yeah, not in a million fucking years. If there's any repairing to do, Mom is the one who needs to do it. Not me."

Barnabas winced when the guest chair's feet left four scrapes on the polished wooden floor. Maybe he should get a rug for that spot. "I'd hoped our conversations over this last year had helped you to move forward in that regard."

Nickie began to pace, clenching and unclenching her fists as a way to deal with the unexpected surge of emotion. "It's...it's not something that can be talked out."

Barnabas nodded in understanding. "Does this mean that you are refusing the assignment? You didn't get to the end of the brief yet."

Nickie stopped and turned to face Barnabas with her hands on her hips. "I'll finish reading it when I get back to the *Granddaughter*. I'll take the assignment. I won't turn down my duty." She looked her uncle in the eyes, her jaw set in that unmovable way that marked her as a Grimes. "But I'm *not* speaking to that woman. If she wanted anything to do with me, maybe she should have paid attention sometime during my childhood."

Barnabas shrugged. "Your decision." He hesitated a moment, unusual for him. "I, um, took the liberty of having your ship refitted for the purpose."

Nickie narrowed her eyes. "You did *what*? Too far!

That's *my* ship!" She turned on her heel and stormed out of the office, making sure to slam the door extra hard.

The sound the stenciled glass made as it shattered was music to Nickie's angry soul. She laughed, calling back as she headed for the elevator, "Hey, Uncle B. Our doors match."

Meredith tsked. *You know you'll have to pay for that.*

Nickie's lip curled upward. *Would you look at that? I just ran out of fucks to give.*

High Tortuga, Space Fleet Base, Aboard the *Penitent Granddaughter*

Nickie managed to hold her shit together until she was safely on the ship. Then she let her frustration loose, kicking over a box she passed as she stormed down the corridor. *Dammit, Meredith! Why does he* always *fucking do this to me?*

What is "this?" Meredith inquired carefully. The spikes in certain areas of Nickie's neurochemistry were more than concerning. *Can you explain?*

You know! Nickie exclaimed. This! *Just as I start to feel like I've got solid ground under my feet, something like this happens, and I'm back to not knowing where the fuck I stand.*

Meredith remained silent, doing what she could to ease the stress on Nickie's brain while she raged incoherently inside her mind.

I don't want to work with the Federation. I sure as hell don't want to see my mother.

Meredith tried to soothe Nickie's anger, but her tantrum continued all the way down the corridor to the elevator by the mess. *Perhaps this is not such a bad thing, Nickie. Maybe it is time to reconnect with your family.*

Nickie growled, startling Bradley and Lefty as the two house bots emerged from the mess. *Keep your traitor thoughts to yourself. I'm not speaking to her.*

The house bots just as quickly ducked back into the mess, emitting high-pitched noises that could only be interpreted as alarm.

Nickie ignored them. She headed for the bridge, seeking the familiar comfort of her captain's chair. She found the bridge empty and dropped into her chair, putting her feet up on the worn spot on the console with a frustrated sigh. *I suppose we're at least getting to help out in the war. I was getting so sick of running around High Tortuga after greedy assholes who get their kicks by turning a quick profit off those who can afford it least.*

Keen arrived, disrupting Nickie before she had a chance to get any real brooding done. "Hey, boss. I hear we're heading out again already. What's the assignment?"

Nickie turned her chair to face Keen. "I haven't read it all yet. Looks like logistics." She frowned. "It probably isn't that bad. Where are the others? I only want to go through this once."

Keen checked the crew off on his fingers as he gave her a rundown. "Adelaide and Durq will be back from requisitions any time now. Grim sent them over with a huge list. You know how he gets about his galley stocks. He's in Stores now, doing inventory."

Nickie swiveled her chair slightly without removing her feet from the spot on the console. "In that case, I may as well tell you the gist of it. We're going undercover as traders."

Keen took the chair beside Nickie so she could stop sitting at that awkward angle to see him. "That doesn't sound too difficult? We've done a few undercover jobs."

Nickie grunted. "Yeah, well. None of those assignments took us to the Federation."

Keen grimaced. "Oh. I see. I get why you're unhappy. How do you feel about going back there?"

Nickie raised an eyebrow. "Who the fuck are you, my therapist? I get enough of that shit from Meredith. I don't need it from my second-in-command."

Keen held up his hands. "Fine, if it's none of my business. But I'm here to talk if that's what you need." He got up from his chair. "I'll go round the rest of the crew up."

Keen left Nickie to her thoughts once again. Although, Nickie wasn't too sure if being left alone with her thoughts was the right thing at that moment.

She didn't *have* to talk to her mother. In fact, Lillian didn't even need to know Nickie was anywhere near QT2, wherever the hell that was. It was too late, so everyone might as well just forget about it.

Nickie sat back in her chair with her hands laced behind her head and closed her eyes to look through the ship's systems in her HUD while she waited for the crew to arrive. She could let it go, since the dilemma was nothing compared to the shock of what Barnabas had done to her ship.

Nickie wasn't sure how she felt about the revamp of the *Penitent Granddaughter*. After all, this was her ship, gained by trickery fair and square. Now the old Skaine freighter had a huge Silver Line Trading Co. logo sprayed onto the side, and everywhere but the bridge had been remodeled to keep up the appearance.

To Nickie, it screamed, "Easy target" in the way that only big company freighters could.

It wouldn't have been her choice.

However, Barnabas had been very clear that they were to remain under the radar at all costs, and the cover from Vietania *was* still good. She opened her brief and read it closely.

QT2 turned out to be a system way outside the safe haven of the border systems Nickie was used to haunting.

The shipyard attached to the QBBS *Helena* was relying on the cargoes of processed metals and other components that Nickie's fake company was going to ship, entirely legally, right under the Federation's noses.

Nickie found the whole thing just a little bit delicious.

Meredith spoke up, sensing Nickie's amusement. *What is it that you find so funny?*

It's the irony, Nickie replied. *This job is so insane. One day I'm breaking up a smuggling ring, the next I'm setting one up.*

I suppose, Meredith drew out her reply, *that you find the unpredictability of your assignment satisfying.*

Nickie smirked. *I suppose I do. It sure beats sitting in a box somewhere doing endless repetitive tasks like some robot. No offense.*

None taken, Meredith assured her, *since I am not a robot.*

Sorry, Nickie offered. *Working for Barnabas, I never know what will happen from day to day. It makes life interesting, you're right.*

I also enjoy the variation in our days. Meredith paused.

Adelaide and Durq are boarding the ship. I will begin the prelaunch processes.

Nickie was barely listening. "This is some frontier shit." She read on, gaining an understanding of what her aunt had been building since stepping down as Empress. "So this stretches... Wow."

Something at the bottom of the brief caught her eye. "That *bastard...*"

I was wondering when you would get to that, Meredith chipped in.

I'm *wondering why you get such a kick out of these moments,* Nickie shot back. *He's made me the fleet captain. What am I supposed to do with that? I shouldn't even be managing myself, let alone a crew, and he wants me to take on a shit-ton of management responsibility. Do I look like a desk monkey?*

What have you learned from Barnabas' management style? Meredith asked.

Not a fucking lot, since he likes to delegate so much. She rolled her eyes as the answer hit her. *Outsourcing, right?*

Meredith made the sound someone would make if a pet did a clever trick. *You have the whole of the former Voidrux Industries infrastructure to work with, and the brief doesn't demand you take the position right away.*

Nickie thought about it for a moment. *I can handle that. Okay. I need a brief that covers the open part of the assignment to give to the crew, then I'll start digging around my new company. I should probably start by finding out what I have to work with before I make any decisions.*

She turned her chair when the bridge door cycled open, admitting the crew.

Nickie flashed a bright grin at them as they filed in and

took their stations. "We have an assignment. Remember me telling you that quick job we did for the General was going to come back to bite us in the ass? Well, here's the bite."

She indicated the viewscreen with a finger. "This is our brief for the moment. We will be reprising our cover as the Silver Line Trading Company, working with General Reynolds and Admiral Thomas to keep the shipyard at QT2 supplied with materials."

The crew murmured as they read through the assignment brief, surprised Nickie had taken an assignment that wasn't even slightly action-y.

"Logistics?" Grim couldn't contain his disdain when he saw their assigned routes. "This isn't quite what I was expecting, Boss. How are you feeling about returning to the Federation?"

Nickie bit back her retort, her decision to keep Barnabas' offer secret weighing on her already.

Outskirts of Yollin Space, Waystation, Aboard the *Penitent Granddaughter*

Nickie paced in front of the viewscreen while the crew waited to receive clearance to dock at the mini-asteroid base. "I always forget what a pain in the ass Federation security is."

Keen snorted. "You've got that right. What's that now, two hours? Sucks to be a civilian. All that waiting in line was a damn shock when I retired from the Marines."

Grim nodded his agreement. "It's like culture shock. When I left the Guardian Marines, it was the same."

Nickie narrowed her eyes at the confirmation of her long-held suspicion that her friend had not always been the lover he often proclaimed himself to be. "You're just full of surprises lately, aren't you, Grimmie?"

Grim shrugged, which Nickie always thought looked funny on a Yollin, and laughed. "My Yollin behind lived for a long while before we met."

Nickie fixed him with a stare. "One of these days, you

and me are going to sit down with an extremely large bottle of that excellent whiskey you're so good at finding, and you're going to tell me all about this long life of yours."

Grim raised his hands. "Maybe. Maybe we'll be stuck here waiting for permission to land for the rest of our days."

Adelaide giggled. "You two are the funniest. This is just standard. I went all the way to the *Meredith Reynolds* with my mom and dad when I was like, fifteen. We waited in line the whole day and thought nothing of it."

Nickie's eyes widened. "Fuck *that*. How did you not go insane?"

Adelaide's eyes lit up. "Oh! Dad made snacks and got out his guitar, and we sang camp songs and had s'mores over the portable heating element. The next day our mom played games, and we all told stories. I had a fight with my sister over nothing. It was a part of the vacation."

Nickie compared Addie's tale of family road trips to the trips she'd taken with Tabitha and her grandad John. "Sounds...great."

"It was!" Adelaide bubbled, missing the note of pity in Nickie's tone.

"We have clearance to land," Meredith announced from the speakers.

Nickie threw up her hands, glad of the distraction. "Finally! Take us in, Meredith."

They disembarked in a large public hangar, where they were met by a two-legged Yollin with a datapad. "Captain Dakkar?"

Nickie waved somewhat awkwardly, wondering why

the Yollin was using her scrapped cover name. "Yeah, um…"

The Yollin looked her up and down. "Funny, you look more like a Grimes to me." His mandibles clicked in laughter. "I'm kidding. My name is Roh'dun, and the General sent me to make sure everything went smoothly at this end."

Nickie raised an eyebrow. "You mean, Uncle Lance sent you to make sure I don't trash the place?"

Roh'dun shrugged. "You can put it that way if you like. I was being polite."

Grim snorted behind her. "Roh'dun, don't annoy her. It hurts too much, as I can tell you from experience."

The Yollin almost dropped his datapad. "*Grim'zee?* The General said to expect a familiar face, but I can't believe it's you!"

Nickie glared at Roh'dun, who nodded, then at Grim. "You two know each other?"

Grim sidestepped Nickie to get to Roh'dun. "We're third…no, fourth cousins twice removed in the matrilineal branch of my family."

Roh'dun grasped Grim's outstretched arm. "That's the side that wasn't so stupid during the Yollin revolution," he joked to Nickie.

Nickie shrugged, having skipped that class.

Adelaide and Keen appeared at the hatch. They hesitated before exiting, attempting to coax a reluctant Durq to leave the ship.

"No luck," Adelaide commiserated as she reached Nickie and Grim.

Nickie looked up at the hatch. Durq was there, peering

around the hangar curiously. She handed her datapad to Keen. "You two take care of the cargo. It's time Durq saw some of the galaxy."

Adelaide grinned. "You go and have fun together. We've got this."

Nickie headed back up the ramp and into the ship. She took a seat on a crate near the hatch and smiled at her timid Skaine friend. "Hey, Durq. You feel like coming out to see the outpost?"

Durq hung around the threshold, looking at his feet. "I want to."

This had been their ritual ever since Nickie had accepted Durq as a part of her life and decided to help him get over his fear.

Nickie grinned, stepping out onto the ramp. "You know, I believe you this time." She held out her hand. "Come on, we'll go get something to eat, yeah? We'll be gone for an hour, two max."

The little Skaine hesitated a moment longer, his foot hovering before he placed it on the ramp. He grasped Nickie's hand like he was drowning and she was a lifebelt.

Adelaide clapped her hands delightedly. "That's great, Durq!"

Durq put one foot in front of the other, his knees wobbling a bit with each step. When they reached the bottom of the ramp, he looked around with delight. "I am leaving the ship! I have got this!"

Nickie squeezed his hand gently. "That's right, buddy. You've got the hell out of this."

That made no sense whatsoever, but it seemed to do the trick because Durq straightened up a touch more and let go of Nickie's hand. "Let's go before I change my mind."

Outskirts of Yollin Space, Waystation, Spaceport

Nickie led Durq out of the spaceport and into the urban crush surrounding it.

Durq's eyes darted around as the clash of many cultures coming together to sell their wares swamped his senses. His already-pale blue skin took on a gray tinge. "Where are we going?" he asked. "This place is busy."

Nickie glanced around the crowded market, sniffing to locate the source of the aroma that had just caught her nose. "There," she told Durq, pointing out a renovated shuttlecraft with neon signage reading Nice to Meat You. She tilted her head at Durq. "What do you think?"

Durq nodded, deciding that as long as they got out of the crowd and somewhere a bit quieter so he could think, he didn't care much what was on the menu. "I suppose so?"

Nickie paused to read the sign on the door. "Bad Company-certified beef? I don't know who Bad Company is but I sure as hell could go for a steak." She looked at Durq, who was hovering behind her, looking for all the world like a lost puppy. "Have you ever tasted beef?" she asked.

Durq's blank expression told Nickie everything she needed to know. She winked as she pushed open the door to the restaurant. "Come on, you're in for a treat."

They went inside and waited to be seated by the Torcellan hostess.

The hostess approached with a bright smile that

quickly faded when she saw Durq. "I'm sorry, we don't serve—" she caught sight of Nickie's expression, "um... breakfast after midday, so get your order in fast if that's what you're looking to eat."

Nickie removed her hand from the grip of her JD Special. "We're not in the breakfast mood," she ground out. "Table for two."

"This way," the hostess told them. She seated them by the window and dumped two menus on the table, not trying too hard to keep the disapproving expression off her face. "Take your time," she told them, turning her back without waiting for a reply.

Durq shuffled in his seat.

Nickie didn't miss his discomfort. He appeared to take the Torcellan's speciesism as though it were his due. She made a face at the Torcellan's back as she walked away. "Stuffy bitch."

Durq gasped when the server stiffened briefly. "I think she heard you," he whispered.

Nickie grimaced. "Good. I hope she fucking chokes on her lemon face." She scooted over to a table in a different section, waving for Durq to join her. "C'mon, she doesn't deserve our custom."

The server for that section came over. "Ma'am? I'm so sorry, you're seated in Camille's section." The young human man smiled at them both apologetically as he spoke, glancing nervously at Camille.

Nickie smiled brightly, leaning in to get a look at the young man's nametag. "Lucas? You seem like a nice guy, and that snotty, speciesist bitch was probably going to spit in our food. I think here will be just fine, thanks."

Lucas looked at the two-legged Yollin behind the counter for approval, receiving a minute nod. "Okay, then!" He returned Nickie's grin with a hearty smile and handed them both an interactive menu. "What can I get you to drink?"

"What do you have?" Durq asked timidly, cringing slightly at the glare Camille was throwing their way.

"All of the usual," Lucas replied cheerfully. "Coke, Pepsi —" He rattled off a long list of other drinks.

Nickie looked at Durq, unable to hide her surprise. "Both?"

"I'll take a Pepsi, please," Durq told Lucas.

Nickie made a face. "I'll have a Coke, thanks." *Don't you say a fucking word,* she told Meredith.

I wasn't going to say a thing. There was an undertone of amusement to Meredith's reply that Nickie chose to ignore.

It's a question of taste, Nickie told her. *As in, Pepsi tastes disgusting.*

They thanked Lucas when he returned with their drinks a moment later.

Durq examined the menu. "I don't recognize anything on here."

Nickie sensed his rising discomfort with the situation. She scooted over in the booth to sit beside him and get a closer look at his menu. "It's mostly meat from different animals," she explained. "I'm having beef, which comes from cows. It's pretty rare outside the Federation."

Durq watched Nickie make her choice, then touched the same window on his menu. Nickie smiled at his safe— but excellent—choice and sipped her Coke.

Durq fiddled with his napkin, suddenly quiet again.

"What do you think of the Federation so far?" It wasn't the most scintillating conversation starter, but idle chat wasn't Nickie's strongest skill.

Durq shrugged, plucking his napkin off the table as Lucas arrived with their food. "I don't really have anywhere to compare it to, except High Tortuga and the ship. It's okay, I suppose?"

Durq's eyes widened when the aroma of his meal hit him, and his nose twitched as he regarded the thick, juicy steak on his plate. "This is the cow-beast you talked about? It smells delicious! I have changed my mind. This is a good place if there is food like this."

Nickie nodded, making a sound of confirmation around her mouthful of meat. She waved her fork to indicate Durq should start eating while she savored her first bite.

"They're from Earth," she told him once she'd finished chewing. "We just ate bistok like everyone else on Yoll until someone brought a breeding herd from Earth."

Durq cut a small piece of his steak and placed it delicately into his mouth. He chewed, slowly at first, moving the meat around his mouth to get every bit of the flavor from it. "Mmmm, ommm... Ohhh."

Nickie snickered at the series of blissful expressions that passed over Durq's face. "There's nothing like a real steak. Or all those weird-ass noises you're making while you eat it."

Durq swallowed, nodding enthusiastically. "I can see why everyone wants to invade Earth so badly. I have never tasted anything so delicious. It would be worth death to get a single taste of the cow-beast again."

Nickie chuckled. "Or we can just eat here again."

Durq nodded. "Oh, yes."

Once dinner was over, they decided to walk back to the *Penitent Granddaughter*. They passed through the marketplace and back into the spaceport, Nickie making noises in all the appropriate places while Durq chattered about his experiences prior to meeting her.

They parted ways at the top of the ramp, and Nickie watched Durq go with a warmth in her chest that had nothing to do with the half a cow she'd just eaten. She was very proud of Durq's progress, and he didn't even think anything of it.

She found herself humming a song to herself as she made her way to her quarters, anticipating the unwinding part of the day since it rarely came around before she dropped off wherever she was working.

It's good to see you happy, Meredith remarked.

Damn right, I'm happy, Nickie replied. *My friend overcame a huge fear today. Maybe he'll be able to do it again soon, maybe not. But he did it.*

The important thing is that Durq has seen that his fear of rejection was real, but he also saw that there are good people who accept others without preconceptions.

Nickie waited for Meredith to open her quarters. *Thanks to Lucas' kindness. I want to do something to reward him. What can you find out about him?* The door slid shut behind her. She kicked off her boots, stripped off her atmosuit, and dropped it to the floor on the way to the bathroom.

I'll check the databases here to see what I can find. Meredith paused before changing the subject. *Should I be worried that this is becoming somewhat of a routine since the ship was refitted? After you were so annoyed at Barnabas for having your quarters refitted and expanded?*

Nickie snorted as she switched on the shower to heat up the bathroom. *Worry all you like. I've got the shower to end all showers. When I get home, the first thing I want to do is to wash the damned day away.* She stepped in and braced herself on the wall while the jets got to work pounding the tightness out of her muscles. *What would be nice is if I could get a bit of privacy.*

Meredith was quiet after that, giving Nickie time to reflect on her day—and the year leading up to it.

The EI would have to get used to Nickie trusting her own counsel. She was past needing to be held up, and Barnabas' offer proved she wasn't the only one who thought so.

Still, she didn't need to be such a bitch about it. *Sorry, Mere.*

You're just upset by being this close to home.

My ship is my home, Nickie stated firmly.

She waited for Meredith's usual rebuttal, which didn't come.

Whatever. She switched the shower over to the sonic dryer and stepped out a moment later, shaking her hair out behind her. She dressed quickly and got into bed, a huge improvement on the hard slab she'd begun with on the ship.

Is there a message? she asked tentatively as she slid under the covers.

Not today.

Nickie shrugged. *I wasn't expecting another so soon. I'll read through the old ones.*

Again? Meredith asked.

Yes, again. Nickie's tone made it clear she wasn't in the mood to discuss it. *Again with the judgment, Meredith. You sound like my mother.*

Someone should, Meredith snarked. *Since you refuse to go and see yours.*

Nickie muted the EI, something she'd worked out since living on the space fleet base. She cupped a hand to her ear. *What's that? Nothing?* She smirked and dropped her head onto her pillows, loading the first message Tabitha had sent into her HUD.

So... You didn't reply. I figure I earned that. Looks like I'll just have to hold up both sides of our conversation until you're ready. That's okay. I can talk enough for us both.

You probably already worked out where I am, and I'll be here when you're ready. Devon isn't too bad. Pete likes it. Did you know we got together? We even had a kid. Bet you can't believe that!

I miss you, Trouble. I hope that I hear from you soon.

Nickie couldn't read any farther than that. Her eyes got prickly when she looked at the attached photo. Her Aunt Tabitha looked the same, just a lot happier than Nickie remembered her, and so did Peter. It was the little boy in Tabitha's arms who brought Nickie's emotions welling up.

She had no fucking business being anywhere near a kid.

Nickie squeezed her eyes tightly closed until the tears

quit threatening to spill. Maybe one day she would earn the right to be a part of that sweet boy's life.

One day.

It wasn't today, but she wasn't going to keep pushing away the person she missed most in the world for another minute.

She opened a reply window and started to write.

Devon, First City, The Hexagon, Penthouse Apartment

Peter walked into the living area to find Tabitha crying into a pillow. "Babe?" He crossed the room in five steps and knelt at Tabitha's side. "What's wrong?"

Tabitha looked up, her eye makeup streaked and running down her cheeks. "I'm okay," she told him, sitting up and scrubbing her eyes. "Really."

"Looks that way." He sat beside her on the couch and held out an arm. "Wanna talk about it?"

Tabitha smiled through her tears. She adored Peter's attempts at sensitivity, even when he got it all wrong. She shuffled over to him and tucked herself into his embrace. "Really, I'm good. Nickie wrote me a letter, and it was emotional."

Peter frowned. "I don't get it. You're crying because you're happy? Are you pregnant again?"

Tabitha slapped Peter's chest and got off the couch. "You have to be a man about it, don't you?" She snorted at the kicked-puppy look he gave her. "I'm not mad at you." She waved her hands, her elation making her want to dance. "This is great! She's accepting the fleet captain position. She's coming home."

Peter grinned, caught up in Tabitha's whirlwind. "She's transferring to Devon?"

Tabitha deflated. "No. Her duty will keep her between the Federation and QT2."

Peter winced. "That kind of sucks. I'm sorry, babe."

Tabitha brightened again. "It's all good. She wrote to me. I'm going to reply in a couple of days. Give her a chance to come to grips with her new assignment."

"That sounds like a plan." Peter got up and wrapped his arms around Tabitha's waist. "Everything is coming up Tabitha, babe."

Tabitha snorted and. "Don't speak too soon," she told him, standing on her tiptoes to kiss him on the nose. "I'm about to chair the first mediation session between Mahi'-Takar's family."

Peter moved to catch the kiss on his lips. "You've got it," he replied, releasing her. "If anyone can argue a generations-old family feud into submission, it's you."

Tabitha raised an eyebrow, pointing her finger at him. "Don't make me murder you before we know I'm going to survive this mediation."

CHAPTER 5 TABITHA AND NICKIE

Devon, First City, The Hexagon, Lecture Room

Tabitha sat with Tu'Reigd, going through some last minute questions she had about his uncles. She shuffled her papers on the table, hearing a large group approaching the lecture room. "You ready, Trey?"

The Bakan heir shook his head. "I'm having second thoughts about whether mediation is going to work. I understand it in theory, but nobody took my family into account when they designed the process. It's all about domination for them."

Tabitha was about to reassure him when they heard a fight break out in the anteroom.

Trey dropped his head onto his folded arms. "I told you they would do this. That's Da'Mahin, pushing my patience again."

"I wish the rest of your family wasn't so uptight about nicknames. And everything else." Tabitha pressed her lips together, seeing that Trey was conflicted. She had chosen the lecture room for its enormous circular table, anticipating the issues that would arise from any seating arrangement that favored a particular Baka. "There's no way that argument is really about who gets to walk through the door first."

Trey snorted, having picked up the habit as quickly as a Yollin learns to shrug since moving into the Hexagon. "It really is. The thing you have to remember is they're all equal in rank, but none of them *believe* they are. Li'Kein, Ll'Eirion, and Li'Orin will listen to reason, but Da'Mahin, Ban'Clai, and Ma' Ruen will fight to keep their dominance over the others. Fu'Ksi will go with whichever faction wins out, which means Da'Mahin's unless Mahi' steps in. It's always the same."

Tabitha had her game plan as to how to handle the brothers pegged. "Da'Mahin isn't winning a thing today, apart from a lesson in how to have your family's back instead of sticking a knife in. We're going to resolve this, Trey. I promise. Are you ready to speak?"

Trey scratched his furry cheek and offered Tabitha a weak smile. "I hope so. I appreciate everything you and Be —Baba Yaga have done for my mother. For my people."

Tabitha ruffled his fur, nodding toward the lecture room door. "No problem, kiddo. You want to do something about them before your mother gets here?"

As if on cue, Mahi'Takar's voice boomed over the clamor in the corridor, and the seven brothers filed sullenly into the horseshoe-shaped room behind their sister.

Tabitha remained seated, waving the dispossessed royal family in. "Take a seat, everyone."

Mahi'Takar brushed past Da'Mahin and swaggered

over to the table. She took her seat at the table, book-ending her son, and glared at her younger brothers until they were seated in relative silence. "Takar'Tu'Reigd. Tabitha."

Tabitha returned Mahi'Takar's nod and indicated Trey with a hand. "Before we begin, I'm going to open the floor to your future leader so you can hear from him what he wants for you as a family and as a people."

Trey did a double-take, then squared his shoulders. "Huh? Oh, right. Yeah." He cleared his throat and ran a hand over his fur to push it out of his eyes. "I want to be remembered as the Takar who freed our people from the influence of the Seven."

His uncles jumped to their feet as one and started yelling at Mahi'Takar.

Tabitha repressed a snicker when Mahi' folded her arms and sat back, her raised chin making it clear she was fully supporting her son.

Trey took it in his stride. He growled and slapped the table. "Look at me, not my mother. You've been mites in her fur for as long as I can remember, and it stops now." He got up and began to pace in the space behind his seat, his hand never straying too far from the short knife on his belt as he laid the law down. "You chose to follow us, to swear to me. I am going to take back our home. I am going to remove Lu'Trein from power. I will not take a single warrior I cannot trust with my life."

He looked at his uncles with a mixture of sadness and resolve. "You have become petty and dishonorable. Your names will be absent from the histories unless you convince me of your loyalty to me, to my mother, and to our people. *None* of you will take my position. I am too well protected with Mahi' and the Mistress at my back."

The seven males backed down, to varying degrees. Da'Mahin's faction glared skeptically, while the smaller three brothers appeared satisfied by Trey's show of force.

Trey continued, standing taller as his teenage slouch dropped away and the leader he was born to be came to the surface for a moment. "It's time to prove that the vows of loyalty you made to me at my birth are worth anything. I have chosen to accept Baba Yaga's offer of enhancement." He held up a hand before any of his family could interrupt. "I am assured that the Vid-doc technology allows me to experience time at an accelerated rate while my body is force-grown. I will not be taking any shortcuts, and Tabitha tells me I can access a much wider range of training scenarios to learn from."

Tabitha took over to give the brothers a brief rundown of the process Trey would undergo. "It's completely safe. Baba Yaga wouldn't allow any harm to come to Tu'Reigd."

Trey flourished his hands. "There you go. What is it to be, Da'Mahin? Keep fighting for power you'll never get and destroy your chance to return home, or work with me to take your brother down?"

Da'Mahin continued to glare for a moment, then his shoulders dropped. "I will honor my vow, Takar'Tu'Reigd."

Trey's expression was unmoving. "Damn right. You will mend your relationship with Mahi', and work with Tabitha to increase your knowledge of the Ooken." He grinned, punching the air. "This is going to be an *epic* fight! They will sing of our glory for generations to come."

Tabitha listened to Trey talk about his hopes for their

family's future and about putting aside their differences for the sake of fighting for their home and people. She couldn't help but contrast Trey's heartfelt appeal to his uncles with the long message she'd received from Nickie that morning.

Times were getting darker, but hope shone through in the end.

Outskirts of Yollin Space, Waystation, Aboard the *Penitent Granddaughter*

Nickie strolled into the mess, full of energy after an unexpectedly good night's sleep to find the rest of her crew nursing strong black coffee and aching heads. "Is there any alcohol left on this rock?" she teased, pouring herself a cup of beautifully over-caffeinated sludge from the pot.

She sipped her coffee and dropped onto the bench between Keen and Adelaide. "Did you all hit every bar in the place?" A smirk played on her lips. "You know, *I* feel great. Maybe because I took it easy, knowing we had a long day ahead of us."

"Okay, already," Keen protested, wincing at Nickie's chipper tone. "No need to rub it in. Besides, can you even *get* drunk?"

Nickie shrugged. "Dunno. It's been a while since I put any real effort into getting wasted." She paused with the coffee cup halfway to her mouth, a look of horror dawning on her face. "Is this it? Am I past it?"

Grim patted Nickie's arm to console her. "I'm sure the party animal we all know and love is still in there under the responsible person you've become. Somewhere..."

Nickie gagged and put the cup down on the table.

"Fuck that. Get me a bottle of brandy, *stat*." She narrowed her eyes and stuck her tongue out at Grim when he groaned. "You ruin all my fun."

Grim lifted his hands in supplication. "What can I say?"

Nickie narrowed her eyes and resumed sipping her coffee. "Time to get to work."

They finished breakfast and made their way to the cargo bays to open them up for the loading crews.

The loading crews were just arriving when Nickie rode the ramp to the hangar floor. "Things are getting pretty slack while Aunt Bethany Anne is away," she teased.

A regal-looking blonde woman wearing four-inch heels and a no-nonsense expression walked in behind the crew and headed straight for Nickie. "You must be Jean's grand-daughter." She held out a perfectly manicured hand. "Giselle Foxton-Thomas, civilian resources manager at the QBBS *Helena*."

Nickie held her face straight while she shook the intense woman's hand. "Yeah, um. Nickie Grimes. You're the Admiral's wife, right? What does a civilian resources manager have to do with supplying a military shipyard?"

"Nothing whatsoever," Giselle confirmed. "However, my husband will be relieved that we have a solution to his supply problem."

Nickie raised an eyebrow as she extracted her hand. "That's me, fixer of supply problems."

Giselle looked askance at Nickie for a moment. "Your grandmother did warn me about your idea of humor." Her lips pressed together in disapproval. "I see what she meant."

Nickie winked and turned to go back aboard the ship. "Then you'll know I'm not joking. See you at the *Helena*."

She grinned to herself as she got back on board the ship, leaving Giselle gaping in annoyance behind her.

Meredith tsked. *Maybe pushing her buttons wasn't the best idea. Never mind that you have to work with her, she appears to be friends with your grandmother.*

Nickie shrugged. *I thought I was nice. I wasn't the one who went into the conversation with a stick up my ass.*

Meredith chuckled. *The Admiral's wife* is *rather militaristic in her manner.*

You don't say. Nickie decided to stick her head in on the crew before heading for the bridge. She found them in the belly of the ship after getting lost in the new corridor layout twice.

Keen was supervising the placement of the crates and pallets that Durq and the house bots were directing in from the hangar below.

Where's Addie? she asked Meredith, knowing the answer already.

Adelaide is in the engine room, Meredith replied, confirming Nickie's prediction. *We are recalibrating the gravitic drives to account for the full load.*

Nickie was more than grateful for Adelaide's growing skills in engineering. She was doubly glad *somebody* was thinking about shit like that because it wasn't on her agenda.

She headed for the bridge and took her chair to plot the course to QT2.

I don't know how we'd manage this assignment without a Gate drive, Meredith remarked.

Fucking slowly, Nickie shot back. *I could have kissed Barnabas when he told me the Gate drive was part of the ship's upgrades.*

Didn't you? Meredith teased. *I remember you displaying a certain amount of affection to make up for your initial reaction.*

Nickie's mouth twitched. *How are the crew getting on with the loading?*

They have almost finished filling the second cargo bay, the EI replied.

Nickie turned her chair, then hesitated before getting up. *And the investigation into the Silver Line company?*

I found something that might amuse you, Meredith told her. *Technically, you own this base. Or you will when you accept the position.*

Nickie spluttered out loud. *Fuck, for real? What else will I "own?"*

I have compiled a breakdown of Silver Line assets for you to read at your leisure, Meredith informed her. *It's going to take you a while to get through all the gains from Luther Voidrux's generous donation.*

Nickie snickered as she scanned the contents index in her HUD. *Donation, huh? That's one way to frame Bethany Anne's hostile takeover.*

Meredith sniffed. *You don't sound concerned about that.*

Nickie shrugged. *What do I care how we got the company? That sorry excuse for a human being was running his workers into the ground for ever-decreasing pay.*

We'll take care of them, Meredith reassured her. *Have you decided when you will tell the crew the whole story?*

Just as soon as I find my feet, Nickie murmured, turning

her chair as the bridge door cycled open. *I can't tell them what's coming if I don't know myself.*

Whatever is coming, at least we will get there in good time, Meredith segued. *The Gate drive is primed and ready.*

Nickie smiled as the crew piled in. *Light it up, Mere. It's been too long since I got to travel without restrictions.*

Leaving Waystation, Aboard the *Penitent Granddaughter*, Bridge

Nickie and Meredith weren't alone in appreciating their new ability to circumvent the public Gate system.

"No more waiting in line!" Adelaide danced around her station, completely ecstatic over the circle of shimmering light on the viewscreen.

Keen and Grim exchanged a glance and burst into laughter as the ship headed through the Gate.

"What?" Adelaide protested. "I've never been on a ship with its own Gate drive before."

Nickie chuckled. "Don't get too excited, Addie. It just means Barnabas can send us farther out."

Adelaide shimmied back to her seat. "All the more reason to get excited. Don't you want to see what's out there?"

Nickie felt her cheeks burn as the guilt of keeping them in the dark about Barnabas' offer surged. "Sure, as long as we're getting paid for it." This was a choice she had to make for herself. There would be time for everyone else to decide when she had options to offer them.

Keen harrumphed. "This is about duty, and don't you

pretend it's anything else, lass. Don't think I haven't noticed you brooding more than usual."

Grim waved a hand. "It's a Grimes thing. She'll perk up once she finds someone to annoy."

Durq looked around at them. "Have you all gone insane? We're headed into a war zone. Have you heard the stories about the Ooken?" He shuddered. *"Tentacles,* Nickie."

Nickie laughed, leaning back into her captain's chair to put her feet up in their customary place on the console. "We are *not* headed into a warzone. We're not going to see any action at QT2. You can bet with certainty that my Aunt Bethany Anne has the place locked down as tightly as High Tortuga and Devon."

Grim chuckled at that, mandibles clicking out of rhythm. "You haven't forgotten how your aunt gets, then."

Nickie narrowed her eyes at her closest friend apart from Meredith. "Time to spill, Grimmie. We have a while to go before we get to QT2."

Grim shook his head regretfully. "Not yet. We're going to need a long night and that bottle of whiskey I promised." He got to his feet and headed for the door. "Besides, we'll be there in less than an hour. Don't you need to do captain-y stuff?"

Nickie did, but she wasn't going to give Grim the satisfaction.

Keen waved his arms to break the building tension. "Grim's story isn't for us to hear. I have the perfect tale to pass the time."

"You mean 'sea story,'" Adelaide modified.

Keen grinned. "You know you love hearing about my adventures."

"What I would *like*," Adelaide declared, "is a few hours in a spa, a decent meal—"

"I don't see you complain while you're eating it," Grim protested.

Adelaide tilted her head at him. "Not what I meant," she told him. "We eat here all the time. I want to get dressed up and eat somewhere different."

Nickie sat up and rolled her knotted shoulders, ignoring the bickering. Some relaxation would be perfect. What *wasn't* perfect was that her mother and her grandma were aboard the station. "Maybe another time. We're not staying any longer than it takes to drop this cargo."

Adelaide pouted. "What, not even a quick tour?"

Nickie shook her head. "Nope. We're headed straight back to Waystation to pick up our next load. The shipyard needs these materials."

Not a thing to do with avoiding your family? Meredith inquired.

Nickie rolled her eyes mentally. *Fuck my life, Mere. What do you want from me? You asked me to show responsibility and I do, and you're still not fucking happy.*

Meredith sniffed as the Gate ejected the *Penitent Grand-daughter* at their destination. *Emotion has no bearing on my assessment, as you well know. However, I am more than able to spot deflection when I see it.*

Nickie rolled her eyes and focused her attention on the screen. "Are all those big-ass guns on those asteroid pointing at us?"

"Looks that way," Keen replied, nervousness causing his voice to sound hoarse.

"That would be CEREBRO's idea of a joke," Meredith reassured them.

"What the fuck, CEREBRO?" Nickie demanded. "Are all of the EI groups assholes?"

The EI group responsible for the QBBS *Helena* laughed. "Our little joke. Welcome to QT2, Nickie. We'll guide you in from here."

Meredith handed over control of the ship and CEREBRO brought them in safely. "We are currently crossing a live minefield," they informed the crew.

Nickie dragged her gaze from the looming station to look at the space around the *Penitent Granddaughter*. Sure enough, the void was strewn with a thick blanket of smallish spheres. "So why aren't we getting blown up?"

The answer to her question became clear when the spheres ahead of the ship parted, making way for them to reach the shipyard.

Durq and Adelaide were speechless as the *Penitent Granddaughter* nosed its way in to dock at a long external strut between two ships almost the size of the battle station.

Keen let out on the whistle. "The military's sure as shit improved since I was last around. I've never seen anything like them."

Nickie shook her head, the corner of her mouth curling in amusement. "You won't have, Space Marine. Welcome to my Aunt Bethany Anne's world."

CEREBRO guided them in through the translucent barrier, directing the *Granddaughter* to one of the smaller protrusions along the strut. The ship turned and descended as mechanical arms came up from the landing pad to cradle it securely.

Adelaide pouted when they exited the ship and the ground crew moved in to unload the *Penitent Granddaughter* and her precious cargo. "This is going to take a few hours. Can't we go and explore just a little bit?" She clasped her hands in front of her chest. "Please?"

Nickie sighed, coerced by Addie's earnest innocence. "Fine. Just be back by the time the unloading is done. Meredith will keep you informed."

The crew cheered and headed as one for the airlock leading to the station.

"Sure you don't want to come with us?" Grim asked.

Nickie grimaced. "No, I'm good here. Once you've seen one battle station, you've seen them all." She waved them off with a grin. "Go and enjoy yourselves. I'll be just fine."

Nickie was soon in her beloved captain's chair. She laced her hands behind her head and settled back in for an impromptu nap. *Meredith, block my comm and seal the bridge.*

Aren't you going to visit your grandmother? Meredith inquired a bit too snarkily for Nickie's liking.

Nickie closed her eyes. *No.* She waited for the rebuke from Meredith. Again, it didn't come. "Nice to see you're finally learning when to shut up," she muttered.

"Actually, Meredith Nicole Grimes, I muted your EI for the moment."

Holy-shit-my-end-is-here. Nickie opened her eyes and shot out of her chair, almost tripping on her feet. Her fear was forgotten when she saw the love behind her grandmother's anger. "Grandma Jean."

Jean's stern expression melted. She held out her arms, tears in her eyes. "Get your skinny ass over here and give your grandma a hug."

Nickie dashed to cover the few steps between them and all but collided with Jean, squeezing her tightly around the waist. "It's good to see you, Grandma."

Jean held Nickie close for a moment, then stepped back to pin her granddaughter with her patented take-no-shit glare. "How are you really? Barnabas keeps me updated on your work, but you haven't reached out, Nickie."

Nickie shuffled under her grandmother's scrutiny. "I'm sorry. I'm good. Really."

Jean raised an eyebrow. "So... You have just forgotten you have a family who loves you?" Her words were hard, but her tone was soft. "A visit to your mother would put her mind at ease. She worries about you."

Nickie turned away. "Yeah, sure. I believe *you* missed me, and I'm sorry for not coming to visit sooner. But my mom only cares about her damned work."

"Lillian sold her company earlier this year," Jean informed her hotly. "Your mother has done nothing except wait patiently for you to pull your head out of your ass. She's been here for the last few weeks, waiting for you to show up."

"Good for her," Nickie retorted. "She can stay in whatever lab is her home in this place."

"You can't avoid her forever," Jean cautioned. "Seven years and more in exile has changed Lillian as well as you."

Nickie snorted. "Thanks for calling it what it really was." She ran her fingers over the back of her chair as a thought occurred to her. "Was it you who sent Grim? I know someone did. I'm not stupid."

Jean shook her head. "Nothing to do with me or your grandfather." She raised an eyebrow curiously when the expression she expected to see on her granddaughter's face did not appear. "You decided to quit hating your grandad?"

Nickie frowned. "No. Not a bit. But I *have* learned to appreciate the training he gave me—even if he had no business training me from such a young age."

It was Jean's turn to snort. "You're kidding, right? Training you was the one thing we *all* agreed on. You needed it, honey. Boisterous wasn't a strong enough word for you as a child."

"Kids *are* boisterous, Grandma," Nickie argued. "It's not a reason to take them away from their friends."

Jean tilted her head. "Would that be the drug-dealer friends or the illegal fights friends?"

Nickie's mouth dropped open, then she nodded. "I guess I have to take that."

"Damn straight, you do," Jean replied. "You don't learn from your mistakes by pretending they never happened."

Nickie nodded, hearing a truth gained through experience in her grandma's statement. "I guess I wasn't the easiest kid."

Jean patted her cheek gently. "The best ones never are. Come on, I'll show you around the station. Have you met Giselle or Qui'nan yet?"

Nickie's lip curled at the mention of the civilian resources manager. "Um...Giselle, yeah. I might have pissed her off a bit."

Jean raised an eyebrow at Nickie. "Just a bit?"

"Okay, a lot," Nickie admitted. "She wasn't the nicest. What the hell did you tell her about me?"

Jean rolled her eyes. "You can get your behind out of this ship and make it up to her at dinner tonight."

Nickie hesitated. Nobody had said anything about dinner. "We're kind of on a schedule here, Grandma."

Jean turned the Look on her again. "Dinner tonight. Don't argue."

Nickie held up her hands in submission. "Okay, not arguing. Can I get my EI back? I need to tell my crew we're sticking around."

QT2 System, QBBS Helena, Shipyard

Nickie got into the small, chunky-tired vehicle her grandma Jean had arrived in. "These are cute," she commented as the roamer set off.

Jean nodded. "Even cuter is that they drive themselves, so my prodigal granddaughter has time to tell me how she's been all these years."

Nickie cringed. This was exactly why she hadn't wanted to see her grandmother. She didn't want to go through this. "You really want to rehash?"

Jean crossed her arms. "Mmhmm."

Nickie's shoulders dropped. "Look, I'm doing okay now, Grandma. Why does any of the rest of it matter? You're not going to be proud of me if you hear what I did for the first few years."

Jean turned in a seat and placed a hand on Nickie's cheek. "Baby girl, I already know what you did and where you did it. I want to hear what you went through, not what

Barnabas managed to get from the authorities in the places you passed through."

Nickie's face burned beneath Jean's palm. She looked down, unable to meet her grandmother's piercing gaze. "It's not news. I was pissed."

Jean snickered. "You are *so* like your grandfather, it's not even funny." She dried her damp hand on her knee. "I'm not judging you, Merry. You paid for your mistakes. I just hope to God you've learned from them."

Nickie turned away and leaned her head against the window, looking out at nothing. "I have," she managed eventually. "I'm trying to be a better person, Grandma."

"You were always a good person, Merry." Jean reached out and tilted Nickie's face toward her with her finger. "You just needed to start making the right choices again. You're doing that, and I'm proud of you."

Nickie pulled away and turned back to the window, her eyes stinging. "I'm doing my best."

"That's all I ever expect," Jean told her gently.

The roamer pulled up in a charging alcove and Jean led the way down the corridor, which was clearly residential, judging by the warm decor.

Nickie took in the soft colors. "This doesn't look much like Aunt Bethany Anne's taste."

Jean shook her head, opening one of the docks. "This was Giselle's station from the construction stage."

Nickie nodded, already done with the subject. She followed her grandmother into her quarters. "No Grandad?" she inquired, seeing none of John's belongings around. "He *is* okay, isn't he?"

"He's out there with Bethany Anne," Jean explained. "I'm based here full-time. He visits when he has a chance."

Nickie decided that being pleased she had her grandma all to herself wasn't a bad thing. She threaded an arm through Jean's and grinned. "Thanks for coming to get me, Grandma."

Jean snickered. "You're a Grimes. You sure as hell weren't going to come out of your cave by yourself."

QT2 System, QBBS *Helena*, Main Concourse

Adelaide wandered along arm in arm with Keen. She took the last bite from the mystery food on a stick she held in her free hand and looked up at the former Space Marine. "Look at all this! It's more than impressive." She waved the bare stick at the finger of rock standing proudly in the center of the concourse to illustrate her point. "Let's go see what that is."

Keen mumbled his acquiescence through a mouthful of his snack and allowed Adelaide to drag him over to get a closer look at the enormous polished black stone Adelaide had pointed out.

Keen paused to read the plaque on the railing that prevented visitors from falling into the "fish" pond encircling the engraved stone. "It's a memorial." He lowered his head in respect for the lost, giving his silent thanks for their service.

"That's so sad." Adelaide joined Keen and the others paying their respects, quietly reading the small plaque attached to the railing in front of her. "All these lives lost."

She turned to Keen, sadness clouding her usually bright face. "What we're doing now is important. It has meaning."

Keen placed his hand on her shoulder. "It does, Addie. Just focus on that, not on lives that are already gone." He indicated the two-legged Yollin by the base of the memorial, painstakingly adding names to the bottom of the list with a hand-held laser device and a pot of gold paint. "You'll see more names than that before this war is done. Best thing we can do is keep up with our delivery schedule. Keep the shipyard supplied."

"Shipyards," a voice came from behind them.

Adelaide and Keen turned as one to the speaker, the blonde woman Nickie had taken exception to earlier.

"Giselle Foxton-Thomas," she reminded them. "Our Queen has ordered two more shipyards built. Fleet orders have been updated to reflect the changes to the shipping schedule."

Keen carefully kept his face neutral. "Has our captain been informed, ma'am?" he asked.

"She has," Giselle replied coolly, choosing not to mention that she'd had CEREBRO pass along the orders through Nickie's EI so she didn't have to speak to Jean's intimidating granddaughter again.

Keen dipped his head. "We'd better get going, ma'am. Our captain will be expecting us."

Giselle nodded, and Keen took Adelaide's arm and propelled her in the direction of the elevators before Adelaide said something they would all regret later.

"Nickie isn't expecting us," Adelaide protested once they were out of hearing range. She pulled her arm from

Keen's grip and put her hands on her hips. "What's the deal?"

Keen waved for her to keep walking. "Nickie wasn't expecting to have her assignment altered without being asked, and she certainly won't have taken it well, coming from Giselle."

Adelaide grimaced and hurried to keep pace with him. "I didn't consider it from that perspective."

Open Space, Aboard the *Penitent Granddaughter*, APA

Nickie laid into the punchbag without mercy. "Stupid. Fucking. *Grrrr!*"

She supposed she was glad of the APA Barnabas had had installed on the mid deck. It was a sharp improvement on the makeshift workout area she'd set up in the old cargo bay, which was now filled with stacked coils of metal and plastic. Nickie had a punching bag that didn't need to be repaired every time she went to town on it, and a fully equipped APA to put it in.

I'm sorry, Meredith repeated for the fourth time. *I can hardly refuse to take communications from Mrs. Foxton-Thomas.*

Nickie growled and started in on the bag again. *It's not your fault, Mere. It's that bitch, Giselle. I told you she didn't like me. Shame I don't own this place too. I could have her reassigned to bio-waste management. Why can't my handler be some dark-eyed hottie with muscles on his muscles?*

Because we live in the real world, Meredith countered. *You have another chance to make an attempt to be pleasant at dinner this evening.*

Whose side are you on? Nickie switched her stance and began adding elbow and knee strikes to her repertoire. *If you ask me, she's too uptight to deal with someone who has no time for all the political "I hate you, but I'm going to smile as if I don't," nicey-nicey bistok shit people like her love so much. No, thanks.*

Meredith snickered. *Her opinion was hardly helped along by the less than stellar first impression you made. Besides, I think you were rude enough that I don't blame her for avoiding further conversation with you.*

Nickie snorted. *What do you know? Your personality is made from ones and zeros.*

Meredith sniffed. *At least I'm consistent.*

Nickie muted Meredith and got back to working on the punching bag. She lost track of time, only surfacing from the zone she'd dropped into when Keen and Adelaide entered the APA.

Nickie looked them over, smirking at their flushed appearances. "What the hell has you two running in here like the apocalypse just landed?"

Keen deflated visibly. "You already know?"

Nickie nodded. "Mmhmm."

Adelaide shrugged. "You're dealing with the changes to our route a lot better than we thought you would."

Nickie burst out laughing. "Oh, I'm plenty pissed, but I'm not running the show. If we want to contribute, this is the role we have to fill." She shuddered. "Ugh, I think I just did the sensible thing again. What's wrong with me?" She began stripping the tape from her wrists and hands. "Look, none of you are contracted. You can leave anytime you like."

Adelaide folded her arms and gave Nickie a stern look. "Let me guess. This is the part where you tell us you don't need us anyway?"

Nickie smirked, shaking her head. "Actually, it's the part where I tell you I value you as friends and as my crew. And that I'd miss the hell out of you if any of you decided to leave, but I'd do my best not to be a dick about it if you chose that way."

Meredith cut in over the speakers. "That's progress."

Nickie glared around at vaguely speaker-height. "I muted you for a reason. You were annoying the shit out of me with your nagging."

Adelaide covered her mouth with her hands. "You can *do* that?"

Nickie snickered. "She's been annoying you, too?"

Adelaide turned bright red.

"I'll take that as a yes," Nickie concluded. "Sometimes we just need to work things out for ourselves, Meredith."

"Well, I never." Meredith huffed. "If nobody wants my advice—"

"It's not that we don't want it," Adelaide explained. "We just don't want it in the form of 'I told you so' all the time."

Meredith's tone turned to ice. "Maybe when we return to High Tortuga, I will join CEREBRO. How would you like that?"

Nickie rolled her eyes and un-muted Meredith. *Is that better?*

It's a start, Meredith conceded.

High Tortuga, Space Fleet Base, Nickie's Office

Nickie entered her office and headed straight for her desk, growling at the protest her chair made when she flung herself down on it.

Her grandma was going to be pissed that she'd skipped out on dinner, but the thought of playing nice with Giselle was a little more than she could stomach right now. Besides, she knew Jean well enough to guess that the awkwardness factor would have been quadrupled by the presence of her mother, whether Lillian was there or not.

There was no way she was going to talk to her mother. Meredith, her grandmother, and even her uncle could try to manipulate her into doing so all they liked. They weren't going to get anywhere.

She took her ball out of the top drawer of the desk and began her old comforting ritual of bouncing it off the wall and catching it while she processed her emotions.

At least they had been open about their intentions. She valued Grim, and she believed he was there to look out for her, but she knew for sure now that their first meeting hadn't been an accident, thanks to her grandma.

Nickie's careful questioning of Grim on the way back from QT2 had helped her check off almost every name on her list of suspects, leaving just one possibility. Her instinct to wring it out of him was countered by the secret she had, however.

She couldn't exactly lose her shit with her Aunt Tabitha.

Thinking of Tabitha reminded Nickie she hadn't read her aunt's last message. She opened it in her HUD and took her time reading about Todd's latest exploits, how Tabitha's students were—or weren't—progressing, and other anecdotes about her life on Devon.

Nickie lingered over her reply, finding it difficult to talk to Tabitha when she felt like she could only say a fraction of what was in her mind. She supposed her guilt about keeping Barnabas' offer from the crew had a part in it, but not so much as to cause the nausea that rose in her stomach when she considered that Grim's reason for sticking around might be down to duty and not any real feeling for her.

Why do you take your reply so seriously? Meredith enquired.

Why do you always butt in when I'm thinking? Nickie retorted. She closed the message window, the moment gone. *I hope you interrupted me for a reason?*

Meredith noted that she was lucky. Surely the original Meredith would have gone completely insane dealing with all of the emotional backlash she had taken from Nickie in the time since she had been reactivated. *I remember when you were so much sweeter than this.*

Nickie snorted. *Yeah? Well, it's getting to the point where I can't remember when you weren't this fucking chatty.*

Meredith took Nickie's barbs with grace. *I'll leave you to think. But I did believe you would like to know that Barnabas is on his way here.*

Nickie threw the ball again. *Dammit. When is he getting here?*

The door opened, and Barnabas caught the ball on its rebound. "Right now, and I don't have to be a mind reader to know you're not happy to see me. Kindly keep your office decorations to yourself this time, if it's not too much trouble."

Nickie glared at him. "Why should I be happy to see

you? Why are you even here? Aren't you missing out on conspiring with my grandma to get me to go and see my mother?" She folded her arms, waiting for an answer to any of the questions she'd just rapid-fired at him.

Barnabas chuckled, making his way to the guest chair opposite Nickie's desk. "That sounds an awful lot like paranoia," he cautioned, getting comfortable. "You should access your EI's therapy functions."

Nickie glared harder. "That would be totally great as an idea—if she weren't one of the main fucking conspirators."

Barnabas folded his hands in his lap, remaining calm. Nickie reminded him so much of Tabitha in her younger years, it was almost painful to see her incomplete. "Do you see a correlation between everyone who is attempting to persuade you to make amends with Lillian?"

Nickie's face was beginning to ache from all the scowling. "You're all giant pains in my ass?" she shot back. "I'm not going to speak to that woman, and none of you can make me. What the fuck is this? Another intervention?"

She got up and stormed out of her own office before Barnabas could say another word. She was done with everybody putting in their two credits' worth on how she should run her damned life.

Nickie's anger ran out before long.

She found herself back in her quarters on the base, out of steam and a little bit deflated. She was well aware of how bratty it was to run to her room every time she heard something she didn't like, but it was either that or find a way to pay another repair bill like the one for their office doors.

Meredith was unusually silent, making Nickie wonder

if even her digital companion was upset with her. She was too angry to care. Still, she was here now, and she had a message to finish writing.

Nickie flopped down on her couch—the only piece of furniture in the center of an ocean of shoes and clothing—and opened her HUD. She noticed a new message icon and opened it, expecting to find some rant or another from Grim about the supply chains in her message box.

It was another message from Tabitha.

Hey, Trouble,

No reply? Guess you haven't been doing much lately. Funny, because Barnabas told me about his offer. You don't want to tell me about it? Hopefully, you will get to see some of Devon soon.

Nickie winced at the mention of the topic she'd skated carefully around in their messages so far. "If you only knew," she murmured, wondering if her aunt's apparent relaxed attitude had more to do with keeping her at arm's length to avoid the real discussion.

She read on.

I told you a little about the situation with the Bakas. These kids are driving me crazy. And by kids, I mean the bunch of grown-ass adults I'm stuck training as my punishment for lying about helping you. You know by now it was me and Pete who sent Grim, right? I hope you're not mad at him, since he cares about you. So does your mom. You two aren't talking, but I bet you're getting enough crap from Jean and Barnabas about that.

So, anyway. These numbnuts. One of them reminded me of someone. I couldn't think who, but it came to me

as I was writing this. Remember Zinshei? Blast from the past, right?

I hear Todd and Pete getting home. Don't leave me hanging too long for a reply, okay?

T xoxo

Nickie felt no better for being reminded of the trip she had taken with Tabitha back when she was fourteen. Her main recollection of it was her mother freaking out when they got back, then handing Nickie over to her Grandad John for a heavy course of his boot-camp-style discipline.

She spent a while wandering around her living area, picking up after herself for no reason other than she'd bought so much clothing since she came to live on a planet with half-decent shopping that she had to arrange it all, sleep on it, or swim through to the bedroom.

A smile touched Nickie's lips as she settled under her covers. It hadn't been the worst trip. Tabitha had given her a taste of what it was to be a Ranger, something she had begged for since, well, forever.

The memory played through Nickie's mind as she drifted to sleep, taking her back to what she now saw was the moment that shaped her most as a person.

The first time she'd seen what it was to live out from under anyone's rules.

Devon, First City, The Hexagon, Underground Hangar

Tabitha entered the hangar from the elevator, Todd's version-umpteen Pod-crib bobbing gently behind her. It was less a crib these days and more a miniature multifunction "racing" Pod, which, thanks to Tabitha and Peter, had dual controls and a sleep mode for when their little tyke had tuckered himself out. Like now.

She tiptoed aboard the ship and crept along the corridor to the bridge, hoping against hope she could get them underway without waking Todd.

No such luck, Todd stirred just as Tabitha left the elevator on the bridge level. He opened his big brown eyes and looked around in confusion. "Where are we?" he asked, rubbing the sleep from his eyes.

Tabitha leaned over and released him from his restraints. "Hey, *mi ángel*. Look who woke up at last! We're aboard *Achronyx*."

Todd smiled and lifted his pudgy hands. "Can I get down?"

"Sure thing," Tabitha told him. She lowered the Pod to the ground, and Todd clambered over the side before dashing off toward the bridge.

Tabitha set the Pod to park itself in an alcove and headed after him. "Ready to take a trip with *Achronyx*?" she called. He would tire himself out again if she let him run free, just like he had on the way here.

Todd ran back to Tabitha and gripped her hand tightly, panting slightly from his exertions. "Yeah! We going far? To see Gramma?"

Tabitha nodded. "Yeah, honey. We're visiting Aunt Lillian, as well as Grandma Jean."

Her son's face lost a little bit of its shine at the mention of his aunt. "Is she gonna kiss me?" He shrugged and smiled. "She pretends to be grumpy, but she's not."

Tabitha smiled, in love with the way her son saw the best in everyone. She wondered for a second if Nickie had changed her stance on her mom since she messaged last. Probably not, but Tabitha had a couple more tricks up her sleeve yet.

Like this visit.

"Is Kevin there?" Todd asked.

Tabitha picked him up and nuzzled his soft cheek. "Probably not, but we'll see him soon. Okay?" She turned a circle, enjoying the peal of laughter Todd gave as she spun him around. "What would you like to do while Mama and Achronyx get us on our way?"

Todd pointed at the corner of the bridge she'd had remodeled as his play area. "Wanna make a...demon." He waved his arms around to demonstrate. "With a swishy tail and big, *big* teeths. She'll scare Aunt Lillian so she doesn't want to kiss me."

Tabitha chuckled and set him down on the thick matting. "That's worth a try, but I never saw anything scare your Aunt Lillian. Show me when you're done?"

Todd nodded in that exaggerated way small children do, then got to digging out his modeling putty while Tabitha got to work.

Tabitha glanced at Todd a few moments later, smiling at the energy he was putting into beating his lump of modeling putty into submission. Becoming a mother had given her an understanding she hadn't had before. It had changed her. Not too much, she hoped, but enough for her to see her hubris in jumping in thinking to fix Nickie like a bit of faulty code.

The weight of unfulfilled duty she'd carried since failing Nickie was a little lighter these days. She'd fucked up, but everything she'd done since to make up for that failure was starting to bear fruit.

"Whoever said hindsight was a beautiful thing had no freaking clue what they were talking about," she muttered softly.

She knew exactly when she'd missed her chance.

The name "Zinshei" had been rattling around in her head ever since she'd last written to Nickie and worked out it was the wily Noel-ni Fu'Ksi reminded her of. The memory of that mission had been popping up whenever she least expected it since then, growing in texture and clarity each time it replayed and compounding the mistake she'd made.

It didn't matter to Tabitha what Pete, Bethany Anne, or anyone else told her. *She* was responsible, whether or not she'd realized it at the time.

After all, she was the one who'd exposed Nickie to the dark side.

High Tortuga, Spaceport (ten years previously)

S.O.S.

That was all Lillian's message had said.

So, of course, Tabitha was on her way from High Tortuga to the *Meredith Reynolds*. She had business to take care of for Stephen regarding Lerr'ek on her return, but she wasn't about to turn down Lillian's plea for help.

I still don't see why we have to take this...junker, Achronyx bitched as Tabitha approached the ship they were taking.

Tabitha looked the generic ship over. *There's nothing wrong with it. It's got everything your ship has.* She scanned the specs in her HUD as the ramp began to extend from the hatch above her head. *Well, mostly.*

Achronyx made a raspberry. *It's got no style. I like my stripe. It gives out a certain message.*

Tabitha snickered at the AI's vanity. *What, that there's a crazy-ass Ranger coming for you? We're completely illegal in the Federation, Achronyx. That's not really gonna hit the subtle vibe we're going for. Sorry, it's the natural look for you until we get back.*

You're not even a bit sorry, the AI grumped. *This isn't fair. How would you like to wear that Torcellan disguise again? For weeks?*

Um, no. Tabitha flicked her hair back and headed up the ramp. *But you get to ride along with me, so you know, it's not a complete suckfest.*

I wish I had eyes so I could roll them, Achronyx stated flatly. *But we're clear to depart, so I might as well stop prolonging the agony.*

Tabitha rolled hers for them both. *You're such an ass, Achronyx.*

Right back at you, he replied. *But you're my ass, so it's okay.*

Tabitha wished there was a way to give him the finger that wasn't essentially just flipping herself off for anyone around to see. *I could have my chip fixed so you're stuck in the ship all the time again if you like?*

Achronyx snickered. *Did I mention that those pants look really good on you?*

Tabitha smirked as she boarded the ship. *Suck-up.*

Yollin Space

They exited the Gate and joined the long, spiraling line at the *Meredith Reynolds*. She finally docked a few hours later using a fake ID and made her way through the station to Lillian's home, keeping herself covered under a heavy cloak.

It was past midnight station time when she reached the

pleasantly-appointed quarters on the residential level where Lillian and Merry lived.

Tabitha frowned at seeing the lights still on despite the late hour. *I was feeling bad about waking Lillian up,* she murmured as she approached the house. *But I don't think that will be a problem.*

She may be working, Achronyx supplied.

Probably, Tabitha agreed. She knocked lightly on the door in case Lillian had just forgotten to switch the light off.

There was movement inside the house, and a few moments later, Lillian answered the door somewhat hesitantly. She peered at Tabitha's covered face. "Who is it?"

Tabitha flicked her hood up for a brief instant. "It's just me. Sorry it's so late. I had to get here the slow way."

Lillian relaxed visibly. "It's okay, I was up anyway. I'm so glad to see you, I thought you were..." She motioned for Tabitha to enter the house. "Never mind. Come in, and I'll fix us some tea."

Tabitha followed Lillian to the kitchen, wondering why Lillian was so calm if she was in the middle of a crisis. "What's the emergency?" she asked, taking a seat at the breakfast bar.

Lillian didn't answer right away. She bustled around at the sink with her back to Tabitha. "Are you hungry? I can make you something."

Tabitha wasn't fooled for a second. "You're trying to distract me. Who were you expecting when I arrived?"

Lillian turned around and floundered, waving her hands as she tried to find a place to begin.

The front door slammed open and shut.

"I'm *home*," Merry yelled. "Are you *happy* now?" The thumping of her feet on the stairs was followed by her bedroom door slamming.

Lillian lifted a hand in the general direction of her daughter's room. "That's my emergency."

Tabitha's jaw almost hit the breakfast bar. "What the hell was that all about?" She'd never heard that edge in her niece's voice before. "I'm not going to lie, I'm shocked."

Lillian leaned back against the counter, her shoulders slumping. "That's Merry these days, Aunt Tabitha. She's going off the rails, and I don't know what to do to fix her." She covered her face with her hands and dissolved into tears. "She started hanging around with these kids… I don't know, she wasn't doing great in school before she met them. Arguing with me about everything, getting into fights."

Tabitha narrowed her eyes and pointed at the seat opposite. "I can't believe this. Why am I only just hearing about it? Sit here and tell me everything. What started it?"

Lillian did as Tabitha ordered. "I don't *know* anything! She doesn't talk to me anymore, and when she does, all I get from her are grunts and one-word replies."

Tabitha wasn't hearing anything out of the ordinary. "So she's rebelling like every other teenager, then." She shrugged. "Just let her dye her hair whatever color and get a few piercings behind your back. She'll soon get over it."

Lillian snorted. "If it were just normal teenage rebellion, I could work with her. It's her anger. It's like one minute, she's my sweet Merry, and the next she's screaming and breaking the furniture." Lillian shook her head, fresh tears forming in her eyes. "I'm scared, Tabitha. I want my Merry, and I feel like the more I try to reach her, the more I'm losing her. She's so *angry* all the time. She's been kicked out of school for fighting. She wrecked a boy's knee."

Tabitha patted Lillian's arm. "We can get her some help. It's not great, but it's not the end of the world, Lillian. Merry can come back from this with a fresh start at a new school."

Lillian shook her head. "That's what I thought. I've taken her to a number of counselors, but she refused to speak to any of them. This is her third school this year." She looked exhausted to Tabitha, her words barely a whisper. "That's why I reached out. You're the only one she'll listen to."

Tabitha sighed, taking in Lillian's dark-ringed eyes and the brittle edge to her voice. She decided she could handle something smaller than the restructuring of High Tortuga. Stephen would understand. She swept Lillian's hair back from her face where it had fallen. "You need a break. I'm gonna take Merry with me for a day or two. I have a thing she can help with. Sleep, get your strength up."

Lillian shook her head. "I can't ask you to do that."

Tabitha wasn't there to take no for an answer. "You're not asking. I'm offering."

Lillian dropped her head onto her arms and raised a tired hand. "Then I accept gratefully. Thank you." Something made her open an eye. "What 'thing?'"

Tabitha waved a hand unconcernedly. "Nothing Merry isn't trained for." She got to her feet, then paused before leaving. "Get some sleep, and meet me at my ship in the morning."

Lillian acquiesced with a nod.

"That's my girl." Tabitha smiled. "It's going to be okay, okay?" She leaned over and kissed Lillian's forehead, then slipped out into the darkened corridor, wondering where the hell she was going to pull a mission from that was suitable to take a teenager along.

The next morning

Lillian arrived at Tabitha's ship an hour later than planned with a sullen Merry in tow. They both looked tired, which Tabitha thought was to be expected after the time Merry had gotten home last night.

Tabitha waved her niece aboard, wanting to speak to Lillian before they left. "That thing I mentioned. It's a child exploitation ring. These scumbags have been luring in street kids with the promise of food and shelter, then forcing them to fight for entertainment."

Lillian's lip curled. "How could anyone do that to children?" She looked at Merry's retreating back with concern etched in the lines around her eyes and mouth. "Are you sure taking her there is a good idea?"

Tabitha nodded as confidently as she felt. "I told you I'd do my best to set her straight again. A short, sharp shock never fails."

Lillian still did not look convinced. "I'm not sure. She's still just a child."

"It worked for me," Tabitha assured her, touching her fingers to the back of her head. "Literally. It also worked for Pete, and for the twins when Gabrielle and Eric went through this with them. Remember when they decided to take a joyride around the outside of the station?"

Lillian's mouth quirked at the memory. "I remember that. It was all Jamie's fault. It was very quiet without them when Aunt Bethany Anne made them work until they'd paid for the mess they made when they crashed."

Tabitha snickered. "See? It worked for them, and every other unruly teenager there has ever been. Actions have consequences, Lillian. Merry's got to learn that sometime."

Lillian glanced at the ship again. "I know. Just make sure she doesn't get hurt too badly, okay?"

"I won't let her out of my sight," Tabitha promised. "And you've got nothing to worry about. She's got her training and her nanocytes. She'll do fine."

Lillian frowned. "She doesn't have enough nanocytes to stop her from dying from a serious injury." She put her hand on Tabitha's forearm. "Aunt Tabitha, I'm only allowing this because I don't know what else to do. It goes against every instinct I have as a mother to let you put my daughter at risk, but she needs to learn what life she'll have if she keeps going down this self-destructive path."

Tabitha placed her hand on top of Lillian's. "It's better we show her now, than her getting dragged down that road later on by some lowlife she's hanging with who makes the lifestyle look attractive. Don't worry. I won't let anything bad happen."

Lillian nodded. "I know you won't."

Tabitha patted Lillian's hand and headed up the ramp onto the ship.

Where's Merry? she asked Achronyx once they were underway.

She is currently decimating your food stores, he replied.

Oh. That's just...great.

Tabitha headed for the galley at a run before Merry found her stash of difficult-to-procure munchies. She found her niece shoulders deep in the cold storage, nowhere near her chocolate.

Merry turned when Tabitha entered and froze with her arms full of sandwich ingredients. "Hey... I was hungry. You don't mind, do you?"

This was a complete turnaround from the screaming banshee who'd blown into the house a few hours ago. Tabitha decided to make the best of it. "Great idea, Trouble. You should get your strength up for where we're going."

Merry looked at Tabitha skeptically. "Where are we going? It can't be anywhere interesting, or my mom wouldn't have let me go."

Tabitha came over and took the sandwich fixings from her. "You're gonna be pretty surprised when we get there if that's your thinking." She found herself grinning despite her earlier resolve and the promise she'd made to be the disciplinarian.

She fully intended for Merry to get her lesson, but it was just so damn *good* that she was old enough to come on a mission with her at last. Couldn't she make the lesson enjoyable?

She knew she should be exerting real discipline right now, but it had never really been her thing. Besides, Merry was a free spirit like her, and she was fun Aunt Tabitha.

Everyone knew *that.*

Merry was done waiting. "Where are we going?" she pressed. "You look like you just won something."

Tabitha winked. "Oh, nowhere special. Just a fight club."

Merry's jaw dropped. "You're *shitting* me. Like a real one? The kind you don't talk about?"

Tabitha's lips twitched. "Bo-*ring*." She pointed at the galley floor. "Down and give me a hundred while I make these sandwiches. Seriously, you should at least make it a good curse if you're going to get corrected for it anyway." She shook her head, grinning as Merry dropped to the floor. "All those different schools you've been to this year, and *that's* the best you can do? Weak, Kid."

Merry looked up from her push-ups. "What do *you* know about that?"

Noel-ni Colony Planet

Tabitha sort of regretted not having the *Achronyx* with her. Maybe the intimidation factor wasn't overkill in this situation.

I told you so, Achronyx grumbled.

She rolled her eyes and muted him. He wouldn't approve of any of this next part anyway. The already seedy mining outpost had gone somewhat farther downhill since she'd last patrolled this way. She could see him bitching the whole time about *this* not being suitable for a child, and *that* being too violent for a child to participate in.

Tabitha kept a firm grip on Merry's arm as they made their way past a succession of bars, a couple of mercantiles, and a brothel on their way to the address she'd been given by the local authorities. "Eyes to yourself," she told Merry, slapping away a red-gloved hand that came snaking out of a window the teen peered into as they passed.

Merry pulled her head back and stuck closer to Tabitha

as they walked. "What's the deal here? Are you Rangering again in secret?"

Tabitha shook her head. "As far as anyone is concerned, we're just two citizens looking to cut loose away from watchful eyes. This is strictly a vigilante gig, no Federation backup. There's been a concerning report about missing children, and the local cops asked the Federation to send someone to investigate. The Federation, meaning Lance, outsourced the investigation to Barnabas because this planet isn't part of the Federation, and here we are."

Tabitha would have taken the assignment even if she hadn't needed the mission as an excuse to teach Merry a lesson. Nothing sickened her more than slavery except the slavery of kids.

And the Skaines, of course, but everyone hated *their* mercenary asses, so it wasn't anything special.

Besides, if the reports were accurate, the owner was an old acquaintance of hers. Curiosity would not allow anything other than her full attention.

Merry stuck close by as they approached the building. "This place is a dump. It doesn't even look like a fight club."

Tabitha winked. "Have you ever been inside a fight club before?"

Merry scowled. "Well, no. But it looks like a gross old bar from out here. It hasn't even got a name." She shuffled from one foot to another. "So, can I get in a fight while we're here?"

Tabitha raised an eyebrow. "I'm not sure which way this is going to go down, so you stay by my side and keep your mouth shut unless I ask you to speak." She fished around in a pouch on her belt and tossed the three small, spherical drones she retrieved into the air. "That's how rookies stay alive."

"What if something goes down?" Merry countered, looking up at the drones. "Can I fight then?"

Tabitha paused outside the door to the building. "If it goes south," she let the moment drag out to make sure her niece was paying attention, "you *still* stay by my side. You remember your training, and you do your best not to get killed."

Merry's already pale face went grayer. "Killed?"

Tabitha nodded matter-of-factly and pulled the door open. "Mmhmm. Just stay aware, and remember everything your Grandad John taught you. Keep your mouth shut, and you'll be fine."

Nickie ransacked her mind for scraps of the lessons she'd done her best not to put any effort into as they entered the foyer, the décor of which screamed "no one gives a shit here," and crossed to the admissions booth.

Tabitha swished her ponytail and flashed her brightest grin at the aging Noel-ni behind the barrier. "Zinshei, great to see you again!"

Zinshei was nowhere near as pleased to see Tabitha as she was to see him. "Ranger." He made the word sound like it tasted bad. "Or should I say, ex-Ranger?" He looked at Merry with barely concealed interest. "Have things gotten so bad for you since the Empire was dissolved?"

Tabitha shrugged. "What can I say? Hard times call for a readjustment of moral lines. I heard from Kibos that you're running something interesting downstairs, and I need fast credits."

Zinshei narrowed his eyes, his whiskers twitching as he

ELL LEIGH CLARKE & MICHAEL ANDERLE

searched for the lie in her words. "Don't we all? I have to say, I wouldn't have pegged you for someone whose tastes ran this way. I have an all-comers event at the end of the next cycle. You should come back then. I'll cut you a side deal, and we'll clean up."

Tabitha waved her hands as she spoke. "Oh, sure. But I have this kid here now, and you know, kids just *love* fighting. Am I right?" She turned and winked at Merry. "In fact, these days you just can't *stop* them from fighting, can you, Trouble?" She jerked her head to indicate that Merry should reply.

"Oh. Um, yeah..." Merry stuttered, caught off-guard. "Love me a good fight. Can't get enough of that um...fighting," she finished awkwardly.

Tabitha repressed her snicker. The child was so far out of her comfort zone, it was almost funny. Just how Tabitha wanted her. "See?" she told the Noel-ni. "She's practically begging. C'mon, Zinshei. For old times' sake?"

Zinshei dropped the thin veneer of civility he'd been holding. "Fuck you." He sneered as he pushed two passes through the barrier and pressed a button behind the counter. "Far be it from me to deprive someone so eager to take part," he replied, a sly expression pulling his lip back to reveal yellowed canine teeth. "Straight through to the back. Show the big guy your passes to access the underground level."

The door clicked open, spilling abrasive electronic music into the foyer. Tabitha grabbed Merry by the sleeve and pulled her through the door into the club, keeping up appearances.

Merry turned to Tabitha with outrage the moment they were covered by the music. "He's lying to us."

Of course, he is, Tabitha soothed. *He's a scumbag, and that's what scumbags do. Don't worry. Old Zinshei might think he's got us, but he's got a nasty surprise coming. Come on, this way.*

The legitimate part of the establishment was packed with people who couldn't afford the illicit entertainments underground. They were still betting, on everything from naked females wrestling in mud to animals fighting inside cages.

Merry pointed out an elaborate construction on one of the tables that was surrounded by gamblers in a heightened state of excitement. "What's going on there?"

Tabitha shrugged, mistaking Merry's reaction to the crowd as fear. *Mental communication now we're in a potentially hostile environment.*

Merry burst out laughing, drawing attention from a few of the people at the table. Rough wasn't the word to describe the degenerate clientele the club drew, but she wasn't scared like Tabitha had thought she was. *Potentially? Meredith is going batshit in here!* Her eyes continued darting over the crowd as Tabitha pushed a path through for them. *She's telling me everyone here is wanted for something or other disgusting and that I need to leave for my own safety.*

Tabitha shrugged. *This is the kind of disgusting place that attracts that kind of assholes. Do you want to see what they're betting on? I'm curious,* she admitted, pushing through to peer over the side of the run.

"Ew!" Merry cried. "They're racing *bugs?*" She held up her hands when the gamblers at the table turned to look at

ELL LEIGH CLARKE & MICHAEL ANDERLE

her. "Sorry," she mumbled, rolling her eyes as she backed away.

They got back to making their way through the crowd, Tabitha in the lead.

Okay, this is officially the worst place I've ever been, Merry bitched when she had to swerve to avoid being crushed by a larger alien for the third time.

Tabitha chuckled. *This is no universe for a short woman. You have to make your own way.* She demonstrated, slicing through the crowd like they weren't even there. *You make it clear you own the space, and it magically empties in front of you.*

Merry flashed a doubtful look but didn't argue, since they were almost at the back now. She gulped at the sight of the Shrillexian guard. *I've never seen so many muscles on anyone except Grandad or Uncle Scott. That must be the "big guy" the Noel-ni told you about.*

The crowd spat them out near the door the Shrillexian was guarding. Tabitha sauntered up to him and held up the passes. She pointed at the door. "This way, right?"

The guard nodded respectfully and opened the door. "Enjoy your evening, valued guest," he intoned flatly as they passed.

Merry kept to Tabitha's heels as they entered a torch-lit corridor leading to a rickety-looking mining elevator. "Yeah, that doesn't look like it's going to send us plummeting to our deaths at all."

Tabitha made a face. "Nah. Killing off your high-rollers doesn't make for good business." She pointed at the floor. "Look, carpet. That proves it. C'mon."

Merry followed her into the elevator, then Tabitha

pulled down the door and set the car to descend to the lower level.

There was another stupid-big Shrillexian at the bottom. He inspected their passes and let them out.

Merry was quiet as they left the elevator. Tabitha noted that her eyes began darting around the roughly constructed underground arena the moment they stepped out. She knew better than to praise her niece for what was second nature, but John would be glad to know his battle to train her hadn't been a waste. The kid was sharp. *Just for fun, what do you see?*

Merry frowned lightly. *I dunno. Um...there's another exit in the back, and there's a couple of beams over there that look like they're gonna give way if someone breathes on them too hard.* She relaxed a little, getting into it. *There's a guard on the cage. Three more on that fat old Yollin over there with the lollipop in his mouth. Meredith's telling me pretty much everyone here is armed. Should we call for backup?*

Tabitha winked, her own assessment of the situation complete. *Sweetie, we don't need backup. But yeah, I'm going to call the local authorities in to round up the gamblers. Do you still want that fight? It's gonna take them a while to get down here.*

Merry grinned, nodding at the Yollin. *Is he gonna die from diabetes if he makes it out of here alive?*

Tabitha suddenly had an appreciation of what it was like to be Barnabas. *Yollins don't get diabetes. How the hell do you even know what that is?*

Merry shrugged. *Dunno. Probably school or something.*

Tabitha smirked. *So you have been paying attention at least some of the time you've been there.*

Merry chose not to reply to that. Her gaze was frozen on the cage in the center of the room. *What's the plan here?*

Tabitha hesitated. *Well, that's where it gets a bit sticky. I didn't have confirmation about the fights until we got down here. I still need proof to give the local authorities before they can get clearance to raid the place.* She indicated the tiny drones above their heads with a look.

Merry's hands clenched and unclenched as she stared at the currently empty cage. *Oh, duh. You want to use me as bait.*

Tabitha winked. *Distraction. It's a classic Ranger tactic. You have to make the most of what you have because it's just you and whatever situation you find yourself in. I mean, it would be nice if just once what the assholes wanted was universal peace, tacos, and an end to injustice everywhere. But no, usually what they want is slaves in some form or another. You've always wanted to be a Ranger, right? This is what Rangers do. Or did.* She waved a hand. *Whatever.*

Merry shrugged and looked away. *Don't know. I guess so? It doesn't matter what I wanted when I was a kid. It's not gonna happen anyway, is it? There are no Rangers anymore.*

Tabitha hid her reaction. *You want to fight, I'm going to get you a fight.* She diverted from her path and headed toward the fat Yollin, who was surrounded by desperate gamblers, all waving their wrist-holos to get their bets in before the impending match began.

The Yollin took an involuntary step back with his rear legs when he saw Tabitha striding toward him. His guards closed in, sensing danger.

Tabitha grinned and waved her own wrist holo along with the rest of the bettors. She bumped the others away to make a space, which she pulled Merry into. "Whoo! Great atmosphere!" she told the Yollin. "Where do I take my fighter?"

The Yollin recovered quickly. "Apologies. We don't get too many humans all the way out here. I thought you were Ranger Two for a second."

Tabitha's mouth twitched. "Wouldn't that be funny? Now, my fighter?"

The Yollin pointed to the exit Merry had spotted earlier. "You may regret bringing a valuable slave like that here. You can get a replacement from club stock when this one dies if you take our guest insurance, but you won't get anything of this quality."

Merry bristled.

Don't say a word, Tabitha ordered. *Look subdued or something while this weasel recites his upcoming rap sheet for us.* "I'll take the insurance. Does it cover me for damages as well?"

"That costs extra," the Yollin admitted, rubbing his hands together. "We can also provide a substitute if you choose not to enter this slave. For a cost, of course."

"Of course," Tabitha repeated. "But I'll stick with what I have."

"Very well," the Yollin told her slightly less agreeably. "Changing area is through the rear exit." He turned his back to find someone easier to part from their credits.

Merry looked down as they walked away, the anger coming off her in waves. *I want to kick his greedy ass.*

Me, too, Tabitha assured her. She took Merry by the arm and led her to the exit. *Let's find out where they're keeping the kids first, yeah? You have to learn to focus your anger.*

How? Merry's inner voice was full of curiosity, laced with doubt. *Seriously?*

Tabitha squeezed Merry's arm gently. *I'm still learning, too. We'll help each other, how about that?* Merry didn't reply, but Tabitha didn't expect her to get it right away. *For now, just take it one step at a time, and remember that we're here to save the kids.*

Merry huffed through her nose. *That I can do.*

Tabitha found herself relieved that her niece could be persuaded to act appropriately for the good of others. It meant she wasn't completely lost since she still had empathy.

She patted Merry's back as they entered the staging area. *That's my girl.*

Noel-ni Colony Planet, Illegal Club, Underground

Tabitha sensed yet another gigantic Shrillexian guard waiting on the threshold of the tunnel beyond the exit.

Merry, however, was caught by surprise when they passed through the makeshift arch and she almost collided with him.

Apparently, Merry didn't possess the flight portion of the brain's self-defense mechanism, evidenced by the way she moved by instinct to attack the guard.

Tabitha grabbed Merry by the shoulder, diverting her before she had to explain to Lillian why her daughter was no longer among the living. "Easy, tiger." She lifted her free hand to the guard in a half-shrug. "What can you do?"

The guard looked at Merry with something resembling fondness. "You got a spirited one there. Make sure she doesn't damage any of the other fighters outside of the ring," he told Tabitha, pointing at a metal sign fixed to the dirt wall behind him. "Owners are responsible for costs."

Tabitha grinned, noticing the guard wore a chunky shock collar under his armor. "Thanks for the heads-up." She looked him up and down. "I've counted six guards just like you. Did Zinshei get you guys as a matched set or something?"

The guard nodded, unfazed by the remark. "He bought us from our parents as infants and raised us as his own."

Tabitha was thrown for a second, but she recovered before her pity made the guard suspicious. She patted the guard's expansive chest, managing to retain her tone of affected boredom. "I might have to think about doing that. Let's go, Sunbeam," she ordered, making a shooing motion at Merry. "Mama's got a new fad to finance."

Merry glared her displeasure with the subservient role but did as she was told, walking ahead until the tunnel led to another room dug out of the dirt.

Tabitha pushed the door open and went in ahead of Merry. They made their way past lockers and benches, the changing area filled with slave fighters from a wide variety of species and their owners. She steered Merry over to the desk by the door.

The female Torcellan behind the desk inspected their passes.

"What kind of human is that?" she asked, waving a finger at Merry without looking at her.

Tabitha frowned in confusion. "What do you mean?"

The Torcellan sighed in frustration. "Is she one of the gifted ones? Or the easy-to-kill type? It makes a difference to the seeding."

"Oh," Tabitha replied, catching the Torcellan's meaning. "Um, she's gifted, I guess?"

She handed Tabitha a ticket and pointed to a free locker by one of the benches. "Fine. You're booked in, so listen for her number being called."

Tabitha glanced at the ticket and led Merry over to the lockers. "Get yourself ready. You might get called any minute."

Merry had an obstinate set to her jaw as she rummaged through the supplies in the locker. "There's no challenge here. Look around. They're just kids like me, only I'm *me*." She rolled her eyes. "Whatever."

Tabitha took Merry by the shoulder and spun her around. "*That's* the kind of dumbass thinking that gets rookies killed. Always be ready for a challenge, and never assume you know everything that's coming."

Merry was about to argue when a pair of full-grown Ixtalis walked in. The majority of the slaves cringed as they strutted through the door like they owned the place. Tabitha assumed the ones who didn't shy away from the pair were newbs who hadn't learned any better yet.

The Ixtalis stopped at the desk to talk to the Torcellan, then looked at Tabitha before turning back to the desk.

"Looks like they're arguing with her about something," Merry remarked. "I could see myself fighting one of them..."

The Ixtalis left the desk and skittered over to Tabitha and Merry.

"Look, Heptix," the female commented to the male disdainfully. "Humans. How...*quaint*."

The male's mandibles rippled with similar distaste. "I saw, Indela. I thought Tolia was playing pranks again."

Tabitha narrowed her eyes at them. "You should show some respect," she told them. "Humans freed your people from their own dumb selves not once, but twice." They were younger than Tabitha had first thought, only just into adulthood, and neither of them wore the slave collars she'd seen on every other fighter in the room. She figured them for rich brats. "Or are you too young to remember the little cult thing?"

The Ixtalis hissed at her reminder of that embarrassing moment in their history. "So, you believe you are a smart human," Indela sneered.

Tabitha looked around them to see where their fighters were. "The pair of you are pretty chatty for two assholes who don't look to have any horses in this race," she returned sweetly.

For once, the translation software dealt with the idiom with a minimum of confusion.

Heptix's mandibles twitched angrily as he replied, "That's because *we* are the main attraction, foolish human. Didn't Zinshei tell you? If your little slave makes it through the rest of the night, we will pull her limb from limb in the finale. You will be powerless to act, or we will be within our rights to kill you, too."

Indela laughed. "It would be just like a human to walk into her own death for the sake of property. How ironic."

Merry lifted her chin and smirked at the raspy, guttural sound coming from Indela's throat. "I know assholes love to look so smart, but that's not irony."

109

Tabitha groaned internally as the two Ixtalis turned their attention to Merry. *I told you to stay quiet.*

They don't scare me, Merry insisted, eyeballing Indela. *I'll fight them right now if they wanna go.*

Heptix came closer and leaned in, his mandibles almost touching Tabitha's nose. "That ticket is useless to you. She," he pointed at Merry, "won't make it past the group stage."

Merry shoved Heptix. "We'll have to see about that. Won't we?"

Tabitha's internal groan morphed into a full-on moan of despair. This was getting beyond her control. She was about to act when her niece spoke up again, her eyes filled with fire.

"Ixtalis bleed and die just like everyone else," Merry stated. "You two are no different."

The Ixtalis laughed again as they strutted away.

"We will see how long you last, little human," Indela called over her shoulder. "I expect the crowd will be disappointed with your miserable death."

Tabitha gave their retreating backs the finger and turned to Merry. *We are out of here. This assignment is a bust.*

Merry shook her hand off. *No freaking way! We can't leave all these kids here. I can take those two. I know I can.*

Tabitha closed her eyes and took a measured breath. *No. Not two adult Ixtalis. That's too much for you, even with your training.*

Merry's eyes flicked to where one of Tabitha's drones was camouflaged against the top of the locker. *Don't those have some offensive capability?*

A slow grin spread over Tabitha's face. Here came the persuasion tactics. *Sure they do. What's that got to do with your ability to take on two opponents, both much larger than yourself, and not get torn to pieces?*

That's what I'm telling you, Merry argued. *Technically, I wouldn't be facing them alone because you'd be helping me.*

Tabitha knew she should say no.

Really.

Oh, come on, Aunt Tabbie. Merry batted her big blue eyes at her. *Pleeeeease? I'll go to school, and I won't fight with the other kids. I'll apologize to my mom and to Mrs. Henderson. I'll even call Grandad! Just let me have one all-out fight.* She curled her lip at the door the Ixtalis had left by. *They deserve it. You know they do.*

Tabitha felt her resolve to be the responsible adult in the situation crumbling. Merry knew she couldn't resist when she called her by her old nickname.

The responsible thing to do was get her niece the hell out of there. But Merry *was* highly trained, and those Ixtalis sure as hell needed a reality check. Besides, if Merry got an outlet for her anger, where was the harm?

Tabitha told herself she could always take out those arrogant brats with her drones if things got too serious. *Fine,* she capitulated. *But only if you listen to every word I say and do exactly what I tell you.*

Merry nodded enthusiastically. *I promise I will.* She rubbed her hands together and sat down on the bench to wait. *Thank you, Aunt Tabbie. I can't wait to take down those bullies.*

CHAPTER 9 TABITHA AND MERRY

The changing room emptied out as the evening progressed until only Tabitha and Merry remained under the disinterested gaze of the Torcellan behind the desk.

Merry was surprisingly calm.

Tabitha had gotten herself into some pretty hairy situations during her own time as a fourteen-year-old hellion, but *she'd* gone through the experiences with her heart in her throat, no matter how well she had fronted it on the outside.

In contrast, Merry sat cross-legged on the bench with her eyes closed, her breathing deep and regular. It was the most peaceful Tabitha had seen her since she'd arrived at Lillian's house.

Dammit, John was right. This is her happy place.

The Torcellan caught Tabitha's eye and jerked her head toward the door, pulling her from her consideration. "It's almost time." She looked at Merry for the first time since they'd arrived, her face filled with ersatz pity.

Tabitha rolled her eyes as she got to her feet. "It's a bit

late to pretend you give a shit." She flounced out, leading Merry. "Asshole."

She unmuted Achronyx as they made their way back down the tunnel to the main room. *Achronyx, it's about to get very messy here.*

Oh, finally, the AI snarked. *I was so bored, you should count yourself lucky I didn't think to start playing with your endocrine levels.*

Tabitha paused. *Have you been playing with my emotions? You'll be in timeout for a lot longer than an hour if I find out you messed with my brain. How soon can you get the local authorities here to back me up?*

Achronyx scoffed. *I contacted them as soon as it became apparent you were having too much fun playing vigilante with Meredith Nicole to remember to do so yourself.*

Bitch at me later, she told him, hurrying to keep up with Merry. *What's the situation?*

I communicated with a Captain Harlow, Achronyx replied. *Former Space Marine—*

Aren't they all? Tabitha interrupted. *We can take care of the niceties once all the scum has been cleaned up here. How long?*

Based out in the center of this sector, Achronyx continued as if she hadn't cut him off. *They're inbound from a call on another planet in this sector. You can expect them within the hour.*

Is that taking into consideration the bottleneck they're gonna encounter at that elevator? Tabitha asked.

I believe so, Achronyx confirmed.

Tabitha wrinkled her nose. *Zinshei's a clever bastard, I'll give him that.*

The Shrillexian nodded to them as they passed him. "Good luck," he offered redundantly, looking at Merry's back with what looked to Tabitha to be regret.

Merry threw a hand up over her shoulder. "Thanks," she called back without turning.

"Don't write her off," Tabitha told the guard, seeing genuine sadness on his face. "She's got hidden talents."

The guard shook his head. "That's not how it works around here."

Tabitha resolved to do something about the guard's situation if she could. She smiled at him, a real smile this time, and followed Merry into the arena.

They were covered in an ultra-fine shower of dust as they entered the main room, the rafters of the makeshift arena literally shaking from the thunderous cheering of the spectators surrounding the cage.

Tabitha kept a firm grip on Merry's sleeve as she made a path through the crowd. *Don't get lost in here. You'd be kidnapped before you could say, "What's that smell?"*

Merry glanced around the crowd. *Really? But they're dressed way better than everyone upstairs.*

Tabitha snorted. *Sure they are. They smell a lot better, too. Money will do that for you.*

Merry wrinkled her nose as they made progress toward the fat Yollin from earlier. *They are a damn sight uglier.*

Tabitha pushed through a group of braying Torcellans. *That's because they are ugly people,* chiquita. *The majority of the people upstairs are just ordinary folks trying to relieve the stress of their crappy lives. They look much worse on the surface than they are in their hearts.*

She jerked her head at the people around them. *These,*

she told Merry darkly, *are the worst of the worst. People who treat the deaths of children as entertainment. That kind of ugliness oozes from them the same way the light shines from an innocent soul like yours.* She frowned, considering Merry's thoughtful look. Maybe this isn't such a good idea...

Don't get any second thoughts about this, Aunt Tabitha, Merry begged.

The Yollin spotted Tabitha and waved her over.

Merry scowled at him, then at his guards.

"I hope that slave of yours has got the fighting ability to back up that attitude," the Yollin told Tabitha as greeting. "She did an excellent job of pissing off my two best fighters. Just look at the mess in there!" He swept a hand toward the cage, which Tabitha and Merry hadn't gotten close enough to see inside yet.

A gap in the crowd gave Tabitha a glimpse of the female Ixtali, Indela. An adolescent Noel-ni lay motionless at the side of the cage, and she held another youth above her head in a two-handed grip.

The Noel-ni bit and scratched, fighting for his life.

Tabitha lost her grip on Merry for a split second.

It was enough.

Merry shook free of Tabitha and made a break for the cage, screaming her outrage. The Noel-ni broke free and twisted to get away from Indela as the Ixtali turned to face Merry. "*You!*" she hissed.

Merry barged up to the guard on the cage door and grabbed him by the front of his uniform. "Open this cage!" she yelled, shaking him roughly.

The guard laughed in her face and moved to brush her aside.

He made two errors at that moment.

The first was not registering the deadly potential of the small blonde human before him. Merry, however young and dainty-looking, had the distinct advantage of a John Grimes education, which the guard unfortunately lacked the benefit of.

He had no way of making up for his other mistake, that being he was just an asshole Skaine slaver standing between a Grimes and her objective.

Tabitha considered stepping in to restrain Merry. However, the Skaines as a whole had never really been her favorites, and she had as many fucks to give about this particular Skaine getting a taste of the payback awaiting him as she had for the rest of the growths on the scrotum of society down here.

The unconscious Skaine landed in the crowd a moment later, and Tabitha caught sight of the two Ixtalis leaving through the enclosed run leading out from the far side of the cage.

She turned to the Yollin, who was striding angrily toward the cage. "I'm not paying for that."

Merry pulled the cage door open and stepped inside. She looked around the other teenagers inside the cage. They were spread out, watching the door to the run. "Why aren't you leaving? Come on, get out of here. "

She spotted the collar on the slave closest to her. "Well, *Gott verdammt*. That sucks, but it's not anything we can't fix."

The slave, a female Yollin, shuffled her two legs and switched hands with her knife. "Shut up and get ready to fight. It's coming, can't you smell it?"

Merry almost gagged as a rank scent crept into her olfactory range. "What the hell is that?"

The Yollin didn't answer.

"My aunt won't let us get hurt," Merry told her. Any opportunity to say more vanished when the doors to the run were pulled back from the inside and the biggest feline she had ever seen came padding out.

Merry assessed the cat for weak points as it paused to sniff the air, its tail whipping as it stalked with utter assurance towards the adolescents. She couldn't see any. It was all claws, teeth, and muscle. *Um... Aunt Tabitha?*

Tabitha snickered. *I take it this isn't the fight you were looking for?*

Not exactly, Merry admitted. *Grandad never told me how to fight a...one of those.*

A "one of those," is a Pandrexan alict, Tabitha informed her, making her way through the crowd to the side of the cage. *As apex predators go, it's not one of the ones you want to get up close and personal with. Want me to get you out of there?*

No freaking way, Merry retorted. *I'm not leaving these kids to die.*

Tabitha compared the hunger in the alict's eyes to the furious determination Merry was projecting. *Fine. But stay sharp and fight smart. That feline has a poisonous barb in its tail. Oh, and you do not want to get bitten by it either.*

The alict stalked a slow circle around the center of the cage, testing the occupants one by one.

Be aggressive, Tabitha warned as the feline approached Merry. *They go for the weakest first. There's something else, but I can't remember what it is.*

It's not going to live long enough for whatever it is to be a problem. Merry growled, dropping to one knee as though she were afraid. She gave a couple of deliberate whimpers to see if it drew the cat's attention.

Tabitha saw Merry's hand slip inside the loose fight club uniform she wore as the alict zeroed in on her niece as an easy meal. *What are you doing?*

It's cool, Merry told her coolly, drawing the blade she'd stolen from the Skaine. *Thanks for the tip.* She glanced at the slave fighters, hoping the alict didn't go for one of them first.

They were moving in to protect her. "Get *back*," she hissed. "I've got this."

They fell back and the alict stalked closer, saliva dripping from its fangs as it contemplated the offering before it. This was a meal that would not bite back. It stopped and sniffed the air hesitantly when it got a few paces away from Merry, its instincts saying something different than its eyes.

Tabitha held her breath as Merry baited the alict, keeping it off the weaker children. *Oh, my God. You have a death wish, don't you? What do you expect me to tell your mom?*

Merry shuffled back and emitted a frightened squeak, enticing the alict to ignore its instinct and attack. *Shh, I'm concentrating.*

The alict tilted its head from side to side, confused by the discrepancy in its senses. Its tail waved as though it were independent of the rest of its body, snaking around to test whether Merry was indeed weak enough to attack.

She let out another small whimper. It was enough to convince the beast.

Merry launched herself into a sideways roll as the alict's

tail whipped toward her, coming to her feet with the short sword raised. The barb hit the floor where she had been a bare second before.

The alict roared and whipped around, spraying blood from the place the end of its tail used to be.

Merry stepped out of striking distance into a back stance, her sword held ready at her right shoulder. It dripped blood on the floor as Merry bared her teeth at the alict.

Tabitha almost cracked up. Merry looked just like John —utterly calm, utterly focused, and utterly deadly. *Where did you get that sword?*

Merry stepped again as the alict slinked around to face her. *I stole it from that useless guard*, she bragged. *If he can't hang onto the sword, then he shouldn't have it in the first place.*

The slaves in the cage moved in cautiously to flank the alict. The Noel-ni who'd been saved by Merry's earlier interruption came from the other side, her claws at the ready, joined the next moment by the Yollin who had given Merry the heads-up earlier.

One by one, the other slaves moved in, brandishing what weaponry they had with the war cries of the long-oppressed given a voice.

Tabitha spotted Merry's mouth moving. *What's going on in there?*

Merry slid over to complete the circle around the alict. *They're asking me what we should do next. What* should *we do? Do we have to kill it?*

Tabitha heard Merry's tone and decided her niece was done. *I can put it to sleep for now with a night-night round.* She drew her Jean Dukes Special and entered the cage too, but she couldn't see a shot through the kids. *Just don't move, any of you. I'm looking for a shot that won't get any of you killed.*

Gotcha, Merry replied. She paused to pass the information along to the other adolescents. *It's sad, really. This creature is magnificent. It would be pretty cool to have around if it wasn't trying to kill us all.*

Tabitha snickered. A fourteen-year-old girl confronted with a fluffy animal would only ever go one way. *Yeah, um, I really hope the next words out of your mouth aren't, "Can we keep it,"* she told Merry. *Because I really can't see your mom letting me take you out on another road trip if you bring home two hundred pounds of poisonous predatory alien feline.*

Good point. Merry sighed. *But I'm looking into its eyes right now, and I've never seen an animal so sad. Can we get it back to its planet, at least?*

Tabitha paled as the nugget of information she'd been unable to recall earlier came loose and presented itself to her. *You're looking it right in the eye? What's it doing?*

I dunno, Merry answered, somewhat dreamily. *It's just lying down like it's tired.* She yawned. *I know how it feels. I'm kind of sleepy as well...*

Tabitha acted immediately. She recalled her drones from around the room and directed them to dive at the spot on the floor directly beneath the alict's head.

The feline dropped to the canvas with three tiny holes in its skull, dead almost as soon as Tabitha had given the order. She avoided slipping on the blood puddle in her hurry to get to Merry's side, but only just.

Tabitha caught Merry by the shoulders and shook her. Her eyes were distant and unfocused. "Merry! Wake up! Fight it."

Merry snapped out of it. She blinked at Tabitha, then looked at the dead alict blankly. "I'm okay. What happened?"

"Sorry, Trouble." Tabitha held her niece in her arms, tilting her chin up to examine her eyes for any residual effects. "That thing I forgot? Pandrexan predators have hypnotic abilities."

The other kids gathered around Merry and Tabitha.

"I told you my aunt would get you out of here," Merry told the Yollin as Tabitha got to work breaking their collars.

A mocking snicker came from the cage door behind them. "Your faith is very touching, child. Unhand my property, Ranger."

Tabitha turned at the sound of Zinshei's voice. "Oh, great! You saved me the bother of coming all the way upstairs to kick your ass." She spread her arms wide to cover the children. "Kidnapping, people-trafficking, forced imprisonment, running an illegal gambling den. Oh, and interplanetary animal-smuggling. You know you're not walking away from this."

Zinshei waved, and the sextet of Shrillexian giants stepped into the cage. "Oh, but Ranger, those were simply side earners that served as the perfect honey trap for the prize I really wanted. *You.*"

Tabitha spit up a little bit inside her mouth. "Sorry to break your heart. I don't know what you've heard, but the interspecies thing doesn't really do it for me."

"Dead!" Zinshei spat. "I want you *dead!*"

She laughed at the Noel-ni's outrage. "Yeah, you're going to be waiting the rest of your life and then some for that to happen."

Merry glanced nervously at the enclosing guards. *Aunt Tabbie?*

"Hold it right there, you sonsabitches. I've got two Jean Dukes Specials and zero tolerance for child abusers. Lay so much as a finger on any of these kids and we'll see how fast an ex-Ranger can drop all six of you fuckers." Her cold smile assured the guards she was speaking the truth.

"Five," one of the Shrillexians stated. "Brothers, join me."

Zinshei seethed, foam flecking the fur around his mouth as he screamed, "So be it, Knarlax. You can die with the rest of them!"

Tabitha grinned, recognizing him as the guard who had taken a shine to Merry. "Good choice. I appreciate it. I'm Tabitha."

"I know who you are, Ranger. I just didn't believe you were crazy enough to take Zinshei on directly." He joined Tabitha, pointing a sword at Zinshei. "No more. *No more.* I will die before I let you murder another innocent for profit."

Tabitha snorted. "I was only kidding about any of us not making it," she reassured her new friend. "The only one dying here today is Zinshei, along with anyone else who wants to continue," she waved a finger in a circle, "this."

Zinshei pulled a device out of his pocket and waved it around threateningly from his safe distance. "What are you waiting for?" he shrieked at the other five Shrillexians. "Kill them!"

Knarlax nodded to his brothers. "Let it be. I will die knowing I fought for what is right."

The crowd was silent at this point, sucking up the drama as the Yollin continued taking bets in the background. The lone Shrillexian braced his blades and prepared to face either his death or his brothers'.

Tabitha's fingers were poised over the triggers on her Jean Dukes Specials, ready to deal death at the first twitch from any of the other five.

Disbelief rippled through the crowd when one by one, the five remaining Shrillexians turned their backs and completed the protective circle around the children in stoic silence.

"*TRAITORS!*" Zinshei shrieked. "Without me, you would have ended up as mercenaries and died on some nameless planet!"

Tabitha blinked tears away, dismissing Zinshei's rant. "It's not like that anymore. Your choices are yours to make from here on out. You're getting out of here," she promised them. "Every one of you."

The brothers simply strengthened their fighting stances, ready for Zinshei's next move.

Achronyx spoke up in the back of Tabitha's mind. *The Enforcement Force is here.*

The Enforcement Force? Tabitha scoffed. *Someone must have been undercaffeinated when they came up with that. How are they dealing with the elevator?*

Six or seven at a time, Achronyx told her. *You're going to have to keep things under control for a little while longer.*

Tabitha glanced at the crowd, which was already looking a little denser than it had been a few moments previously. *Those the plainclothes officers I can see out there?*

They are, Achronyx confirmed. *As soon as there are*

enough officers in the downstairs level to deal safely with the guards accompanying the spectators, they will act.

And how much longer is that going to take? Tabitha demanded.

Almost there, he asserted. *You can keep Zinshei busy for a little while longer, can't you?*

Tabitha clicked her tongue. *I suppose. I don't have much choice, do I?* She considered the options. *Looks like I need to start a fight.* She spoke out of the side of her mouth. "We need to buy some time."

Zinshei was running out of steam in his impotent rant at his former guards. The Shrillexians stood fast at Tabitha's side, weapons raised, and ignored him. "If you won't obey me, then all of you can die!"

Zinshei glared at her with utter hatred. "I've wished for the day I could be rid of you for so long. Every time you rear your ugly pink head, I lose out." He pointed at the dead alict. "Do you know how expensive it was to transport that alict off Pandrex?" He lifted the hand holding the device.

Tabitha shot the device out of Zinshei's hand. "I don't, but I *do* know the crime carries a very harsh sentence. I hope you like digging rocks in the ass-end of nowhere because that's where you'll be spending the next couple of decades."

Zinshei barked a cold laugh. "Not likely. Your days of costing me are over."

Tabitha kept one eye on the drone feeds in her HUD and continued riling Zinshei. "Any day I can cost you a few thousand credits is a good one, I'm not gonna lie." She tilted her head and smirked. "You know, I'm kinda going to miss busting your dumb ass every few years. What am I going to do for laughs now?"

Zinshei snarled. "I wish I could have spaced you decades ago, Ranger. There was always the matter of your badge." His snarl twisted into an emotionless grin. "I don't see a badge anymore."

"Not cool." Tabitha shook her head and raised her Jean Dukes, enjoying the discomfort the view of the inside of the barrel of was causing him. "And there was me thinking we had some simpatico after all these years."

"Enough of this. No more avoiding the inevitable." Zinshei twisted his head from side to side. "WHERE ARE MY IXTALIS?"

Indela and Heptix appeared at the door to the run and advanced into the cage with their long Ixtali knives raised.

Merry picked up her stolen short sword and came to stand by Tabitha's side. "Aunt Tabitha, is this the kind of situation where I'm allowed to curse without getting a punishment?"

Tabitha shrugged as the two Ixtalis climbed the cage. "Why the hell not? I won't tell if you don't."

Merry grinned and leaned toward Indela and Heptix. "Hey, assholes! Fuck *you*!" She straightened, holding her sword with a little more confidence than she had the moment before.

Tabitha couldn't suppress her laugh. "Keeping it simple, then?"

Merry nodded, her eyes on the Ixtalis. "Why mess with perfection?"

Tabitha wished she wasn't in the position of needing to drag the situation out until there were more than her, the

Shrillexians, and a bunch of kids against half the people in this room and their guards.

Her worst fear came true when some of the patrons at the front of the crowd sent their bodyguards in to protect their favorite fighters.

Achronyx! she hissed. *Where is the damned enforcement whatever?*

A few more minutes, Achronyx replied. *They are almost in position.*

That doesn't help me now, does it? Tabitha had no choice but to let the fight go ahead. She holstered her Jean Dukes Specials and slipped her hands into the grips of the twin kukri blades she kept sheathed at the back of her belt as the cage filled even more.

Indela choked out that nasty laugh of hers and skittered towards Tabitha and Merry, leaving the Shrillexian brothers to take care of the bodyguards who were rushing to support the two Ixtalis.

Merry was ready. Her adrenaline should have been spiking, but she wasn't feeling anything but cold outrage. She glanced at Tabitha, seeing the hesitation in her aunt's stance. *Aunt Tabbie, I've got her. Take care of those brainless muscleheads, okay?*

Tabitha didn't waste time arguing what made sense. Merry had no chance of getting out of this unless she did something about the bodyguards. She passed Merry her kukris and drew her JD Specials again.

Fight smart, and if that bragging bitch puts her back to you—

I know, Merry dropped the sword, grinning as the grips on the kukris molded themselves to her hands. *The cluster of tendons on the inside of the rear ankle.* Indela was upon her in the next moment, cutting off their time for planning ahead.

Merry slide-stepped in, feinting a jab with her left blade as she brought the right around to cut into the Ixtali's thigh.

Indela skittered back out of range, hissing.

"'Sup?" Merry taunted. "Is it different when your opponent can fight back?"

Indela backed up, reversing up the mesh feet-first. She sprang suddenly, knives flashing. "You can fight, but you will die."

Merry ducked and whirled under Indela's knives, the momentum from her turn giving her the perfect arc to slash open Indela's robe and slice into her soft under-carapace. The Ixtali hissed in pain when Merry flicked the left blade as she completed the spin.

"How dare you!" Indela shrieked as her robe dropped away, her mandibles writhing with rage and shame.

Merry danced around Indela, cutting here, jabbing there with the blades. "How dare I? How dare *you*? An easy death would be too good for evil like you." This was going further than she'd ever been, but the dead Noel-ni on the floor cried out for Justice.

Tabitha worked around the two, keeping the bodyguards, and now a shit-ton of Zinshei's guards, away from the adolescents. She focused a drone on Merry as she fired from her position, noting that the Ixtali wasn't looking like she was slowing down despite the blood loss she was suffering at Merry's hands. She needed to end this.

Achronyx spoke up in her mind. *There are enough law enforcement officers in the crowd.*

A screech cut the air, halting both Achronyx' report and Indela's attack. Tabitha turned to Heptix, who was on the floor under the stamping feet of the three children.

"Brother!" Indela's hands moved seemingly of their own accord, then there was a clatter as the young Yollin hit the deck with a knife's hilt protruding from her thorax. "I'll kill you *all!*" she screeched, striding over to retrieve her knife.

Merry saw red. She leapt onto Indela's back and opened her throat with Tabitha's blades before the Ixtali could take another life. "Take that, you murdering sack of bistok shit!"

She jumped clear as the Ixtali dropped to the blood-soaked canvas, clutching her ruined throat uselessly as her life force sprayed through her fingers.

Merry dropped the kukris and vaulted the bodies on the floor to get to the Yollin. She knelt by her side, knowing it was too late when she saw the bloody foam coming from the wound in her chest. She wrapped her arms around the Yollin as best she could and looked into her still-defiant eyes.

"Thank...you," she gasped, straining to force the words out with her final breath.

Merry's chest constricted as the light left the Yollin's eyes. "*No!* Don't die! We *saved* you!" Her vision was blurred by tears, turning Tabitha into an outline in her peripheral vision. "How could this happen? People don't die, not the good ones."

Tabitha knelt by Merry and laid a hand on her niece's shoulder, her heart just as heavy. "You okay?"

Merry looked up from the Yollin's body. "I didn't even know her name."

Tabitha nodded, pressing a hand to her hair. "But you

fought for her all the same. That's all we can do." She wiped a spot of blood from Merry's cheek. "I can't wait to tell your mom all about this. You acted when it mattered and saved lives. You did awesome, Trouble."

"I won't forget her, not ever. You have to fight for the living, right?" Merry leaned over to brush the Yollin's eyes closed with her fingertips, then released her gently to the floor. "She'd better get a proper funeral."

She turned her head to look at the survivors standing in the carnage, feeling a sense of purpose at long last. She didn't want to be a soldier or on a team with rules like the Enforcement Force. Those guys were severely constrained in what they could do. If it wasn't for her and Tabitha, all of these kids would still be slaves, or worse, dead.

"Do you think my mom would let me come stay with you? We could be vigilantes together."

Tabitha gave Merry the eyebrow, her focus on the riot taking place outside the cage. "You want to what, now?"

"Come on," Merry protested. "Look, I've learned something important out of this. Rules are for—"

A blaster hissed and Merry crumpled to the floor, bright blood blooming on her club uniform.

Zinshei spoke into the silence. "Take from me, I take from you, Ranger."

Time halted on its axis for Tabitha. She whipped around and saw Zinshei's shaking hand on the blaster that shot Merry. She didn't remember raising her Jean Dukes Special, but there it was at a right angle to her body, and there was Zinshei with a smoking crater instead of a head.

Her brain refused to connect the two pieces of information.

She scooped Merry up and ran from the cage. All hell was breaking loose around them, but her only thought was to reach the elevator and get Merry to the ship.

The crowd parted in fear of the crazy red-eyed human.

Tabitha didn't care who recognized her.

She arrived at the elevator with Merry in her arms and was met by a pair of EF officers carrying what they probably thought were big guns.

Before Tabitha had a chance to order them out of the way, they stepped to the side and let her through. She was inside the elevator on her way up to the ground floor before she realized the Shrillexians were still with her.

She blinked, coming out of the autopilot that gotten her this far. "You guys didn't have to do this. You're not slaves anymore."

"You freed us," Knarlax told her. "We're going see you out of here, and see *her* safe." He nodded at Merry. "She is a true warrior and does not deserve to die today."

Tabitha held Merry tightly to her as she looked around at the brothers squeezed around her in the elevator like super-aggressive giant alien versions of her Tontos.

A single tear slid down her cheek. "Thank you," she managed through her emotions. "I'm going to make sure you guys are taken care of. This place will be yours to do something good with."

The brothers did not know how to respond to that.

They rode the rest of the way in silence and escorted Tabitha and Merry to the front of the club, where Achronyx had their ship waiting overhead.

Tabitha jumped for the half-extended ramp and pelted to the ship's medical bay.

"Pod-doc One is ready for Meredith Nicole," Achronyx informed her.

Tabitha murmured desperately to Merry as she placed her on the Pod-doc mat and force-closed the lid. "Hold on, Trouble," she begged as the viewing window fogged over, anesthetizing her niece.

The Pod-doc hissed, making her jump. "How bad is it?" she asked Achronyx, hardly daring to hear the answer. "Just tell me."

"She will be fine," Achronyx assured her from the speaker. "Her nanocytes had already begun to heal the initial injury. The Pod-doc is remedying the blood loss and repairing the damage to her internal organs as we speak."

Tabitha sagged against the lid. "*OhthankGod.*" The words spilled out of her in a rush as the adrenaline dump hit. "I thought I was going to lose her. What was I thinking, bringing her here?" She looked into the viewing window, seeing that a bit of Merry's color had already returned.

"You had me scared for a moment there, Trouble. How does your mom cope with you full time?" She snorted softly as the panic faded.

A short, sharp shock was what she had promised Lillian she'd give Merry, and there was no denying she'd fulfilled her promise. Maybe Lillian would cope a little better from now on.

Tabitha left to get herself cleaned up before Merry was done in the Pod-doc. There was a message from Lillian waiting when she got out of the shower.

Not sure if I want to open this, she admitted to Achronyx.

I didn't think you would, at least until you and Meredith Nicole have your stories straight. But you can't exactly ignore it,

Achronyx told her firmly. *Lillian just wants to know how her daughter is, which is her right. You should call her.*

Tabitha read the message quickly. *Did you already read this? That's pretty much exactly word for word what Lillian wrote.*

Achronyx made a noise that could be taken either way.

Bad AI. Stay out of my messages. You just earned yourself a timeout. Tabitha muted Achronyx before he could argue with the convenience of her complaint as she headed for the bridge to get the ship launched without the side of snarky judgment Achronyx was serving.

She called Lillian once they were underway.

Lillian appeared on the screen from the shoulders up. "Aunt Tabitha! How's it going?" She looked around for Merry. "Is everything okay? Where's Merry?"

Tabitha held up a hand to stay Lillian's worry. "She picked up an injury on the mission, but don't worry, it's not serious. She's in the Pod-doc getting healed."

"What kind of injury?" Lillian demanded.

"Nothing that won't be healed by dinnertime." Tabitha saw some of the color return to Lillian's complexion. "We're on our way back, actually," she told her. "The assignment went well."

"'Which one?" Lillian asked, narrowing her eyes at Tabitha's vagueness."

Tabitha winked. "Both, of course. This is me you're talking to, don't forget. I don't suppose you still make that cassoulet I like? A story always goes down better with a good meal."

Lillian chuckled and waved a hand. "Well, that settles it. Everything must be just fine if you're begging for my home cooking. Get yourselves back here. I'll have dinner ready for when you arrive."

Tabitha dropped the call and leaned back, lacing her hands behind her head. "I think we can call both objectives of this mission a success," she murmured to Achronyx, feeling sure of herself again now that it was just the two of them.

She remembered she'd muted Achronyx when he didn't reply. "Sorry."

"You can make it up to me," Achronyx replied. "As to whether you can call this a win, it will remain to be seen."

Tabitha laughed, waving his gloomy prediction off. "Nah, Merry's gotten it out of her system. It will be smooth sailing with her from now on."

High Tortuga, Space Fleet Base, Nickie's Quarters, Present Day

Nickie woke up with a smile. Tabitha's message had brought back some good memories. She sat up and stretched, looking forward to the day ahead. *Morning, Meredith.*

Good morning, Nickie, Meredith replied. *How are you feeling? You were tossing and turning for most of the night.*

Nickie shrugged. *I had a dream about that trip I took with Aunt Tabitha when I was fourteen. She mentioned it in her message.*

Meredith made a disapproving noise. *I'm surprised your aunt chose to reminisce about such a traumatic experience.*

Nickie snorted as she got out of bed. *Are you shitting me? That trip was one of the best times I ever had as a kid.*

The first time you took a life was one of the best experiences of your childhood? Meredith's voice held an undertone of amusement.

Nickie narrowed her eyes. *Nooo, but the time my best*

aunt took me to a freaking fight club when I should have been royally grounded for breaking some grabby asshole's knee was.

I remember it happening a little differently, Meredith told her dryly.

You always do, Mere. Nickie half-shrugged as she selected a black shipsuit from the hanging row of identical black shipsuits, atmosuits, and overalls in her closet.

You can't deny that you were affected by it, Meredith refuted. *I was there too, remember?*

Nickie looked at the bomb site in her closet and sighed. *You know, I should update my work wardrobe. Atmosuits are so last year.* She dressed quickly and grabbed her boots. *I remember you freaking out the whole time. Does that count? Why would I be affected? I was born and raised to this life—against my will, if you remember. The most traumatic part was getting home afterward and dealing with my mom freaking out that I got hurt.* She bent to lace her boots. *Like she gave a crap.*

Nickie, that's not fair, Meredith ventured. *Your mother loves you. We've talked about this.*

Nickie snorted as she left her quarters. *No, Meredith. You've talked about it. Endlessly. And then you complain when I mute you.*

Meredith sniffed. *You'd better not mute me again.*

Nickie smelled victory. *Are you gonna get off my back about my mother?*

Fine, Meredith conceded. *We have too much to get through today for tantrums.*

Nickie grinned. *Good. I'm so glad you get that and have decided not to make things difficult for us.*

Meredith huffed. *It's not too late for me to join CEREBRO.*

If that's what you want, I won't stop you, Nickie teased, calling the EI's bluff. *I mean, you've been talking about it an awful lot. If it's what you really want, who am I to hold you back?*

Meredith chose not to respond.

Nickie headed straight for the office to file her flight plan. She was just leaving when a familiar voice rang out from across the hangar.

"Nickiiiiiiiieeeeeee!"

She twisted toward the sound of her name, and her jaw dropped when she saw that her ears weren't playing tricks on her. "Fuck *me*, it's Rickie!" She hopped the railing and met him halfway across the floor under the fuselage of an inactive ship.

Rickie grabbed her around the waist and spun her. "Lookin' good, kid." He dropped her when she punched him. "Easy, tiger. How's it hanging?"

Nickie grinned, gesturing at her crotch with both hands. "I haven't grown a dick since the last time you asked that." She ignored Meredith's groan. "It's going good."

Rickie put a hand over his eyes. "You haven't changed a bit."

Nickie shrugged. "You'd be surprised. Anyway, where did you go? One day you were on the *Meredith Reynolds,* and the next you just…ghosted."

The sparkle dropped from Rickie's eyes. "Can't tell you, kid. I'd have to…" He drew a finger across his throat, screwing his face up. "Seriously."

"What, you?" Nickie teased. "Yeah, right. Everyone knows you can't keep your mouth shut for shit." She winked, since Rickie had held onto a secret or two about her during her wild youth. "You couldn't take me if I cut off both arms and blinded myself, old man."

Rickie's amiable expression returned. "Old man? Strong words for a pretty little thing like—*oof*!"

Nickie smirked. "You were saying?"

Rickie rubbed his ribs. "I was going to suggest we meet up to spar, then get something to eat afterward and catch up. It's been a minute."

The words fell out without her brain engaging. "Careful, that sounds almost like a date."

Rickie looked at Nickie fondly for a moment, then laughed and reached out to ruffle her hair. "Funny. Where the hell have you been all this time?"

"Wouldn't you like to know?" Nickie trilled sweetly, grabbing his hand.

Rickie got out of the resulting wrist-lock and twisted Nickie into a half-nelson. "You've improved, but you'll have to try a bit harder than that, kid."

Barnabas walked into the hangar just as Nickie bloodied Rickie's nose with the back of her head. He spotted the two of them roughhousing and was next to the ship in the blink of an eye. "This," he waved a finger between the two of them, "is not happening. You two stay the hell away from each other."

Nickie and Rickie shared a confused glance.

Barnabas shook his head at their blank looks. "I've already got a headache that won't go away. I do *not* need it in stereo." He turned in a whirl of robes and stalked off, muttering something about "damn kids being the end of him."

Nickie watched him go, failing badly at keeping the

smirk off her face. She turned back to Rickie once Barnabas was out of sight, seeing an identical bemused expression on his face.

They looked at each other and cracked up. Nickie touched the back of her head and grimaced at her fingertips. "Ew, you got blood in my hair. Gross, Rickie."

"Serves you right for headbutting me," Rickie managed through his laughter. He glanced after Barnabas. "What the fuck was *that* all about?"

Nickie wiped a tear away, trying to get her breath. "Dunno. You know those crazy-assed vamps."

Barnabas spoke up in her mind. *The "crazy-assed vamp" can still hear you, Meredith Nicole.*

Nickie burst into fresh giggles. *Sorry, Uncle B. You know I love you, really.*

You love being a pain in my ass, child, Barnabas returned before dropping the link.

Nickie cringed, still laughing. "Shiiit, he heard me!"

Rickie looked around, his laughter trailing off into a nervous chuckle. "He did?"

Nickie waved his concern off as she pulled herself together. "Don't worry about it. He's a sweetie, really."

Rickie snorted. "Yeah, I'm not seeing it. So, dinner? Sparring? What's your choice?"

She shrugged. "Your choice. Wanna meet up when I get back from this run?"

Rickie's face fell. "You're headed out today?"

"Uh-huh," she confirmed. "In a couple of hours. Dammit, are you not gonna be here when I get back?"

Rickie shook his head. "Nah. I'm based on Devon. I've

141

gotta get going now, but maybe you can swing a run to the *Guardian* sometime soon?"

"Maybe," Nickie muttered, doing her best not to notice how nicely he filled out those fatigues he was wearing as he left.

Another reason to take Barnabas' offer? Meredith reasoned. *Your brain is practically swimming in dopamine and norepinephrine.*

Nickie pressed her lips together. *Butt the hell out, Meredith. What does that even mean?*

It means you like him, Meredith replied. She paused for a second. *I recall you going through a period of infatuation with Captain Escobar when you were younger. We should talk about that.*

Um, no. We really shouldn't, Nickie retorted. *I should get my ass on the ship and get out of here before Barnabas thinks to lecture me any more about hanging with Rickie.*

Unfortunately for Nickie, Barnabas was waiting at the foot of the ramp when she got to the *Penitent Granddaughter*.

Fuckdammit! I told you, Meredith. Here comes the lecture, and I have to just smile and take it. Nickie plastered a smile on her face and walked up as though nothing was out of the ordinary. "What's up, Uncle B? Come to see me off?"

Barnabas pursed his lips. "Not quite. There's been a small change to this assignment. You have enough crew to run two ships, yes?"

Nickie raised an eyebrow, wondering where he was going. "Maybe. Why? This isn't your way of pushing me into taking your offer, is it?""

"One of the newer crews did not return from their last

run." Barnabas tucked his hands into his sleeves. "There is a second ship waiting for you at Waystation, which is to be transported to QT2."

Nickie made a face. "They went AWOL?"

Barnabas shrugged. "That remains to be seen. However, the crew's absence does not preclude the delivery of their load. I trust you can take care of it?"

Nickie reflected on the change in Barnabas. It wasn't so long ago that he was hovering over her shoulder watching her every move. She nodded. "This is... Um, yeah. We can take care of it."

Barnabas patted her arm. "Good." He smiled that serene smile of his. "It's good to feel this trust, and you've earned it, Merry."

Nickie laughed. "Way to ruin the moment, Uncle B. Stay the fuck out of my head." She smiled at Barnabas before heading up the ramp. "Thanks. It means a lot."

Barnabas chuckled. "Go on now. Come see me when you return."

Nickie nodded, too choked up to reply. She headed up the ramp onto the ship, the walk to the bridge giving her a chance to clamp down on emotions she didn't have the luxury to indulge in right now.

The crew was already at their stations when Nickie arrived. She clapped her hands as she crossed the floor to her captain's chair. "Looking good, everyone! Let's get this show on the road. Take us out, Meredith."

Nickie turned her decision over in her mind as High Tortuga receded on the viewscreen.

"We are clear to Gate," Meredith announced once the

ELL LEIGH CLARKE & MICHAEL ANDERLE

Penitent Granddaughter was a suitable distance from the Interdiction.

"I love this bit!" Adelaide squeaked.

Nickie spun her chair around to face Adelaide as they entered the event horizon. "You're going to love this next bit even more," she told her engineer.

"Oh?" Adelaide's expression faltered for a second. "Is this one of those times where you *say* we're going to love it and then we don't?"

Nickie snickered, thinking back on how many times their assignments had tuned out that way. "You know, Addie, I'll leave it to you to decide. How does adding a ship to our fleet sound?" She winced internally at the slip.

Adelaide tilted her head, curiosity lighting her face. "That will depend completely on what new ship you have for me."

Nickie lifted her hands. "No clue. Barnabas just told me about it as I was getting ready to board."

Keen looked up from his station. "So it should be a decent ship, probably a Federation one. No worries, Addie."

Outskirts of Yollin Space, Waystation

The *Penitent Granddaughter* emerged from the Gate in the Yollin backwater where their designated supply depot was secreted. Roh'dun was waiting for the crew as usual when Meredith brought them in to land.

Grim embraced his somewhat distant cousin, and the two of them left with their heads close together in conversation. "Won't be too long," he called back. "Roh'dun has sourced some interesting galley supplies, and we're going to take a look while we pick up perishables for the second ship."

Nickie left the rest of the crew to their routine tasks and headed off to find the depot manager. She found the corporal after searching the warehouses behind the offices.

Corporal Weisman turned from her conversation with the group of workers she was speaking to, smiling when she saw Nickie. "Hey! Good to see you. You're taking the double load, right?"

Nickie nodded and had Meredith send over her orders from Barnabas. "Hey, Judith. It's too bad about all this. My crew can handle taking up the slack." She raised an eyebrow. "What do you think happened?"

Corporal Weisman shook her head. "I don't know. Nothing good, that's for sure. I can't see Jennie's crew going AWOL." She sighed. "I don't suppose we'll find out either way since there was no sign of them when the investigative team went to find out what had happened. Just the empty ship."

Nickie tilted her head in sympathy. "I didn't realize you knew them personally. You should get in touch with Barnabas."

Judith smiled. "I already spoke to General Reynolds. If they're out there, we'll get them back." She looked sad for a moment. "It hasn't been easy on Jennie's wife. They just had a baby."

Nickie closed her eyes. "Damn. I'm sorry for being flippant. I hope it works out for them."

"Me, too." Corporal Weisman gave Nickie the access codes to the second ship. "Thanks for taking this on."

"Not a problem," Nickie assured her as she left to get the crew together. *Meredith, round the crew up and have them meet me at,* she checked the orders Corporal Weisman had given her, *the* Lucky Run. *Can't be too lucky if the crew just vanished like that. That shit's just weird.*

I have to concur, Meredith agreed. *I've sent over your orders, and everyone is on their way.*

Adelaide, Durq, and Keen were already at the QBS *Lucky Run* when Nickie arrived at the hangar where the ship was berthed.

Grim turned up just as the ramp touched down, panting behind a line of antigrav carts.

"What the fuck is all that?" Nickie demanded. "I thought you were going for supplies, not buying the whole fucking outpost."

Grim looked instantly guilty. "I, um...they had some exotic produce, okay? You'll thank me when you're eating it later on."

Nickie scowled at Grim's back as he shepherded half the carts aboard the *Lucky Run.* He returned a few minutes later to take the rest over to the *Penitent Granddaughter.*

Nickie saw something squirming in one of the carts as he passed. "Yeah, no. I'm gonna cook for myself tonight."

Grim snorted softly and continued on his way. "I'll believe *that* when I see it." He held up a finger over his shoulder without turning back to look at Nickie. "Emptying a can into a bowl and giving it five minutes in the convection unit does not count as cooking."

Nickie gave Grim's back the finger and went to find Adelaide.

As expected, she found her in the engine room. "Hey, Addie. How's it going?"

Adelaide jumped at the sound of Nickie's voice, banging her head on the top lip of the compartment she was currently waist-deep in. She grinned at Nickie, rubbing the sore spot. "Oh, hi! Ship's looking good. She's seen some action recently, but she's in good shape."

Nickie patted Adelaide on the back. "That's what I like to hear."

Adelaide made a face. "There's just one tiny thing…"

"Spit it out." Nickie frowned, expecting to hear that there was a major problem she could do fuck all about.

Adelaide winced. "Um…we're going to be pretty stretched running both ships. The *Lucky Run* needs a skeleton crew of five."

Nickie grinned. "That's not a problem. I can run the *Penitent Granddaughter* by myself, and you all can take the *Lucky Run*. I'm headed back there now, so I'll let Grim know he's needed here."

Adelaide nodded and ducked back into the compartment. "Sounds good!"

Nickie headed straight for the galley when she got back to the *Penitent Granddaughter*, knowing that was exactly where she would find her old friend. She had planned to use the time to get Grim's story out of him, but it would have to wait.

"Looks like I'm going to miss out on your dinner after all," she told him. "They need you on the *Lucky Run*."

Grim turned from the storage unit. "What a shame."

Nickie made a face at the tank of live creatures he'd left on the counter. "Yeah, totally. Next time, maybe."

Grim gave her a knowing look but didn't press. "You'll be okay without me for a while."

Nickie raised an eyebrow, her hands dropping to her hips. "I managed perfectly fine without you for over two decades."

"Did you?" Grim asked.

Nickie glared at him. "I think I'll be okay for a few hours."

"Okay, then." He came out of the storage unit with a medium-size crate, which he placed the tank into. "There are a few precooked meals in the cold storage. Don't want you going hungry."

Nickie's mouth twitched. "Thanks, Mom."

Grim shook his head fondly. "See you at QT2."

Nickie wiggled her fingers at him. "Bye, Grimmie." She left the galley and made her way to the cargo bays to check her load before she left the depot, then headed for the bridge and her chair.

Are we good to go? she asked Meredith.

Almost, Meredith replied. *Grim is boarding the* Lucky Run *and...yes, we are good to go.*

Nickie settled back and put her feet up on the console. *Then what the hell are we waiting for? Let's* go, *already.*

You're rather gung-ho about this run, Meredith noted as the ship lifted off.

Nickie laced her hands behind her head and closed her eyes. *I've got a good feeling about this one, Mere. Now shush, I'm taking a nap.*

Open Space, Silver Line Route

Nickie was just considering getting impatient when the Gate spiraled open and the crew came back on the Etheric comm. *About fucking time,* she bitched. *What took you all so long?*

Damn Gate drive went on the fritz, Adelaide grumbled as the *Lucky Run* came to a stop near the *Penitent Granddaughter.*

Nickie chuckled. *Chill, Addie. Do you need us to stop while you finish any repairs?*

It's fixed now, Adelaide told Nickie. *I can get us there. It's just three more jumps.*

Something feels off to me, Keen mused. *I mean, Addie checked everything as soon as we got access to the ship, and there were no problems then.*

Adelaide wasn't mollified one bit. *Well, we will have to wait to get to the* Helena *to do complete diagnostics, since the EI on this ship is too basic to be of any help.*

Which proves my gut theory, Keen continued. *Nickie, did*

your uncle tell you much about the circumstances the crew went missing under?

You know, I clean forgot to ask. Nickie pursed her lips when Meredith brought a blip on the scanners to her attention. *Addie, are you sure the Gate drive will last the three jumps to QT2?* she asked distractedly.

Well, yeah, Adelaide confirmed. *I wouldn't guess with our lives.*

Oooo-kay, then, Nickie interrupted. *Gate away.*

Do what, now? Grim asked.

Get out of here, she told them, her attention on the blip, which was approaching too fast and straight to be mistaken for anything but a ship. *I'll catch up with you shortly.*

What's going on, Nickie? Keen demanded.

Nothing for any of you to be concerned about, Nickie assured them. *Just a ship that shouldn't be here.*

Grim still sounded worried. *You think it's something to do with the missing crew?*

Nickie snorted as the ship came into viewing range. *You don't? Because I'm looking at a damn pirate ship. The* Lucky Run *would have been sitting pretty for them right about now if not for Addie.*

It can't be a coincidence, Grim conceded. *Okay, we're out of here.*

The crew wasn't happy.

We are not leaving you, Keen argued.

Did I say you had a choice? Nickie stated. *Grim, get them out of here. Now!*

But we're a team! Adelaide cried. *We can't just leave you to face whoever that is on your own!*

Grim, however, had already initiated the Gate drive, recognizing the tone in Nickie's voice. It took him back, oh, about seven years or so. *Take care, Boss.*

Thanks, Grimmie.

Keen paced the bridge as the *Lucky Run* came out the other side of the Gate. "I don't like leaving Nickie."

Grim shook his head. "It's probably best that none of us sees what's about to go down on that ship. She's been building up a head of steam since that asshole prince."

Durq's lip curled. "Ugh. I *never* liked him."

Open Space, Aboard the *Penitent Granddaughter*

Nickie returned to the bridge, having completed setting her traps. The house bots trundled behind her like a row of bulky metal ducklings following their mama. *Is Adelaide's security system ready to go?*

It is, Meredith informed her.

Nickie smiled as she shepherded the house bots into the corner. "You guys sleep now. You'll be safe here."

The bots obeyed, except Bradley, who flashed a heart on his screen before shutting himself off.

Nickie snickered at the bot's cute trick and headed for her console. *What's with the tone about Addie's system?*

No tone, Meredith replied.

Nickie wasn't buying a second of it. *Well, you could have fooled me.* She scanned the ship from her console, checking each strand of the web of death she'd set up with the help of the house bots and Meredith.

We have a breach, Meredith announced suddenly.

Nickie confirmed Meredith's report. *Let the fuckers come. I'm more than willing to teach the stupid sons of their own aunts and uncles exactly what happens to pirates who mess with a Grimes.*

She dropped into her captain's chair and got to work. *These are going to wish for my grandfather's mercy.*

I wasn't aware that mercy was one of the things enemies celebrated about John, Meredith pondered.

Nickie felt calm descend. *Exactly.*

Meredith made *that sound,* the one that increasingly reminded Nickie of her mother. *Just try not to make too much mess, okay?*

She shook her head. *Not a chance. Let them in, Meredith.*

Last chance to have me just fry them on the hull.

I won't repeat myself.

If you're going to be an ass until you get your own way.

Nickie growled, *Meredith!*

Okay, fine. The EI complied. The airlock cycled open and the slightly bewildered pirates spilled into the *Penitent Granddaughter.* Nickie watched them enter hesitantly at first, then with increasing boldness when no challenge came.

Shall I stop them? Meredith asked.

Let them go, Meredith. Nickie's fingers dipped to brush the pouch on her belt that held Tabitha's original drones. She'd done a lot more with a lot less. Crude work sometimes required only the simplest of tools.

Nickie, you're angry.

Meredith's insinuation that she would allow anger to affect her performance didn't sit at all comfortably with Nickie. *Hell yeah, I'm pissed. There's a woman at home with a new baby who doesn't even know if her co-parent is ever going to return. The only way any of these bastards are getting off my ship alive is if they have information about the missing crew.* She paused as a thought hit her. *And then only if that person isn't too much of a dumbass to keep that info to themselves. Are you done worrying?*

Meredith wasn't done. *Are the grenades necessary?*

Um, yeah, Nickie replied, clipping them onto her utility belt.

Oh.

Nickie ignored Meredith's tone as she activated her armor's helmet. *Why do you sound so nervous about that? It's better to have them and not need them than need them and not have them.*

One could argue that nobody aboard a spaceship actually needs a grenade, Meredith countered.

Nickie rolled her eyes. *Or a full pirate crew roaming the corridors? Just open the hatch, Meredith.*

Meredith opened the access panel to the ventilation system above Nickie's chair.

Thank you. Nickie jumped up and pulled herself into the duct. *Lighten up, Mere. There aren't that many of them.*

Really? Meredith's tone made her position clear. *Because I wouldn't call you against fifty or so pirates bent on stealing the ship a fair fight.*

Nickie made a face as she crawled along the duct to the access corridor outside the bridge. *I know, right? I'd feel sorry nobody warned them what they were headed into if they weren't, you know, fucking* pirates, *Meredith.*

Nickie got to the access in the corridor outside the bridge and loosened the panel, watching the pirates progress on her armor's HUD. *How many took the bait?* she asked.

It's amazing what psychological effect a flashing green light has upon most species, Meredith commented.

Nickie rolled her eyes. *Mere, do me a favor? Switch off fucking therapy mode and get in the game. How many went into the elevator?*

Meredith huffed. *Well. I was about to tell you that most did, but we have a couple of splinter groups. One is headed for the cargo bays. The other appears to be on their way to the bridge.*

Fuck. Nickie paused and considered her options. *Okay. Pen the main group in at the bottom. I'm going to take care of the assholes up here first, then the ones trying to get at the cargo.*

Nickie split the view in her HUD, cycling through the cameras to track both the strays near the cargo bays and the bright sparks who had thought to come up to the bridge. She perched above the open vent and waited for the first to die to arrive, concentrating on feeling like a black widow in her web.

Powerful.

Deadly.

She focused on that feeling and tried like hell to spread it around some.

The pirates entered the access corridor, all cursing and bravado until they hit the edge of the disquiet Nickie was projecting.

Nickie grinned at the confirmation that her practice in

the Vid-doc was paying off. *Thank you, Eve.* She wrinkled her nose when they kept walking slowly toward the bridge. *Dammit, it's still not full-on fear, is it? I mean, I don't want them to shit their pants like people do when Aunt Bethany Anne switches the fear on, but awkward silence? It sucks.*

You couldn't even do that much before, Meredith reminded her. *You know, if we went to Devon—*

I swear I'll find another way to mute you, Nickie threatened.

Or you can just keep practicing, Meredith backtracked.

Nickie ignored her. The pirates were almost past the point of no return. *I'm going to have to go down there and take care of them. Open the bridge, Meredith. See if that tempts them in.*

I do not agree with this.

Which matters how much right now? I'm not taking damages, Meredith. Team Asshole there needs taking out before they break my ship.

The bridge door began to cycle open, drawing the newly-christened Team Asshole in just as Nickie wanted.

She held her breath and waited for the largest asshole to take the final two steps and put all five of them in range.

The pirates looked up, sensing danger. It was too late.

Nickie dropped from the vent, landing on Asshole Number One's shoulders. She locked his head between her thighs and shot Assholes Two and Three, flinging her body weight forward to snap One's neck as she dropped into a forward roll.

Assholes Four and Five apparently had a brain cell to share between them and had run for the outer corridor while Nickie was taking care of the first three.

Nickie came to her feet and flicked her hair out of her eyes. "Do yourselves a favor and give up. Who knows? I might not kill you."

Right away.

The pounding feet gave her the answer.

"Fine, play it that way." Nickie hopped back up into the vent. *It's time to test Addie's security,* she told Meredith.

But the mess...

Nickie shrugged. *The bots can take care of it. Run it.*

She brought up the corridors on that level in her HUD, wincing as the tiny drones Adelaide had made located the final two assholes and gave the rooms they were in a fresh coat of red paint.

Nickie wiped her hands. *Next. Is the main group still secure?*

Penned in, like you asked, Meredith confirmed. *They're not too happy, though.*

Nickie nodded and turned to jump down from the vent. *Tough shit. If they don't like it, they shouldn't fucking be pirates.*

I don't disagree, Meredith replied. *However, they are going to break out of that elevator eventually.*

Nickie ran for the elevator at the end of the main corridor. *If they do, then we have already tested the security system. I'm sure Addie would be interested to know whether her drones are as effective as my aunt's in close quarters.*

She got into the elevator and waited until Meredith halted the car a couple of decks from the cargo bays. *We good?*

Of course.

Nickie climbed out of the maintenance hatch in the

ceiling and steadied herself before drawing the pistols made for her by her grandma. *Let's go.*

The elevator began to move again, slowly this time.

Nickie heard voices getting closer, matching what she saw in her HUD. *That sounds like Skaine.*

It is, Meredith confirmed.

Nickie repressed a giggle. *Fuck my life. Can you hear what they're saying? This shit's hilarious.*

She turned up the volume in her ear as the quartet of Skaines turned into the corridor. Nickie mentally named them Spooky, Snarky, Suck-up, and Stick-up-the-ass. Not too original, but she hadn't played this game for a while. *Come on...*

It would be much faster to reveal yourself.

Nickie's lip curled. *I know. This skulking doesn't suit me at all, but this is a marathon, not a sprint. Drawing smaller groups into kill zones is the right move here. Open the door.*

"Look," Spooky quavered. "Another one opening by itself. I reckon this ship is haunted."

Snarky laughed cruelly, and Nickie heard the sound of an open palm on flesh. "Shut up, idiot. It's got an EI, is all."

"I agree with Bloat," Suck-up sucked-up. "It's the EI."

"It's neither," Stick-up-the-ass told them all. "But I still don't like it. This is a merc ship. Where is the crew? The slaves?"

Close the door, just slowly, Nickie told Meredith.

"Get in there before we're trapped here!" Snarky ordered.

Nickie was rewarded a moment later when two Skaine hands were thrust into the door to prevent it from closing. *I wish I had time to play with these fuckers.*

The elevator is still holding, Meredith offered.

Nickie almost fell into the elevator. *Who the fuck are you, and where's Meredith?*

You are operating as you should be, so I have no reason to advise caution. Damn, I should have saved the "welcome to the fold" speech for this moment.

Nickie put a hand to the ship. *Fuck. That was a* day.

Um, the Skaines down there? Meredith reminded her.

Nickie snapped out of the memory. *Shit. Yeah.*

She'd hoped for all four, but the gods of shit going just how you want it to were only half-listening that day. Stick-in-the-ass and Suck-up poked their heads into the elevator, and Nickie shot them off.

Fuck it. I haven't got all day.

She dropped into the elevator and shot Snarky.

Spooky stood there with her hands in the air, her head turned to the side and her eyes squeezed tightly shut.

"Aw, dammit," Nickie groused. "You're not even a fucking pirate, are you?"

The female opened one eye and shook her head rapidly.

Nickie noted her glance at Snarky. "That was your boyfriend?"

She nodded again.

Nickie rolled her eyes. "Fuck my life." She crossed to the Skaine and shoved her into a storage compartment. "Stay there until this is over, and I'll try to help you."

The Skaine took in Nickie's glare and pointing finger and nodded mutely.

"I mean it," Nickie told her. "If you decide to join up with the others, you'll die with them. Do I make myself clear?"

She closed the compartment, then thought twice and opened it again. "Do you know anything about humans being kidnapped?"

The female's eyes widened, and she nodded again. Her mouth opened to speak, but nothing came out. She tried again, her voice as wobbly as Durq's. "They're at Bloat's place. He wanted to sell them, but nobody will touch humans. Even I know that."

Nickie pointed again. "Change of plan. Come with me." She pulled the surprised Skaine out of the storage compartment and into the elevator. "You just saved me a hell of a lot of work, Missy."

"That's not my name," the female told Nickie as the elevator ascended to the bridge level.

Nickie shrugged. "A name's a name, right? I mean, you can call me Nickie, but all the other motherfuckers on my ship are going to die knowing a scary-ass bitch named Grimes killed them. It's all subjective."

The elevator opened on the bridge level and Nickie escorted Missy to the small holding cell in the outer corridor. "It's for your own safety," she explained at Missy's odd look. "And, you know, mine."

Once Missy was locked up tight, she secured herself on the bridge.

Adelaide's security system? Meredith asked hopefully.

Well, yeah. Nickie dropped into her chair and pulled up the controls for the elevator holding forty or so pissed-off pirates. *That's a complete U-turn on the system.*

Meredith chuckled. *When the system gets us to QT2 within the hour, I'm not going to argue, mess or no mess.*

Nickie let out a huge yawn as she sat back. *Yeah, me*

either, Meredith. She closed her eyes and opened the elevator doors to let the pirates out into the empty bottom deck. *Release the drones, and wake me up when we get there.*

QT2 System, QBBS *Helena*, Shipyard, The *Penitent Granddaughter*

The crew waited outside the ship for Meredith to drop the ramp.

Adelaide shifted from one foot to the other, impatient to get aboard. "Come *on,*" she muttered.

Grim put a hand on her shoulder. "She's just fine, I keep telling you."

"Then why isn't she responding to the comm?" Keen demanded, just as agitated as Adelaide.

"Nickie will be asleep," Durq predicted. "Otherwise she would have picked up."

The ramp touched the ground and the four headed aboard with varying degrees of haste, Grim bringing up the rear.

They all paused on entering the ship.

Grim almost bumped into Keen. "What's going o...*ohhhhh.* That's a hell of a mess. Meredith?"

There was no reply.

Adelaide ran for the bridge, yelling at the top of her lungs as she went. "*Nickiiiiiiieeee!*"

The others followed close behind, scrambling for the elevator.

Grim was first out. He ran as fast as his two legs could carry him until he reached the carnage in the access corridor.

Adelaide hid her face in her hands. "None of those are…"

"No," Grim told her. "Look, the door is opening."

The four walked onto the bridge somewhat hesitantly, Adelaide and Durq taking cover behind Keen and Grim.

Keen almost shot Lefty when the house bot whirred inquisitively. "Dammit, Lefty."

Lefty whirred again and got back to cleaning the dried blood on the center console.

The noise was enough to make Nickie stir. She murmured in her sleep and settled back when her senses told her she was safe.

Durq smiled softly and left the bridge. "I knew she was fine. No one gets the better of our captain."

Adelaide and Keen looked at each other, then at Nickie, who was lying blood-soaked and fast asleep with a faint, satisfied smile on her lips, then at Grim.

Grim snorted. "Like I said, nothing to worry about."

CHAPTER 13 NICKIE

QT2 System, QBBS Helena, Shipyard

Jean regarded the damage to the *Penitent Granddaughter* with a critical eye. "Sweetheart, you might want to consider upgrading. This ship's better days are so far in the past I wouldn't want to embarrass her by talking about them."

Nickie's heart fell. "Grandma, *no*! I love this ship."

"Really?" Jean flicked a finger at the partially-burned name on the hull. "What's with this? I keep meaning to ask."

Nickie felt her cheeks burn. "Um..." She considered making something up. *No, fuck it. I'm not going to lie.* She shrugged. "I did it because I was pissed at Grandad, but then I kind of grew into it. It's my ship, Grandma. It's my home."

Jean sighed. "Don't give me those sad eyes, child. I'll fix your ship."

Nickie flung her arms around Jean, jumping up and down. "Thank you, Grandma!"

Jean snorted. "Don't thank me yet. I'm going to have to squeeze it in around Bethany Anne's orders, so you might have to stick around a minute or two."

Nickie pursed her lips, thinking of Missy. "That's fine. My crew could do with a break after the briefing. If we're staying, I'd better get my shit together and report to Barnabas."

Jean patted Nickie's cheek, pride in her smile. "That's my girl. Want to do something once you're done with duty? You owe me for deciding not to turn up for dinner the last time you were here."

Nickie floundered for a second before coming up with a way to make it up to Jean without getting stuck talking about her mom the whole time. She smirked as she gathered Jean in for a hug. "That would be great. I have *just* the thing in mind for us to do together."

QT2, QBBS *Helena*, Shipyard, Aboard the *Penitent Granddaughter*

Grim was getting dinner on the table when Nickie arrived in the mess.

Grim spotted Nickie slipping in and grinned. "You're just in time!" He placed the large covered dish he was holding on the table and waved her over. "Come and sit before it gets cold...er."

Nickie took her seat and looked under the cloche at the mass of shiny-looking tentacles. *Fuck my life.* "Looks great, Grim. Mmmm."

"Just wait until you taste it," Grim promised. Threatened?

Nickie wasn't too sure.

Adelaide, Durq, Keen, and Missy looked on in silence as she cut a bite-sized piece off and put it into her mouth.

"Is it good?" Adelaide whispered while Grim's back was turned.

Nickie moved the piece of meat around her mouth and bit down. Her ability to reply was lost to the party in her mouth.

"Well?" Adelaide pressed, glancing at the whatever-it-was with a mixture of hunger and horror. "Are those tears of pain or happiness?"

Nickie pulled the dish toward herself. "Mmf, no. You wouldn't like it at all. You should totally let me take care of the whole thing." She cut off another piece as Grim returned with the side dishes.

He took one look at Nickie and shook his head. "And you were so anxious to eat anywhere but here tonight."

"I take it all back." Nickie waved her knife at Grim. "Sit, eat."

Grim sat by Nickie, and the crew got to work on the meal.

Nickie looked around the table, her gaze lighting on the female Skaine. She looked terrified, and more than a little bit confused by Durq's presence among the mostly human crew. "So, Missy…"

The female's head ceased its constant roaming and snapped to Nickie. "Y…yes?"

Nickie gestured for Keen to pass the dish down the table. "You're not hungry?"

Her eyes flicked to the dish, then back to Nickie. Hunger and confusion—or maybe gas? Nickie didn't claim to be an expert on Skaine physiology beyond how to dismember them —on her face. "Not really. What are you going to do to me?"

Nickie rolled her eyes. "Nothing. Durq, can you tell Missy we're not going to eat her?"

Durq winced when the female squeaked in fear. "Really, we're not. What kind of name is Missy for a Skaine?"

The female sneered and spoke in Skaine. "It's not my name. Just what the human keeps calling me."

Nickie's expression hardened at the disrespect. "The human's name is Captain Grimes," she cut in, also in Skaine. "I am the niece of Ranger Two, and this is *my* ship you're aboard. A touch of gratitude for not just blowing your head off with the rest of those assholes you had the shitty sense to hook up with wouldn't go amiss."

Missy nodded, subdued. "I apologize, but my name is…" She uttered a string of syllables that made both Nickie and Durq snicker.

Nickie waved her fork at the female. "I'd stick with Missy if you're planning on hanging out with us for a while. I'm not gonna lie, humans would have a field day with that."

Adelaide, Keen, and Grim got the translation from Meredith a moment later. The guys cracked up, and Adelaide looked confused for a moment longer before covering her mouth with both hands.

She turned to Nickie. "Meredith doesn't lie, does she?"

Nickie shook her head, biting the inside of her lip so she didn't laugh at the beetroot shade her unworldly engineer had turned.

Adelaide's eyes widened. "Wow."

Missy had other concerns. "If you're Ranger Two's kin, what are you doing with a Skaine on your crew?"

Nickie blew Durq a kiss, which he caught. "Because *he's* an absolute sweetheart. Missy, my aunt and I know better than anyone that not all Skaines are dicks. I heard that asshole hit you, and to me, you're no different than any other young woman who got in over her head." She waved her fork at Missy. "I give exactly no fucks about wasting your asshole boyfriend, but I'm gonna help you if you want to quit being bum-gum. Your help finding our missing people would go a long way toward building trust between us."

Missy considered Nickie's offer. "Okay, I'll tell you where the humans are. What then?"

Nickie shrugged. "It's up to you what you want to do once you've shared what you know with my boss."

Grim snorted. "*You* have a boss, Boss?"

Nickie lifted a shoulder. "I'm sure Barnabas sees it that way. It doesn't hurt to humor him. The point is that Missy here knows where the crew of the *Lucky Run* is being held. The dead Skaine on cargo deck B, Missy's ex, was the one who kidnapped them."

Everyone turned to Missy, who nodded hesitantly. "He really was a dick," she admitted. "My parents wanted me to go to school in the Federation. I wish I'd listened."

Nickie sat back in her chair and dropped her fork onto her plate. "Then it's settled. You come with us when the ship gets back from my Grandma Jean's workshop, and we get you to school if that's your jam."

Adelaide looked up from her food, her fork hovering

halfway between the plate and her mouth. "When the ship gets back from where?"

Nickie winced internally as she turned to Adelaide. "From my grandma's workshop," she repeated. "She's giving the old girl an overhaul."

The color drained from Adelaide's face. "I've put a lot into this 'old girl,' and I don't want some other engineer taking liberties." She paused a second. "Even if that engineer *is* Jean Dukes. It's like inviting a stranger in to look at your," her eyes flicked to Missy, "underwear or something."

"Or something?" Nickie teased. "Grandma Jean can get it done fast, and we need it done fast."

Keen wiped his mouth and dropped his napkin onto his empty plate, a wry smile twitching under his mustache. "I think what Addie was trying to say before her pride overcame her sense is that she would appreciate the opportunity to learn from the master."

Nickie drained her cup and got to her feet. "If you want to spend your leave hounding my grandma's teams, I'm not going to stand in your way. You might wanna avoid my grandma, though."

"Leave?" Grim echoed hopefully. "I could use some time."

Adelaide tilted her head. "Why should I avoid Jean?"

Nickie nodded at Grim. "We need a break. You're all free until the ship is repaired." She pushed her chair in and turned to leave. "As for Grandma, she *always* gets grumpy after a shopping trip."

QBBS *Helena*, Main Concourse, Commercial Quarter

Nickie held up two pairs of shoes, unable to decide between them. "Which ones?"

Jean glanced at Nickie and shrugged. "They're exactly the same."

Nickie groaned, putting both pairs back on the display. "Are you kidding? Grandma, you can strip any piece of machinery and reassemble it by eye, but you can't tell two completely different shoes apart?"

Jean rolled her eyes. "They're shoes, so who cares? You sound just like your mother. Why the two of you can't just get along is beyond me. You're..." she paused to reconsider what she had been about to say, "nothing alike. But still. You should call her, she misses you. And I hate shoe shopping."

Nickie's arms dropped to her sides. "Dammit. There goes my good mood."

Jean's eyebrow went up. "Meredith Nicole Grimes, you drop that attitude right this second and apply some of the good sense you've gained these last few years to look at things from your mother's point of view."

She turned on her heel and left Nickie standing in the middle of the store with her mouth hanging open.

Maybe you should have chosen a different activity, Meredith suggested.

Maybe you should have spoken up earlier. Nickie hurried after Jean. "I'm entitled to my attitude," she argued, falling into step beside her. "You don't know what it was like after you left, just me in that house and her always at work."

Jean grunted. "Poor you, having a parent who worked her ass off to put a roof over your head, clothes on your back, and food in your stomach. It must have been *so* hard for you."

"What about having someone at home when I got in from school?" Nickie retorted. "That would have been good, too."

"It would have been," Jean agreed. "If you had *gone* to school. Your mother raised you right despite the challenges she faced as a single parent."

Nickie rolled her eyes. "Sure, make her sound like the perfect mother. You weren't there, Grandma. She's cold, and she's *always* been cold."

Jean snorted. "I'm not saying Lillian is perfect by any means. God knows she drives me crazy." She stopped Nickie with a hand on her arm. "But she loved you from the moment the doctors put you in her arms, and she's never stopped for a second."

Nickie pushed away from Jean, her eyes stinging. "Grandma, don't."

Jean's voice was soft. "She's your mom, but she's also a human being. Did you ever stop to consider how she felt about losing your father the way she did?"

Nickie's protest froze in her throat. "She never told me anything about him except his name and that he died before I was born."

Jean threaded her arm through Nickie's and steered her past a bar and into a quiet coffee shop. "That I didn't know." She headed for a booth in the corner and sat down. "He was a scientist. Did you know that? Your mom was never going to fall for anyone who wasn't brilliant."

Nickie slipped into the booth across from Jean and dropped her bags on the seat beside her. "Why are you telling me all this now? Like I said, it doesn't matter. I never knew him, and my mom never bothered to tell me anything about him."

Jean frowned, concern in her eyes. "Then it's time you got some understanding. You can't keep blaming your mother for her choices." She held up a finger before Nickie could interrupt. "You can't keep blaming her for yours either."

Nickie's shoulders dropped as she recognized the truth in Jean's words. "Well, shit."

Jean pressed her lips together. "I'm not done yet. You aren't the only one who lost someone, but you sure as shit weren't left holding a baby when you did. Your mother didn't have the luxury of being able to throw the Empire's biggest temper tantrum when your father died. She had you to take care of."

Nickie shrugged. "I don't want to talk about my mom," she admitted. "She hurt me, Grandma." The urge to run was almost overwhelming, but Nickie made herself stay in the booth. "I don't need to be reminded of what a disappointment I am."

Jean snorted. "You were never a disappointment. An ass, yes. You get that from your grandfather. Not your looks, though. You might think you look like John, but there's more than one blue-eyed, blond man in your gene pool, and you have his eyes."

Nickie traced the lines on the tabletop with her finger. "What was he like? My, um...dad?" She stumbled over the word, the taste of it strange in her mouth.

Jean smiled sadly. "I didn't know him that well. They met on a research station they were both working on while your mom was going through her 'save the universe' phase. We spoke in the background of Lillian's calls. He was kind. Smart, like your mom. Regular human, not enhanced."

"I figured that from the weak-ass dose of nanos I got," Nickie conceded. "How did he die?"

Pain flashed across Jean's face. "There was an attack on the station, some enemy of the planet below. The station was destroyed in the crossfire."

Nickie was suddenly angry for the man she never knew. "Who attacked? Was my mom hurt?"

"It doesn't matter," Jean told her. "Bethany Anne resolved it, as Bethany Anne does. Your mother only escaped because she was away on an expedition with her team." She placed a hand over Nickie's briefly before reaching for the menu. "I thank my lucky stars every day that she wasn't aboard that station. What would I do without my girls, hey?"

Nickie gave her food order and put the menu to the side. "You and she don't do anything but fight like cats."

Jean's eyes wrinkled at the corners. "Sure, and we love every minute of it. I've come to realize the only important thing is that we stay connected, even when we're mad at each other. You're home, and that's all I care about."

Their food arrived a few minutes later, giving Nickie time to chew over her thoughts as well as the sticky ribs on her plate.

Did she feel like she was home? She wasn't sure if "home" was anyplace other than her ship these days. Where she was suited her, no matter what everyone else in her life seemed to think. She was happy out on the edge where she could act without too much oversight.

Jean broke the silence. "How did your briefing with Barnabas go?"

Nickie dropped the bare bone onto her plate. "He put it off until we get back to High Tortuga. I don't know why. He's only going to lecture me into breaking something of his." She shrugged at Jean's quizzical look. "I don't know whether to take his offer. He's bugging me about it by not bugging me about it."

Jean waved her fork, spilling rice back onto her plate. "This isn't about the offer."

Nickie shrugged. "I need to talk to my crew. There are some communication issues between Grim and me," she confessed. "I've been holding onto my full orders until I know for sure what his motivation for sticking around is."

Jean's face softened. "Oh, Nickie. That's not going to resolve anything."

Nickie nodded, poking around on her plate with her fork. "I know, Grandma. I'm not the one avoiding the issue, but I don't want to push if it's going to break up what we all have."

High Tortuga, Space Fleet Base, Barnabas' Office (one week later)

Barnabas caught a glimpse of the main arena in the center of the Hexagon as Tabitha chased her escaping son. "Don't you sit still for one minute?"

Tabitha laughed, the camera feed from her drone bobbing to keep up. "Which minute do I have for that? The one between my eyes opening and closing each night? My child has inexhaustible energy, Barnabas. There is no rest."

Barnabas chuckled at her good-natured bitching. "The joys of parenthood are bountiful, I'm led to believe."

Tabitha's grin transformed into a frown. "One second, Barnabas." She turned to her left and got the mom voice out. "Todd *Michael*, you get down from those ropes right *now*."

The child in question did as he was asked. However, the set of his lip reminded Barnabas so much of Tabitha's sulky side, he couldn't help but snicker.

Tabitha turned her frown to the camera when Barnabas cracked up completely. "Not funny."

"'Lexis and Gabriel are allowed to go in the ring," Todd protested, encouraged by Barnabas' apparent approval. "I'm big too!"

Tabitha knelt by Todd, doing her best to keep her stern expression fixed in the face of his adorable petulance. "Alexis and Gabriel are teenagers, honey. You have a ways to go before you're as big as them."

Barnabas snickered at Todd's petulant tone, enjoying the go-around from his long, *long* come-around. "He reminds me of you, Tabitha. Hard-headed."

Tabitha pouted, scooping Todd up to carry him to the elevators. "Oh, you'll get your turn with him. Probably when he's all teenage and hormonal."

"Saints preserve me." Barnabas groaned as he sat back in his chair. "Will I ever be free of stubborn children bent on driving me back to my old ways?"

Tabitha raised an eyebrow. "Nickie giving you trouble?"

Barnabas shook his head. "The opposite, actually. She prevented a pirate attack and got a lead on Jennie's crew in the process."

"That's great!" Lillian appeared on the camera as Tabitha walked into the apartment. "How is she?"

Barnabas' face softened. "She's doing well, Lillian. I'm just sorry she hasn't gotten past her anger at you yet."

Lillian's eyes dropped. "She's doing well otherwise?"

Barnabas smiled. "Better than any of us could have hoped, given the circumstances."

Lillian nodded. "Then I'm not going to push her. I don't want her to run again."

Tabitha reappeared minus her tiny terror and did something to switch Barnabas' view so it was stable. "Have you told her you're based on QT2 these days?" he asked.

Lillian shook her head. "She knows. She hasn't reached out. She will when she's ready, and until then, it's enough to know she's doing okay."

Tabitha nodded in agreement. "Maybe it won't be so long. She's still pretty guarded in her messages, but she's coming around, right?" She looked at Barnabas. "Right?"

Barnabas lifted his hands. "I wouldn't know."

Lillian narrowed her eyes at him. "What, you haven't even peeked into her mind to see how she's feeling? I don't believe that for a second."

Barnabas' mouth twitched. "I did check her sanity when I found her um…wrestling with Rickie Escobar."

Tabitha squealed. "Oooohhh! I remember when she had a crush on him!"

Lillian rolled her eyes, chuckling. "Don't remind me. All I had to do was mention his name when she was sixteen, and she'd turn bright red and run. It was almost painfully cute." She made a face. "*Wrestling?*"

Barnabas nodded. "In the middle of the hangar, no less. So, of course, I looked."

Tabitha waved her hand in a circle. "And?" She shrugged at Lillian's reaction. "What? If our favorite loud-ass tempts her to come home to us, let's not complain."

Barnabas wrinkled his nose. "There's a small snag in your plan, Tabitha."

"Rickie wasn't looking at her that way," Lillian guessed.

Barnabas pointed at her. "Got it in one."

Lillian shrugged. "He never did. I know Rickie is a pain

in the ass, and also in the head—but he's a good man. He looked out for her as much as he could when she went off the rails. A couple of times, I only knew what party to go drag her out of because she had told him where she was."

"Which is why this could be perfect!" Tabitha argued. "Think about it. We get her and Rickie together, and then she comes home to us."

Barnabas rubbed his temple. "You're not going to let this go, are you?"

Tabitha winked. "Hell, no. I'm gonna go find Rickie and grill him just as soon as Trouble wakes up from his nap."

Barnabas sighed. "I wouldn't meddle if I were you," he cautioned. "Besides, Nickie's infatuation appears to have passed."

Tabitha waved him off. "Don't sweat it. As far as Rickie will know, I'm just a concerned aunt asking after her niece."

"And I'm just a harmless monk," Barnabas returned dryly. "Now isn't the time to throw a relationship at Nickie. She'll find someone if and when she's ready. Without our help."

Tabitha pouted as she headed out of the room. "Buzzkill. You're right, though."

Barnabas nodded sagely. "I generally am."

"You're an ass, is what," Tabitha told him, ending the call.

Barnabas waved a hand to collapse the screen, then sat back for some contemplation while he had some peace and quiet.

Which was apparently something that didn't exist in *this* lifetime.

The door bounced open before Barnabas had even begun to regulate his breathing. "Good afternoon, Nickie."

Nickie strode in and dropped into the guest chair with all of the usual care she showed his beloved antique furniture. "You ready for the briefing?"

Barnabas opened his eyes and sat up in his chair. Contemplation would have to wait. "Yes, which is why I asked you to stop by when you got back. I have a new assignment for you."

Nickie frowned. "I already have an assignment, and I haven't even decided if I'm going to accept it yet. Is this about all those dead pirates? One little fight, and you have me going back to High Tortuga?"

Barnabas waved away her interruption. "No, no. Quite the opposite, in fact. I had a very interesting discussion with the Skaine you picked up."

"Missy," Nickie supplied.

Barnabas pursed his lips. "Ah, that explains the discrepancy. Apart from the name she gave, everything she told me checked out."

Nickie broke into a grin. "I think I'd go with a nickname too if my name was—"

He held up a hand. "Indeed. Back to the matter at hand."

Nickie got to her feet. "You want me to get the missing crew back? Just give Meredith the coordinates, and I'm gone as soon as I've informed my crew of the schedule change."

Barnabas shook his head. "I'm splitting you off from your crew for this. They will continue on their regular route, and you, my dear, are heading a little deeper into the Federation."

Nickie groaned and sat back down. "The Federation? Is this another attempt to get me to fangirl over unity and togetherness?"

It *might* have been—if Barnabas hadn't already decided to pick his battles with her. "No, this is an attempt to extract our people from an extremely hostile situation using the best tool I have at my disposal for the job. You."

"Call me a tool and ask me to do something for you, sure," Nickie grumbled. "Can I at least take Grim with me?"

Barnabas inclined his head. "If you must. There's a ship waiting for you in Hangar Three. I've also arranged with Lance to provide some additional resources. It's a short diversion to pick them up on your way."

Nickie's lip curled. "Why do I think I'm not gonna appreciate whatever you've arranged?"

Barnabas lifted his hands, a smirk touching his lips. "Not a clue. Meredith has your brief, so good luck."

Nickie got to her feet and headed out of the office.

Barnabas waited for the usual slam but was rewarded with the soft *snick* of her closing the door quietly instead. He almost felt bad about the surprise awaiting her at the outpost.

Almost.

High Tortuga, Space Fleet Base, Hangar 003, QBS *Sayomi*

Adelaide gazed at the Shinigami-class ship enviously. "It's just so..."

"Pretty ship, huh," Nickie agreed, putting an arm around Adelaide's shoulders. "But it's only a loaner. Besides, Grandma sent a message with the ship that said if we mess with it, she'll personally see to it nobody on the crew will be able to eat solid food for a month."

Adelaide took a step back. "Yeah, um, I'm good on the *Penitent Granddaughter*, thanks."

Nickie released Adelaide. "I thought you had a great time learning from Grandma? She was impressed with you."

"She was?" Adelaide pressed her lips together and nodded. "I did. I learned that she makes *you* look even-tempered and that she's a million times smarter than me. The woman scares the crap out of me."

Grim chuckled as he passed the two of them on his way to the QBS *Sayomi*. "You and me both, and I've known her a hell of a lot longer than either of you."

"Just how long *is* that, Grimmie?" Nickie asked.

Grim shook his head and made his way up the ramp. "Impatience will get you nowhere," he chided gently.

Nickie watched him go, the discomfort she'd felt since the truth about Grim had begun to surface bubbling up. "He's not getting out of it this time," she muttered, turning back to Adelaide. "We'd better get going. Are you guys going to be okay without us?"

Adelaide snorted. "Are you kidding? The ship is in the best shape I've ever seen her. The run is going to go smoother than ever." She bumped Nickie with her shoulder. "Besides, I was going to ask you the exact same thing."

Nickie nodded, the weight of the mission ahead settling over her. Was this how it felt to be responsible? She shook it off. "Me? I'm just fine. It's Captain Jennie we need to think about."

Adelaide pressed a hand to Nickie's shoulder. "If Jennie

and her crew are still alive, you'll bring them home safe and sound. I know it."

"I'm going to do my damnedest to make sure of it." Nickie smiled and moved toward the *Sayomi*. "See you when we get back."

Nickie headed up the ramp, considering the best approach to get Grim's story out of him while they were alone. Her head down, she almost crashed into him as she walked onto the ship. "Shit, did your legs stop working or something?"

Grim lifted a finger to point at the translucent human shape floating in the center of the corridor. "What the hell is *that*?"

Nickie considered the black-eyed apparition for a moment and shrugged. "Fuck if I know. Why don't we ask?"

The apparition spoke, her long, blond hair lifted by a nonexistent wind. "I am Sayomi. Welcome aboard my ship, Captain Grimes."

Nickie raised an eyebrow and nodded at Grim. "Avatar." *Fucking kooky EIs.*

Shinigami-class ships house AIs, Meredith told her.

Okay, then, Nickie modified, *fucking kooky AIs. Same difference.*

I don't know, Meredith countered. *I wouldn't annoy a being Eve created from Shinigami. It could get painful.*

Sayomi turned in midair to glide away, her robes swishing gracefully around her. "If you would follow me. We will be departing shortly."

Nickie adjusted the weight of the bags she was carrying

and set off after the avatar. "Thanks for the ride, Sayomi. You heard the nice AI, Grim. Let's go."

Grim hesitated for a moment, looking at Nickie. "Are you sure about this?" he whispered. "She looks like something out of one of those human movies where everyone dies horribly."

Nickie shook her head minutely, glaring at Grim to shut him up before he offended Sayomi and his fears became reality for them both. "Show some respect and you'll be fine. Besides, do you think I'm gonna let you die before we have that conversation you've been putting off for so long?"

Grim shuffled along behind Nickie. "I'd like to think you wouldn't let your dearest friend die at all."

Nickie snorted softly. "That remains to be seen."

Federation Outpost

Nickie looked around the landing pad, pointedly ignoring Grim.

Grim wasn't falling for her mood. "It's not the right time."

"When will that be?" Nickie retorted. "Or am I just supposed to carry on as though I trust you until you decide that time comes?"

Grim looked hurt. His reply, however, was soft. "I'm not denying that our meeting was no accident, but I didn't have to stick around. I chose to stay because we forged a bond. You can trust *that*. Besides, I'm not the only one playing my cards close to my chest, am I?"

Nickie's stomach did a somersault. "We have a mission to get through."

Grim's reply was cut short by the appearance of a uniformed man in his mid-thirties who slipped out of the crowd and came up to her with his hand out. "Hey, you must be the Grimes we've heard absolutely nothing about. I didn't know there was a girl Grimes."

Grim sucked in a breath.

Nickie ignored his hand and poked him in the chest. "Do I look like a fucking 'girl?'"

The man's mouth quirked to the left. "If I say you're definitely all woman, will it get me punched?"

Nickie grinned, the tension broken. "Shit, I don't even know. Try it and find out."

Grim chuckled. "I wouldn't."

Nickie shot him a glare. "Just because *you're* on my shit list doesn't mean I'm pissed at everyone." She turned to the man and smiled. "I take it you're Lance's guy?"

The man nodded. "The name's Jack. Jack Harrison. Anything you need while you're here, you just ask for me."

Nickie wasn't planning on staying long enough to need anything. "Good to meet you, Harrison, but it's going to be a short acquaintance. I'm only here to take on a delivery. Let's get it loaded so I can be on my way."

Harrison looked up at the ship, then down at his wrist holo, confused. "You *are* Captain Meredith Nicole Grimes, right?"

Nickie nodded, not liking the doubt she saw on his face. "Uh-huh. What's the issue?"

"You're down for an overnight, Captain." Harrison tapped his holo, and she received a ping from him.

"My delivery is live cargo?" She was going to have some serious words with her uncle when she got back to High Tortuga.

Harrison snickered. "Cute. You might wanna call my team something other than that if you want them to put any effort into keeping your ass safe on that planet."

Grim darted in front of Nickie and stuck out his hand before she could refuse the team's help altogether. "We're glad to have you along. Grim'zee, call me Grim."

Harrison took Grim's hand and shook it, smirking at Nickie's look of fury. "Good to meet you, Grim. Come on, I'll introduce you to the guys before I show you to your quarters. There's usually some kind of chow going in the team rec room at this time of day."

Grim nodded amiably. "Sounds good to me. Boss?"

Nickie rolled her eyes at Grim's way of making friends with every stranger they met and swept a hand in front of her. "Whatever. Lead the way."

She allowed them to walk ahead while she considered the best way to murder someone who could hear you thinking about it. *Mere, do you think I could get the drop on Barnabas?*

I don't think going after your uncle is the wisest decision, Meredith told her. *Besides, it's not really Barnabas you are annoyed with, is it?*

I don't know what you're talking about, Nickie grumbled. *Of course, I'm annoyed with Barnabas for messing with me. Now I have to babysit Uncle Lance's guys as well as get Jennie and her crew to safety. Fucking Grim. It would be nice to have backup I can trust on this.*

You're being hard-headed again, Meredith admonished.

Grim has your back. Are you sure you're not taking your frustration out on him because you don't feel comfortable asking your Aunt Tabitha for answers?

Nickie glared at Grim, who was chatting animatedly with Harrison as they walked. *Nope. That's a different bone I have to pick. He deserves it for lying to me.* She wrinkled her nose, stifling a yawn as she followed Harrison and Grim into a small rec room. *I hope this doesn't take too long. All that awkward silence on the trip over here was a bitch, and I'm wiped.*

Meredith hesitated a beat before replying, *You've had a lot to process recently. It takes energy.*

Nickie groaned internally. *This isn't the time to bring up my mom, Meredith.*

I didn't mention your mother.

Nickie chose to accept Meredith's denial in the name of getting peace and fucking quiet on the subject.

Harrison briefly introduced Nickie and Grim to the team before showing them to their quarters for the night.

Nickie wrinkled her nose at the mostly bare living area. "Kind of reminds me of my ship. Before the upgrade."

"The *Sayomi* was this basic?" Harrison asked in surprise.

Nickie snorted. "Fuck, no, and if my Grandma Jean ever heard you compare this place to one of her creations, you'd be wearing your testes for earrings. I snagged a Skaine battleship a while back, and it's been a project."

Harrison made a show of looking pained. "Wow, that's a harsh comparison. I mean, it's a bit spartan, but it's serviceable,"

"It's great," Grim interceded. "We appreciate it, don't we, Nickie?"

Harrison frowned when the temperature in the room

dropped sharply. "I'll, um, leave you two to get settled. Those two are the bedrooms, and that's the bathroom," he told them, pointing to the three doors. "Sleep tight."

Nickie nodded. "We'll convene on the *Sayomi* first thing." She took one more uninterested look around the living area once the door closed behind Harrison, then headed for her room with the food she'd snagged from the rec room.

"When are you going to be done ignoring me?" Grim called after her.

"I dunno," Nickie retorted. "Probably when the time is right."

Grim stopped dead in the middle of the room. "That's not fair," he protested. "Nickie!"

Nickie slammed the door behind her, crossed the three steps to the cot on the left wall, and sat down heavily on the edge.

Screw Grim. He could keep his secrets.

She opened the container of what looked like some-thing-with-rice and forced herself to take a bite. It tasted like cardboard next to Grim's cooking.

Fuckdammit!

Would you like to talk about it? Meredith asked.

No. Yeah. Fuck it, I don't know! She dropped the mystery rice dish on the locker by the bed and lay down without getting undressed. *I just want some answers. I don't think it's too much to ask from someone who claims to be my friend.*

Meredith made a soothing sound. *I don't want to keep reminding you that Grim's loyalty isn't in question here. You know deep down that you can trust him.*

Nickie huffed. *Then why the fuck won't he tell me how he*

ended up in that bar when we met? I'm pretty damn sure Aunt Tabitha had something to do with it. I need to know, Mere.

I don't have access to his thoughts or I would tell you, Meredith told her gently. *But I would hazard a guess that his appearance wasn't the first time she sent someone to keep an eye on you.*

Nickie frowned. *Fuck it, I'm gonna ask.* She opened her HUD and selected the message icon.

However, no words appeared. Instead, she stared at the message window without seeing it.

Is something wrong? Meredith's tone was full of concern.

No, it's okay. Nickie blinked away the tears that had suddenly ambushed her. *I just want... I want...* She switched her attention back to the message window and started a new message.

Hi, Mom.

Beyond Federation Borders, Approaching Pirate Hideout, QBS *Sayomi*, Bridge

"This ship is unbelievable," Harrison marveled as the *Sayomi* Gated in, invisible to all the security around the outer edges of the system. "This is the closest we've gotten to the planet without being made."

Nickie sat up in the captain's chair when he entered the bridge. "You're being generous, calling *that* shitsplat a planet."

Harrison lifted a shoulder and walked over to the couch by her chair. "It's a gigantic pain in my ass, no matter what anyone calls it."

She glanced at him. "How much of a pain in the ass?"

Harrison grimaced. "Let's just say I'm impressed by the ease with which we're getting in. We've been trying to work our way into the place for almost a year, and the most we've been able to do is observe."

"Why not just take the whole planet out?" she asked. "Seems like the logical thing to do."

Harrison shook his head, slipping his kit bag off his shoulder. "That would've been my first course of action. Higher-ups decided differently."

"Can't say I'd be happy coloring within the lines like that," Nickie admitted.

Harrison half-shrugged as he opened his bag and began laying weapons out on the couch. "As much as it pisses me off to play nice, it's working."

Nickie raised an eyebrow. "Yeah? Sounds like you've found a workaround for the security."

He nodded and got to work strapping the contents of his bag around his body. "My team knows their work. What we lack in physical presence, we more than make up for with all the active tech we have floating around on the planet."

Nickie was familiar with the type of operation. "Assholes attract other assholes. It makes sense to take advantage of that. Let them think they have a safe haven."

Harrison put a foot up and bent to slip a blade into his boot. "Uh-huh. But in reality, we know almost everything they're up to, which means we keep on top of things out here."

Nickie definitely didn't look at his ass. "So you knew about the kidnapped crew?"

Harrison stood up and turned around, rubbing the back of his neck with one hand. "Um, no. That one got by us. But we know where Bloat's gang is based. You did a good thing taking him out."

Nickie leaned against the console and crossed her arms. "Waste of good oxygen fucking deserved it," she told him. "Fuckface was beating his girlfriend when I shot him."

"Skaines have girlfriends?" Harrison teased. "Who'da thunk?"

Nickie put her hands on her hips. "Well, yeah. You need a girl Skaine and a boy Skaine to make a Skainlet." She demonstrated with a few gestures, making Harrison laugh. "Didn't your dad ever have 'the talk' with you?"

Harrison's face stilled. "He might have done that if he hadn't died when I was a kid."

Nickie grimaced. "Shit, didn't mean to hit a nerve." She bumped his arm with her shoulder on her way past to the elevator, wondering what in hell brought on *that* little sharing-is-caring moment. "Come on, we've got a bunch of people waiting for us."

Nickie led Harrison to the cargo bay Sayomi had designated as the operations room, where Grim and Harrison's team were finishing up preparing for their part in the mission ahead.

The fifteen men and women stopped working when Nickie and Harrison walked in. Harrison came to life in the presence of his team. He raised his clasped hands above his head and made his way through the avenue they created for him, stopping to give every one of them a word of encouragement.

Nickie snickered when he slapped the ass of the largest man as he skirted the drop doors on his way to the table, the rest of the team falling in behind him and fanning out to take their seats.

Nickie smirked, feeling the love from everyone in the room except Grim.

Her friend looked as uncomfortable as ever to be wearing armor, despite the fact that the armor Sofia had given him was nothing like as heavy as the traditional bulky–ass Yollin exosuit he'd worn when they first met.

Nickie dropped into the chair between Grim and Harrison, smirking when he flinched at her unexpected attention. "'Sup?"

Grim glanced at Nickie but didn't let the reprieve from her silence stop him from bitching. "I keep telling you I'm a lover, not a fighter," he moaned. "This armor chafes."

Nickie's smirk widened into a grin. "At least it's not gonna cook you."

Harrison knocked on the table to bring the briefing to order. "Ladies and gentlefuckers, we have around forty people—"

"Forty-three," Nickie supplied.

Harrison swept a hand to indicate that Nickie should take over. "Feel free to share with the group. Brace yourselves, we have the honor of a Grimes among us."

The Federation soldiers turned as one to stare at her.

Nickie clapped to silence the murmurs that went around the table. "Your commander tells me you're shithot. There are forty-three of Bethany Anne's people somewhere on that planet. Let's keep the focus on them, not on my fine ass."

"We're all Bethany Anne's people," Harrison murmured.

"Whether we want to be or not," Nickie agreed. "I'm happy to sign autographs afterward if any of you are still feeling starstruck." She winked at Harrison, then dropped the friendly grin as the chuckles died down. "Now, I understand we're in a delicate position regarding the op you've been working this last year. I want you to know I have no intention of screwing your effort."

Harrison raised an eyebrow. "I have to admit it's been a concern, even though the General cleared whatever action was necessary to get the crew back. How do you plan on retrieving them without causing a scene?"

Nickie lifted a finger. "I wasn't done. I *have* no intention of causing a scene. But make no mistake, I'll leave a trail of crispy criminals a mile wide if that's what I have to do to get that woman and her crew home to their families."

Harrison nodded. "Understood. It's in our best interests to make sure you know what you're walking into. Let's get you the information you need so we can get underway. Greatreeks, the images." He nodded to one of the younger men on the right of the table. "Jason is our eyes down there," he told Nickie.

Jason tapped his wrist holo as he got to his feet and walked around to the projection screen, where a window came up. "Bloat's gang is...was based out of this fine establishment. I suppose they'll lose out to Scrag's lot now he's dead. Maybe Doxie's."

Nickie's lip curled when she saw the rusty sheet metal building. She noted that the whole neighborhood had a similar aesthetic—neon signs and sadness. "Shit, what's that place held together by, the collective failed hopes of its patrons? I'm gonna take it there's no weather down there."

Jason shook his head. "The atmosphere is entirely artificial."

She nodded. "What do you have on the gang, and the bar in general?"

Jason tapped his holo again and several new windows were overlaid on the first, each containing a mugshot. "These are all known gang members, Bloat's lieutenants."

The windows were replaced by another set, then another. "These are persons of interest to us. We're monitoring… pretty much everyone on the planet, but the drones we're working with don't react well to EM fields."

Harrison pushed an envelope-sized packet across the table toward her. "You could actually help out by taking a few inactive drones in for us."

Nickie nodded and accepted the packet, her focus on the mugshots. "Mmhmm. Shouldn't be an issue. Wait, go back." Her eyes were instantly drawn to a familiar face among the scowls, missing teeth, horns, and antennae. "Hello, handsome," she murmured.

"Is this really the time to trawl for guys?" Grim asked.

Nickie shot an elbow into his ribs. "Don't be a dumbass. I just found my way in."

Harrison looked hopeful. "Yeah?"

"You mean *our* way in," Grim modified breathlessly, rubbing his side.

Nickie grinned. "Not gonna work. You're so uptight, I might as well take Grandad John in with me."

"If only," Grim muttered.

"It would change this operation, that's for sure." Nickie pushed her chair back and got to her feet. "Change of plans," she told Harrison, pointing at the dark-haired human on the screen. "Find that guy."

"That's simple," Jason chirped cheerily. "That's Darius Prior, small-time con artist and petty thief. I could go on. I've just sent the command out to the network. Soon as we find him, you'll be the first to know, Captain."

Nickie waved him off. "I know *all* about Darius and his delusions of being some badass fuckboy. A scumbag never changes his spots." She shook her head at the blank looks. "I'm gonna play him to get inside that bar. You need to be ready."

"Ready for what?" Harrison asked, concern touching his face.

Nickie shrugged. "How the fuck should I know? I'm making this shit up as I go. Just get me Darius' location and be ready."

She heard Grim consoling Harrison as she stalked out of the cargo bay.

"Is she your first Grimes? Mmhmm. I thought *someone* would have warned you..."

After a quick trip to her quarters, Nickie headed back to the elevator. "Transport bay," she commanded, feeling less than commanding with half her body on display.

Sayomi appeared from the shoulders up on the screen above the panel. "You look nice, Captain."

"Didn't realize I was talking to you, Sayomi. Thanks." She looked down at her street clothes: a buttoned cutoff top over tight, tight jeans and her everyday boots. "Heels would have been better, but I'm not learning *that* lesson again."

"A wise decision," Sayomi intoned as the doors opened on the bay. "I wish you success. Remember, I am a call away if you are in need of assistance."

Nickie narrowed her eyes at Sayomi's wicked grin. "By 'assistance,' I take it you mean the total destruction of everything for miles around the target?"

Sayomi inclined her head. "I cannot but be who I am."

Nickie grinned. "I'm trying to keep the destruction to a minimum, but I'll keep your offer in mind."

"In the meantime, I have a Pod ready and waiting for you."

"Thanks, Sayomi."

Meredith spoke up as Nickie left the elevator. *I've informed Grim that we're leaving.*

Nickie clenched her teeth to stop the muscle in her jaw from twitching. *Why would you do that?*

Were you really thinking of going in there alone?

Nickie pushed the door to the transport bay open. *I wasn't thinking of it, Meredith. I* am *going in by myself.* She picked up her pace, hoping to get to the Pod before Grim made it down there.

He was waiting by the open Pod with his arms folded across his chest. "Really, Nickie?"

"Whatever." Nickie marched past him into the Pod, his sigh when she refused to meet his eyes causing her chest to constrict. She dropped onto one of the benches and waved him in. "Just get aboard if you're coming. You can wait in the Pod."

"Taking us down now," Meredith announced from the speaker once the doors were closed.

CHAPTER 16 NICKIE

Pirate Hideout, Pod

Nickie worked hard to maintain the silence as the Pod sliced through the thin atmosphere.

It came to a stop twenty feet above one of the unlit buildings.

"Open the door, Meredith." Nickie paused in the open hatch, leaning out to see the lights on the main drag below.

She made the jump, the rush of wind that enveloped her gone as quickly as it had hit her. She landed silently on the roof.

I'm not happy about staying up here, Grim grumbled over the Etheric comm.

Nickie looked up at him, gripping the Pod as though his life depended on it. She lifted her hands, then turned and stepped onto the lip of the roof. *Sorry, Grimmie. No time to wait.*

Nickie switched the Etheric comm off to cut off Grim's protests and hopped over the edge of the roof, making her way down to ground level in blissful silence.

A quick glance around showed Nickie she was alone in the alley opposite the bar. *Meredith, I need access to Harrison's eyes.*

Working on it, Meredith replied. *Done. Looks like it's getting busy. Are you sure about using Darius? You two didn't part under the best circumstances.*

Nickie scanned the drone feeds in her HUD, testing the temperature of the crowd on the street. *Trust me, he'll be more than happy to see me once he gets that I'm not here to kill his lying ass.*

Meredith chuckled. *If you say so.*

I do. There he is. Nickie reached around and tightened her bra a notch, then popped another button on her top before slipping into the crowd and heading toward her prey.

Never hurt to make sure.

She found Darius outside the bar, talking to a couple of hooded figures. *He's not as hot as I remember.*

Meredith sniffed. *He wasn't anything special in the first place.*

Well, he's useful now. Nickie fixed an excited expression on her face and ran over to where Darius now stood alone. She leapt into his arms, almost knocking him over. "Darius! I *knew* it was you! Where've you been? You look good!"

Darius was too dazed to notice her drop one of the drones Harrison had given her into the pocket of his long coat. "Nickie? What are *you* doing here? I thought you died in that Federation raid on Balakis."

"So does the Federation," Nickie lied smoothly, tracing his jaw with a fingertip. "I wasn't too happy to leave *you* behind…"

Darius' eyes drifted downward. "I wasn't too happy to be left behind. Or to get six months' hard labor after your little vanishing act left me high and dry."

That's what you get for selling stolen rejuvenation packs, asshole. Nickie pouted and dropped her hand to stroke his chest. "Poor baby," she purred. "Let me make it up to you. We can start with a drink."

Meredith snickered when Darius let his lower brain make the decision. *My bad. You were right. He hasn't changed a bit.*

Told you. Nickie slipped her arm through Darius' and steered him toward the bar entrance. *Now all I have to do is act like a dumb blonde, and we're golden.*

The heavies on the door looked right through Nickie, too caught up in fawning over Darius to register her as a threat.

Nickie squeezed his arm as they entered the building. "You must be doing pretty well for yourself."

Darius puffed his chest out. "I'm doing great. I fell into a lucrative logistics opportunity after I got out."

"Oh, yeah? How, um, interesting." Nickie repressed the urge to vomit. Instead, she fluttered her eyelashes while smiling vacuously at Darius

"It is if you know the right people," he explained, grinning at her like he was the second coming.

Dumb fuck didn't even manage the first one.

"Tell me more," Nickie simpered, somehow maintaining her syrupy tone instead of breaking his face when he put his hand on her ass.

Darius was happy to oblige, which gave Nickie the opportunity to get a read on the place with the part of her focus that wasn't on saying "Wow," "Ooh," and "How *smart!*" in all the right places.

She'd been in so many dives like this during the early part of her sabbatical that they were almost generic to her. There were the regulars crowding the taps and the barflies all over anyone who looked even half-willing to buy them a drink.

And the gangsters.

They huddled together, doing their business in the shadowy booths behind walls of muscle, away from prying eyes.

Darius stopped in his tracks when his name was called from one of the booths a few steps from the bar. "One minute," he told her, dropping her arm. "Wait here."

Nickie saw the Skaine who had summoned Darius glaring at her. "I'm gonna get us drinks." She turned to the bar, surreptitiously releasing the rest of the drones.

The bartender noticed Nickie waving for attention and served her quickly before moving on to the next patron. She sat and sipped her drink while she listened in on Darius' conversation with the Skaine.

It took a moment for her to isolate the two voices from the background noise. The Skaine sounded two seconds away from murder—and also somewhat afraid.

"*You* told me you could do something about Bloat's…indiscretion."

"And I can," Darius assured him. "The plan is going forward. I just need one final piece in place to ensure nothing leads back here. This isn't the Federation, Doxie. There's nothing to prevent Baba Yaga from coming here for her revenge."

"Nobody wants *that*," Doxie agreed. "Fucking Bloat. My mother always said that no-hope, rotten idiot would get himself killed and leave me up to my neck in shit."

"She'd know," a new voice piped up. "She did give birth to him."

"I shoulda listened to her," Doxie moaned. "Fucking family. You try to look out for them, and the next thing you know, there's a bunch of fucking *humans* in your basement. Just find a way to get them out of here before somebody turns up looking for them. And Darius?"

"Yes?"

The Skaine's tone was dispassionate as he spoke. "You don't need me to remind you how I feel about being lied to. I want a resolution, and you have one chance to be that resolution before I consider you to be part of the problem. Do we have an understanding?"

Nickie smirked into her drink as Darius mumbled his reply. *Meredith, are you getting this?*

I am, Meredith replied, *and so are* Lieutenant Commander Harrison's *drones.*

Good. Now let's see... What's the fastest way to get Darius out of here? I want to know exactly what plan he has for the crew and how I can fuck that up for him.

Darius returned a moment later, his confident grin belied by the ashen tone of his skin.

Nickie slid his drink along the bar, and he downed it in one gulp. "Someone giving you trouble?" she asked, feigning concern.

Darius looked askance at her. "No one. It's nothing." He caught the bartender's attention and waved for one of the bottles on the top shelf.

He grabbed the bottle, waving his wrist holo carelessly in the bartender's direction, then turned to Nickie. "Wanna take this party somewhere quieter?"

Nickie drained her glass and put it back down. "Thank fuck for that."

He didn't take long at all, Meredith remarked.

I remember that being one of the reasons I didn't try too hard to save his ass last time around. Nickie's mouth quirked as she squeezed Darius' bicep. "Let's go."

Darius smirked and moved in to nuzzle her ear. "Still impatient, I see."

Nickie forced her jaw to unclench and smiled brightly. "You know me. Who has time to wait around? I thought you were gonna drag this out all night."

The cocky grin returned to Darius' face. "Baby, I plan to drag this out *all* night long."

This time Nickie almost did throw up.

"Are you okay?" Darius asked. "You look sick."

Nickie grinned, waving a hand at Darius. "Yeah. Just my body arguing about yet more alcohol. You know how it is."

He laughed. "I know there's a damn sight more than alcohol in your body right now. How you're so healthy-looking is a mystery."

Nickie winked and skipped a few steps ahead. "Maybe I had a few of those rejuvenation packs stashed away for rainy days."

"Rainy days, sure," Darius snarked, picking up speed when Nickie disappeared into the corridor that led to the ground floor rooms. "Not to pull your ass back from the brink when your latest bender takes you there?"

Nickie turned back, smiled sweetly, and gave him a

double middle finger salute. "Same fucking thing, isn't it? Now, what did you have in mind? I'm getting bored."

Darius waved the bottle vaguely at the ceiling. "I have a room upstairs."

Meredith sniffed. *A room that's probably got more bugs than half the people in this place.*

Nickie snorted. *Wow. Judgmental much, Meredith?*
Just saying.

Darius frowned, his hands dropping to his sides. "You don't like the idea?"

Nickie shrugged. "Didn't say I didn't *like* it." She nodded at a plain door. "I'm impatient, remember?" She took his free hand and pulled him through the door into the small maintenance closet. "It's gonna be a squeeze, but that's half the fun, right?"

Darius dropped the bottle on the nearest flat surface and came at her with greedy hands. "Sweetheart, half the fun with you is not knowing what crazy shit you're gonna pull next."

Nickie welcomed him into her arms. "You don't get this much hotness without at least a little bit of crazy," she giggled, walking her fingers down Darius' chest toward his waistband.

Um, isn't this going a little further than you planned?

Nickie snickered in her mind. *Nope.*

"Is that good?" she asked, tilting her head up at him.

Darius groaned. "Mmhmm…"

Nickie raised an eyebrow. And her knee.

Darius' moan of pleasure morphed into a wheeze of pain as his legs gave way on contact.

"How about now, you dirty no-good lying sack of shit?"

she demanded, kicking him as he fell to the floor in the fetal position.

Darius curled up tighter with each blow she landed.

"Logistics opportunity, my enhanced left ass-cheek. You're a fucking *smuggler*, Darius. And not even a decent one. Those are people's *lives* you're playing with." She laid a boot into his ribs for good measure. "Get up, you fucking coward. Were you going to look those people—those human beings—in the eye when you 'got rid of them?' Explain to Jennie that her child will never know her because *your fucking profits are all that matter?*"

Darius pulled his head out of his arms. "No! I got dragged into this!"

He's lying, Meredith told her.

Oh, I know that. It's easy to tell—his mouth is open. Nickie bent and grabbed Darius around the throat. She lifted him easily, pinning him to the wall with her face bare millimeters from his. "The only reason you're still fucking *breathing*," she ground out, "is that I need your sorry ass alive to get my aunt's people the fuck out of here and back to their families."

Darius looked at her like she'd just shit on his favorite shoes. "'Your aunt's people?'" The outrage melted away, replaced by fear. "Oh, fuck. I can't believe it. You went home."

"Fucking right, I did," Nickie snarled, her breath hot in the narrow gap between their faces. She shook Darius and released him. "Now listen up, because I want you focused on your investment in my plan, and I'm only going through it once."

Darius' hands dropped to his groin, his knees buckling as the aftershock of Nickie's nutshot went through him. "You wanna suck up to the Federation, that's your business. I don't have any investment in your plan."

"Course you do," Nickie told him cheerfully. "You're gonna be the first to die if anything goes tits-up, so I'd call it an investment in your continued ability to breathe."

Darius glared at her, his knees still trembling a bit. "What the fuck, Nickie?" He leaned against the wall and groaned in pain again.

Nickie flourished a hand. "You could be a little more grateful. I'm being nice here."

"*Nice?*" Darius gaped at her in disbelief. "How is a knee to the balls *nice?*"

Nickie looked at him with pity, tapping her nails together. "You still have them, right? In fact, considering that you don't have any way to come through on your promises to that Skaine, you should be on your knees thanking me for pulling your dumb ass out of the shit."

"How do you know about that?" He narrowed his eyes, straightening his clothing angrily. "You were listening."

"No kidding." She smoothed her hair with a hand. "You can thank me later by making sure I never see you again. Until then, this is how it's gonna go. I'm gonna get my ship, you're gonna wait five minutes after I go to tell Doxie you got the humans a no-strings ride, and make sure you look like you just got fucked within an inch of your life, or he might just work out what kind of worm he's dealing with."

Darius glared at her as he obeyed. "It's not gonna be a stretch to pretend."

Nickie straightened Darius' shirt collar, ignoring the flinch when she pushed a comm bud into his ear. "Attaboy. It's showtime. The sooner you get what I came for, the sooner you can go back to fooling yourself that you're King Dick around here."

Darius sneered at Nickie. "Fuck you, Nickie. I should've remembered what a bitch you are."

Nickie snorted, wiggling her fingers over her shoulder as she left. "Should've, could have, and I'd be a bitch all the same. Now be a good little lowlife, and remember—I'm listening."

Nickie shuddered, hurrying to leave the bar. *Fuck my life, Mere!*

Meredith's snickering devolved into what Nickie would have called a belly laugh if EIs had bellies. *Never mind your life. I thought for a moment that you were going to—*

Nickie cracked up, drawing a few looks from the people in the corridor. *Ew. No.* She ignored the looks, making her way past the guards on the door onto the street beyond. *Besides, it was* priceless!

Priceless, indeed, Meredith offered dryly. *But do you think Darius will follow instructions?*

Nickie shrugged as she left the street for the alley. *It's going to suck much, much worse for him if he doesn't, but I fully expect him to try to pull something stupid.*

As if on cue, the comm bud she'd given him went dark.

You should turn your comm back on, Meredith advised. *Grim will be worried.*

Grim's always worried, Nickie complained, activating her comm as she began the climb up the building.

What happened in there? Grim cut in. *Did you find out where the crew is being held?*

Nickie rolled her eyes. *Yeah, they're in the building, underground. Darius is going to deliver them to me.*

Grim didn't try to hide his relief. *That's great news! What's our next move?*

Nickie scanned the wall for the next handhold. *Get with Harrison. I want his team all over the handoff site.*

There was a pause before Grim came back. *He's on his way.*

Nickie hauled herself onto the roof of the building, squinting up to where the Pod hovered overhead. *Good. Hit me up when you're all in place. I've got a knife in the back to keep watch for.*

Will do, Grim replied as the Pod shot upward. *Just...be careful, okay?*

Nickie dropped the link and crouched by the edge of the roof, where she had an unobstructed view of the bar front.

He's behaving like someone who has something to hide, Meredith noted as they listened to the audio from the drone she'd hidden on Darius.

Uh-huh, Nickie replied. *This would be easier if I was feeding him lines. If he fucks it royally, I'll step in and negotiate for Jennie and her crew myself. Otherwise, I don't want to blow Harrison's efforts.* She wrinkled her nose in frustration. *At least the Skaine won't get too suspicious, since Darius was already shiftier than quicksand to begin with.*

True, Meredith conceded. *I've had word from Sayomi. Harrison and his team are in position.*

Nickie touched her ear as Meredith fed the team's comm into her HUD. *That was fast, guys. Welcome to the party.*

Harrison chuckled in her ear. *We don't fuck around, Captain Grimes.*

Shame, Nickie teased. *There I was, hoping you were good with weapons.* She grinned to herself when Harrison's team catcalled over the open channel. *Our asset is currently persuading everyone's favorite neighborhood kingpin that I'm a good bet for solving their little human problem.*

"Ass" describes him better, Meredith snickered.

You're *an ass,* Nickie told her fondly. *Where's Grim?*

He's coordinating on the Sayomi.

Avoiding the fight, you mean. Nickie's annoyance almost made her miss the end of Darius' explanation. *Shit, they're almost done talking. I'm going back in.*

Ready and waiting for your word, Harrison confirmed.

Good to hear. A few minutes later, Nickie was back in the bar, sidling up to Darius at the booth with a wide-eyed pout. "Baby, where did you go? I thought we were gonna blow this place, and then you disappeared. I can't wait around forever, you know."

Darius turned to the others at the table and rolled his eyes at the petulant tone in her voice. "Females. What are you gonna do?" He stiffened momentarily when she slipped into the booth beside him and put her hand on his leg. "I told you I had some business to wrap up first, remember?"

Nickie applied a touch of pressure to the nerves around his knee with her nails to remind him which one of them needed to respect the other in this situation. "I don't mind.

Who are your friends?" She flashed a bright grin at the gangsters around her. "You don't need him anymore, right? I'm pressed for time in a way a few thousand credits isn't going to make up for if I have to wait much longer."

The Skaine waved Darius away, much to his disgust and Nickie's amusement. "Yes, take him." He waved one of his Zhyn guards after them. "Escort them down to the holding floor. Give them whatever help they need to get the humans aboard the female's ship."

The Zhyn nodded and gestured for Darius and Nickie to follow him.

Nickie raised an eyebrow when the guard avoided eye contact with her. "Aren't *you* just the friendliest!"

The Zhyn continued to pretend she didn't exist, which suited Nickie down to the ground. She kept up the spoiled human act while the Zhyn led them out back of the bar and down two flights of stairs to the sublevel where the crew was being held.

"What's the deal here?" Nickie asked the guard while they paused at a heavy iron door. "I mean, no one is stupid enough to think slavery is a viable way to make a profit anymore."

The guard glared daggers at her before turning to the iris scanner.

Nickie shrugged. "Fine, don't talk. Darius, make him hurry up. I told you, I'm not waiting around forever." She wrinkled her nose as she looked around in disdain. "This place is gross."

You missed the scanner, Meredith told her.

His fucking head was in front of it, Nickie retorted. *Did I suddenly develop x-ray vision?*

The guard pushed the door open and entered the holding floor ahead of them. A brief burst of many voices in conversation leaked out but ceased immediately when the guard stepped onto the floor.

Nickie shoved past Darius to get through the door before him. *Meredith, there are more than humans here. There's what, twelve cells here, and they're full.*

What can you do that won't endanger any of them?

Nickie thought about it for a moment. *That's not an issue.* A smile played across her lips. *I think the question is, whose account will I get the most joy from raiding to buy their freedom?*

Meredith snickered. *I wouldn't like to be you when Barnabas finds out what you've done.*

Then he shouldn't have pranked me first. Get me access, and connect it to my wrist holo. "Hey, I want to speak to your boss about buying all these slaves."

The Zhyn guard headed straight for a bank of switches on the wall opposite the cell floor without acknowledging Nickie.

She walked over and grabbed the guard's arm. "Hey! I'm talking to you. Are these slaves for sale or not?"

Darius found his voice at last. "It's okay, Verril. She's probably just after squeezing a few more credits on top of what I'm paying her to take care of Doxie's little embarrassment."

The Zhyn reacted at last. He turned and grabbed Darius by the throat. "You don't talk about the boss like that. He looks after us like Bloat never did." He looked Nickie up and down. "The stock is for sale to those who can afford it. You do not look like someone who can afford it."

"Like fuck, I can't," Nickie retorted. She dipped her fingers into her pocket and pulled out the thousand-credit chip she'd put there while dressing. "Don't be fooled because I'm slumming it here with Darius. We'll take care of the humans." She flipped the chip for the Zhyn to catch mid-air. "But call your boss and tell him I want to talk business."

The Zhyn examined the chip, then nodded to Nickie as he pocketed it. He touched his ear and murmured for a few moments. He turned back to Nickie. "Boss says six mil for the lot."

Nickie made a show of examining the slaves in the cells. "Hmm. That doesn't give me much margin. Tell him my offer is four-nine."

The guard passed along her counter offer, then nodded. "Payment first. Boss' orders," he told her.

Nickie swiped her wrist holo against the Zhyn's.

He glanced at his wrist holo, then nodded toward the other end of the cell block. "Congratulations on your purchase. This way."

That might have been a little extravagant for your means, Meredith remarked.

Fuck, yes, Nickie replied. *Uncle B. can replace it. He'll thank me when Lance is happy I didn't trash his operation.*

Jennie and her crew were in a less than cooperative mood when the Zhyn released them. They huddled together and advanced on Nickie, Darius, and the Zhyn.

Nickie groaned internally. *Meredith,* do *something.*

The Zhyn raised his blaster just as the crew received Meredith's assurance they were being rescued in their implants and backed down. He growled and waved them into line. "That's what I thought. Outside, all of you."

Captain Jennie narrowed her eyes at Nickie as she passed. Nickie winked at Jennie in return.

The Zhyn jabbed Jennie in the ribs with his blaster. "Keep moving."

CHAPTER 17 NICKIE

Federation Outpost, Team Base

Nickie held her glass high to avoid losing her drink to the dancing around her. She swayed her hips to the music as she crossed the rec room, nodding to Jennie and Jason. She paused when she met Harrison's eyes.

Meredith had something to say, as usual. *Will you admit you're attracted to Harrison now that the mission is complete?*

Nickie looked away. *Aren't you satisfied with getting Jennie's crew back and rescuing all those other people? The Polaris has only just left, for fuck's sake. Give me a minute to breathe before you start nagging.*

Jennie is fine, Meredith countered, *and the people you rescued are all being taken care of and returned to their homes. It wouldn't be such a bad thing to let your hair down, would it?*

Nickie groaned internally. *Shut up, Meredith! I'm not interested, okay?*

Harrison had that look as he approached her. Tipsy, and a little bit hungry. "You want to disappear a while? I think we can escape without anyone noticing."

Nickie spotted Grim sitting alone at a small table in the corner. Her old friend had two clean tumblers on the table in front of him. Seeing Nickie, Grim produced a large bottle and set it between the glasses.

She nodded toward him, glad of the excuse to let Harrison down easily. "Doesn't look like the stars are in alignment."

Harrison took one look at her thoughtful expression and nodded in understanding. "I hope you two work it out. You're good people, and you deserve it." He leaned in to whisper, "But if you get done early, you know where my quarters are."

Nickie winked. "You know, maybe I will. But right now I've got a long-overdue explanation to hear." She brushed past Harrison and made her way over to Grim.

Grim looked up as she arrived at his table. "Hey."

Nickie rolled her eyes and dropped into the seat opposite him. "Wipe that sorry-ass look off your face, Grim. This isn't a trial. I just want answers." She grabbed the whiskey bottle and unscrewed the cap, sighing as she poured them both an extra-large measure. "I guess I owe you a few as well."

Grim tilted his head. "No, you're entitled to your feelings. I'm sorry for making you wait for answers."

Nickie raised her glass, forgetting her own confession for the moment. "I've worked most of it out. I just need to know one thing."

Grim touched his glass to hers and took a sip. "What do you want to know?"

Nickie hesitated, finding the admission difficult to put

into words now that the moment had arrived. She sipped her drink to buy another second. "I just want to know why you stuck around."

Grim choked, spraying his mouthful of whiskey everywhere.

Nickie pushed her chair back to avoid getting an unwelcome facial. "What the *fuck*, Grim?"

Grim coughed, clearing his throat of rogue alcohol. "Sorry, it's just…" He wiped his mandibles with his sleeve. "You're kidding, right? I thought you found out Tabitha sent me and you were going to make me leave. That's why I've been putting you off. You're my best friend, Nickie. I stuck around because I *wanted* to."

Nickie couldn't process the sheer weight of her relief. She put her drink down and gripped Grim's hand. "I have to tell you something. I don't want you to overreact, okay?"

Grim nodded, extracting his somewhat crushed fingers. "Okay?"

Nickie grinned. "Barnabas—"

Meredith cut in. *I'm sorry to interrupt. Sayomi is preparing her ship to leave. You have maybe ten minutes to get there.*

Nickie jumped up and grabbed the bottle. "Shit! Come on, Grim. We've got to run, or we're gonna miss our ride home."

Federation Outpost, QBS *Sayomi*, Bridge

Nickie ran onto the bridge, pausing at the top of the staircase to look for Sayomi's avatar. "Sayomi? What's going on?"

The AI appeared before her, wearing armor instead of the ghostly accouterments Nickie had seen her wearing so far. "There has been an Ooken attack on the Silver Line network. I am the closest ship to the location."

Nickie grimaced. "Another attack? Fuck. What can I do?"

Sayomi shook her head, the shine in her eyes the only thing that differentiated them from the rest of her face. "You will remain aboard. I'm not averse to confining you if you decide not to comply. The Ooken aren't anything to mess with unless you have one of the highest levels of enhancement."

Nickie raised an eyebrow. "I'm not far from that. I can heal myself."

Far enough away that you probably won't survive, Meredith warned. *Don't make me snitch to Sayomi.*

Nickie dismissed Meredith's nagging. "How often are the routes being attacked?" she asked, following Sayomi down the stairs.

The AI waved a finger at one of the secondary consoles as she walked past to stand in front of the wraparound screen. "See for yourself, Captain, I have provided all the data you have clearance to access. We will Gate shortly."

Nickie took a seat and skimmed the reports. "These all look like chancers trying their luck. Robberies, not massacres."

Grim caught the end of Nickie's sentence as he entered the bridge. "What massacres?"

Nickie shook her head. "I was saying that there haven't been any massacres."

Grim glanced at Sayomi's back. "So why the rush to leave? We were just getting started with the party."

Nickie nodded at the screen. "Take a look."

The *Sayomi* exited the Gate in the center of a debris field—the remains of a ship.

"Are we too late?" Grim asked, joining Nickie to examine the devastation.

"Which ship is that?" Nickie asked, waving Grim off for the moment.

Sayomi shook her head. "That information is for fleet command only. I need you to step back, Captain Grimes."

Nickie clenched her fists, refusing to give in to her emotion. There was only one way she was getting in on this. She closed her eyes and said goodbye to her freedom. "Are you able to take an affidavit?"

Sayomi inclined her head. " I am. Do you wish to record one?"

Nickie nodded. She opened her eyes and lifted her chin to meet the AI's dark gaze. "Ready? I, Meredith Nicole Grimes, hereby accept the position of Silver Line Fleet Captain," She paused, wondering if she was coming across as too stuffy. It wouldn't do to give the impression she intended to become anybody's golden girl. "Offered by that eternal pain in my ass, Barnabas, on behalf of Queen Bethany Anne Nacht. I want it recorded that I'm accepting this duty because there are lives at stake and it's mine to claim." She pressed her lips together. "That get me clearance, Sayomi?"

Sayomi's eyes flashed red. "Affidavit witnessed by Grim'zee P. Bonesticker and sealed. Thank you, Fleet

Captain Grimes. You have clearance to access classified material."

Nickie grunted and returned to the secondary console. "Give my EI everything you've got."

Grim's mandibles fell open in shock when Nickie's eyes turned white. "What did you just *do?*"

Nickie extracted herself from the torrent of data and flashed him an apologetic look. "I'm sorry. I didn't want to tell you Barnabas offered me the rank until I knew for sure you were gonna be sticking around."

Nickie, Meredith intervened, *You should see this. We're on one of the side routes to Devon. That was a supply station, not a ship.*

Nickie held up a finger while she skimmed the details of the war so far, paying extra attention to the parts that had information on Ooken physiology.

"I have located an Ooken ship signature at the far edge of this system," Sayomi informed them, interrupting Grim's spluttering reply. "We are in pursuit."

Silver Line Route

Nickie remained glued to the viewscreen as the ship ate up the kilometers between them and the Ooken ship. The *Sayomi* came into range, giving Nickie and Grim their first look at the enemy that had Bethany Anne breathing fire.

The dreadnought was almost half the size of the rogue moonlet orbiting dangerously close to the system's Kuiper belt, making it easily twice the size of the *Sayomi*.

"What are you going to do?" Nickie asked.

"This," Sayomi replied. She fired on the Ooken, sending

out two blue-white streaks that lit the void with bright contrails.

Nickie held her breath as one of the missiles exploded against the dreadnought's shielding.

The dreadnought bucked under the impact, veering off-course.

Nickie's lip curled. "Is that it?" She ate her words when the Ooken ship was rocked by another explosion, this one inside of the shield.

"Nice!" Grim exclaimed.

"Etheric-enabled missiles," Sayomi explained as though it were completely normal for an explosive to vanish into another dimension and reappear.

The dreadnought spiraled, leaving a trail of twisted metal and shredded components behind.

Nickie leaned over the console, gripping it tightly in her excitement as the Ooken ship careened toward the moonlet. "What are we waiting for? Let's go finish them off before they get back and tell the other Ooken where they are."

Sayomi shook her head. "They already know. These invaders share one mind, so you can be assured there will be a reaction from the hive. We should scan the wreckage of the station for survivors, then get the hell out of here before the Ooken send reinforcements."

Grim nodded. "That's the most sensible thing I've heard since I got on this ship."

Nickie gave the crash site a crestfallen glance as it receded in the viewscreen, half-regretting the missed opportunity to pit herself against a superior opponent for the first time since she was a kid.

Are you sure you're not chasing adrenaline? Meredith asked as Nickie turned away from the screen.

Not even a little bit, Nickie replied. *I was born for this.*

Silver Line Route, Station Wreckage

Nickie paced the bridge, much to Grim's annoyance. He didn't want to stay in this system for a minute longer than they needed to be. Unfortunately, he wasn't in command of the situation. "How long is this going to take, Sayomi?"

Sayomi flashed red eyes at him. "I have been scanning for less than a minute. What is it you expect me to have—" She tilted her head. "Oh, wait. There is a heartbeat."

Nickie frowned, her eyes darting to the remains of the station's superstructure. "A human heartbeat?"

Sayomi nodded, adding an overlay to the image on the viewscreen. "This is the infrared scan. There looks to be a portion of the station that is still mostly intact."

Nickie couldn't make out anything that looked humanoid on the infrared. The overlay on the sealed part of the wreckage was mostly shades of indigo and green, with splotches of fading orangey-yellow where the life support systems were winding down. "You sure it was a heartbeat?" she asked Sayomi.

Sayomi flourished a hand, and the image zoomed in on a small dark-orange blob. "It is faint. I believe the human is injured."

"Are there any Ooken there?" Nickie asked.

"No," Sayomi responded.

Nickie nodded. "Then we'd better move."

Sayomi raised an eyebrow. "'We?'"

Nickie slapped Grim's back, ignoring his wince. "Yeah, how else do you expect whoever that is to make it out of there? This is the shit we live for. Isn't that right, Grimmie?"

Grim sighed. "I'll go get my exosuit back on," he intoned wearily as he set off for the armory. "Don't go out there without me."

Silver Line Route, Station Wreckage

The Pod landed on the burnt hull of the station. Nickie and Grim exited the Pod and looked around for an easy entry into the wreck.

"This way." Nickie set off along the hull toward a nearby airlock.

Grim scrutinized the lock pad. "You can open that, right?" He shuddered, his voice sounding strange to him inside his helmet. "I hate armor, and nothing is going to make me change my mind."

Nickie rolled her eyes as she moved past him to get a closer look. "Would you be saying that if you were standing out here without any?" She bent to examine the opening mechanism, reading the hololabel instructions as soon as the words resolved into English. "Manual lever is in the... Got it." She straightened up and wrenched the mid-panel on the right-hand side of the hatch clean off.

She grinned at Grim in her HUD cam and pulled the lever down. "Bingo."

Grim frowned as the hatch cycled open. "What's a bingo?"

Nickie shrugged and slipped inside. "No idea."

They passed through the airlock on the other side and made their way into the corridors beyond.

Grim gagged at the tableau of indiscriminate butchery they stepped into.

"Don't throw up in there," Nickie warned, feeling rising nausea herself at the sight of the bodies piled around the airlock. She managed to hold onto her cookies for the moment, touching her Etheric comm to activate it. *Sayomi, you reading us?*

Loud and clear, the AI responded. *Your target location is approximately two kilometers from here. Take a left and follow the corridor until you reach the elevators. I will guide you from there.*

Grim looked around uneasily, squinting a little under the harsh emergency lighting. *This is unbelievable. This was a station just a few hours ago. How powerful* are *these Ooken?*

Nickie couldn't argue with Grim's disbelief. *I'm beginning to think very,* she murmured, noting that apart from the odd chunk of tentacle among the bloodbath, there were no Ooken among the dead. *Bethany Anne needs to know about this.*

I have already sent the report with my scan data, Sayomi informed them.

Nickie trod softly, making no noise as they progressed past open doors toward the elevators. *You wanna talk about my new job?* she asked Grim, thinking to take his mind off his nerves.

Grim moved similarly stealthily, his concentration on

his surroundings and picking his way through the organic slurry without slipping. *What, now?* he blurted.

What better time? Nickie reasoned. *This is the kind of shit I'm going to be working to prevent. I need someone I can trust to take care of the company while I'm captaining. What do you say?*

Grim hop-skipped over a puddle, skidding as he landed. He steadied himself against the wall. *I think that's more Keen's cup of Coke,* he told her. *If you're going to keep fighting, then it looks like my mother's favorite son is going to war.*

Nickie smiled, scanning ahead as she walked with her Jean Dukes Specials at the ready. *That doesn't sound too bad. Just the two of us, flying around delivering an ass-kicking to the Ooken.*

Grim shook his head. *If you think Bethany Anne is going to give you free rein for destruction...*

Nickie turned back and waved her JD Special over the carnage around the airlock. *To prevent this from happening? Sure she will. She can't grow her military fast enough. I've seen the company books, I know how much cargo is being transported to the shipyards. She needs every fighter she can get, and I'm one hell of a fighter if nothing else.*

Okay, Grim acquiesced, accepting her resolve. *We've been strictly support so far. What made you change your mind?*

Nickie wasn't entirely certain. *Maybe it's just time to grow up and do what's right. I've spent too much time being selfish, thinking of myself instead of what I can do for others.*

Grim patted Nickie's upper arm. *You haven't been that person for a long time, Nickie.*

The conversation ended when they came to the junction where three elevators sat opposite them on the corridor going crossways.

Nickie wondered why Sayomi had directed them to the dead cars. *Where do we go from here, Sayomi?* She looked around the empty corridors on either side, feeling a twinge of foreboding when the AI hesitated before replying. *Please tell me we don't have to haul our casualty up the fucking elevator shaft.*

I could, Sayomi told them, *but I don't see how lying to you will benefit this rescue mission in any way.*

Grim groaned aloud, moving to pull the doors of the central shaft apart. *Anything but heights. Have mercy on an old Yollin!*

Nickie rolled her eyes at his bitching. *You know damn well you're going to go down that shaft. Why complain?*

Grim shrugged, letting go of the door once it clicked past the safety mechanism. *Because it makes me feel better, that's why.*

Nickie punched his upper arm before reaching for the maintenance ladder inside the shaft. *It would be too quiet without you,* she teased, stepping down onto the rung.

Grim whimpered as he swung his bulky body onto the ladder. *As much as I hate to inflate your already enormous ego, life has taken a turn for the better since I met you.*

Nickie looked up, then wished she hadn't when her pause almost got her a faceful of Yollin ass. She resumed her descent quickly, putting some space between them on the ladder. *Don't know what the fuck you're talking about with my ego, loverboy. Don't think I missed you sneaking off every time we dock at Waystation. Have you been finding a little excitement of your own?*

Grim hesitated.

Nickie snorted. *Grimmie's got a girlfriend...*

Did you see Durq and Missy getting chatty after dinner the other night? Grim sidetracked, hoping she would take the bait.

Nickie let Grim's secret romance be for the moment. *You think those two are gonna hook up?*

Maybe, Grim conceded. *They were definitely getting along well.*

Doesn't mean anything, Nickie disputed. *Watch yourself. We're coming to the end of the ladder.* She turned her head to get a look at the floor below and jumped past the last few rungs.

Grim clambered down a few moments later and paused to rest his hands on his exosuit's knee plates. *Yollins are not built for this kind of maneuvering.*

And yet you managed it. Nickie waved him over, seeing that neither of them could reach the exterior doors from the depression they were in. *I need a boost to get the doors open.*

Grim stood patiently while Nickie climbed up on his shoulders and forced the doors apart.

She hauled herself out, then spun around on her stomach to reach back into the shaft to pull Grim up. "Put some effort into it," she teased as he gasped for breath. "You're going to have to take a desk job at this rate."

Grim fell forward out of the elevator shaft onto his hands and knees, then rolled over on his back and lay there for a second to get his breath back. "I'd rather have another session in a Vid-doc and come out with the body of a god."

Nickie rolled her eyes. "Wouldn't we all."

"You're already enhanced," Grim pointed out as he got to his feet.

"Yeah," Nickie agreed as they resumed their trek into the wreckage. "But if I could summon a damn energy ball, I'd be a happy woman."

Ooken Outpost, QBS *Defiant*, Bridge

John opened the report Sayomi had sent him in his HUD

The first part was straightforward enough: she had answered a distress call from a station a couple of systems out from Waystation. He frowned at the next part, the furrow in his brow deepening with every word he read. The last sentence made him grunt in surprise. "The *fuck?*"

Eric's eyes flicked to John and then back to the outpost on the viewscreen. "Hey, what's up?"

John closed the report and engaged the *Defiant's* weapons systems. "My granddaughter has somehow ended up in my ship at the site of an Ooken attack."

Eric's eyes widened. "Nickie? *Shiiit.* Can she handle it?"

John's jaw tightened as he released the missiles. "Sayomi stranded the Ooken ship and headed back to search for survivors from the station. Nickie and Grim went in to rescue a survivor."

Eric grimaced. "You don't think she's taken on too much? What if she comes across an Ooken?"

John sighed, wishing he wasn't so far away. "I have to trust that she's ready. Still gonna worry about the kid, though. She's always been a hothead."

They watched the staging post explode, leaving the readings to the ship's AI.

"Wanna get back?" Eric asked once the show began winding down.

John nodded. "Yeah, that would be good."

Silver Line Route, Station Wreckage

Nickie halted at the bulkhead blocking their way. "Is this an exterior wall?" she asked, confused.

No, Sayomi replied. *It is the failsafe between this segment and the next. A safety measure meant to enable the sections to remain sealed should a catastrophe occur.*

"Only one survivor," Grim commiserated. "I'd say it didn't work in the case of an attack on this scale."

"One is better than zero," Nickie countered. "Sayomi, how do we get past the bulkhead?"

There is an air duct located above your heads, Sayomi supplied. *It will bring you out fifty meters from the casualty.*

Nickie and Grim looked up at the meter-square vent cover.

"Doesn't the duct negate the bulkhead?" Nickie asked.

It does. Sayomi confirmed. *However, there is also an independent secondary life support system in each section that is activated when the bulkhead seal is broken.*

"I'm not going to fit through there," Grim complained, frowning at the vent cover.

Nickie shrugged. "Wait here. I'll be back before you know it."

Grim sighed, moving into position to help Nickie up into the vent. "Fine. Just be careful, okay?"

Nickie pulled the vent cover free and crawled into the duct on her stomach. She pulled herself toward the junction leading to the other side of the bulkhead, glancing nervously at the narrow bands where the cutoff panels were located on the boundary.

The access panel to the other side fell away with a clang, startling Nickie with the sudden loudness. She slid out feet-first, landing softly on the floor below with her weapons raised.

Sensing no threat, Nickie dropped her arms and walked a few steps along the dark corridor before remembering she didn't know where she was going. The smell of blood was still strong in the air, making it impossible for her to find the injured survivor that way.

Fifty meters, huh? she remarked to Sayomi. *Which way?*

Keep going, Sayomi instructed. *You are almost there.*

Nickie advanced, her senses straining for any sound that would guide her to the survivor. She came to a hole in the wall where there had previously been a door.

She stepped over the door, which lay flat on the other side of the ruined portal, and entered the mess beyond.

The spartan dining area had been completely overturned. Tables smashed, and food, plates, cups, and cutlery everywhere.

And the bodies.

Nickie's nausea returned with a vengeance when she saw the half-chewed and discarded corpses strewn around the mess.

The people here had fought hard for their survival and lost.

Nickie's eyes were drawn to a heap of red fur and

bright blue flesh over by the kitchen. She gripped her JD Special and approached cautiously.

The Ooken twitched a tentacle as she leaned over to examine its body. Nickie fired three kinetic rounds into its skull, and the tentacle dropped back to the floor. She caught another movement in her peripheral vision and turned to see a foot disappear behind the island in the kitchen.

Nickie holstered her weapon, calling softly as she stepped over the dead Ooken. "Hey, it's okay. My name is Nickie Grimes. I'm going to get you out of here."

A disheveled teenaged head peered over the island, his hands gripping the edge to support his weight. "What about the monsters?" he asked in a shaking voice.

Nickie met his frightened eyes and flashed the most confident smile she had as she skirted the counter. "I'm a Grimes, kiddo. The monsters are scared of *me*. Besides, they're gone."

"Really?" He looked at her skeptically for a moment before coming out from behind the counter with a cleaver in his left hand. "I'm Toby."

Nickie looked Toby over for injuries. "You hurt?"

He held his right arm, showing her the useless elbow joint. "I can walk."

Nickie wrinkled her nose. "Yeah, no. I need you to climb and crawl. Let me think about it for a minute." She looked around to see what she could use to haul him up into the duct, then pushed a table over before undoing her belt. "Let me lift you up," she instructed. "Here."

Toby allowed Nickie to help him onto the table, then she joined him and fastened her belt under his armpits.

"Hold that there with your good arm. I'm gonna jump and then pull you up after me."

Nickie hauled herself into the duct, then turned around and leaned out to grab the belt. "You good?"

"Um, I think so," Toby told her nervously.

"Just watch your arm," Nickie reminded him. She braced her feet and pulled the boy up into the duct.

She looked at Toby's slightly clammy face with concern. "You sure you're okay?"

"I'm fine," Toby assured her. "One time, I crashed a roamer and broke my femur in two places. This is nothing compared to that."

Nickie snickered, taking her belt back for the moment. "If you say so. Follow me. We're going to crawl along this duct to where my sidekick is waiting."

"You've got a sidekick?" Toby asked.

"No, she hasn't," Grim called from up ahead, his voice echoing in the duct. "She has a long-suffering friend who indulges her far too much."

Toby grinned. "Where can I get one of those?" he asked Nickie.

Nickie snickered at Grim's exasperated sigh. "You can have mine for a while if you like. I warn you, he loves to complain."

She went slowly to account for Toby's injury, monitoring his progress in her HUD cam. "We're almost at the access now, Toby. You're doing great."

Toby paused his slow shuffle to catch his breath. "How close? I don't know how much farther I can go."

Nickie unhooked her belt from around her body and left it for Toby. "Ten feet. Wait here and get the belt back on. I need to get out at the access to turn around, but I'll be right back for you."

Toby nodded, and Nickie scrambled for the access.

Grim only just avoided being Nickie's landing mat. "Seriously? You couldn't yell or something?"

Nickie was already back in the duct. "How you doing, kiddo?" she asked Toby. "Ready to get out of here?"

Toby pointed to the belt, which was still on the floor of the duct. "Are those grenades?"

Nickie nodded, unclipping the grenades from the belt and dropping them into the pouch with her drones. "Yeah, but it's keyed to my genetic code, so don't sweat it."

Toby eyed the pouch as Nickie clipped it to her armor. "Okay, so how do I get down?"

Nickie checked that the belt was secure under his arms and moved carefully backward until her HUD cam showed her the edge of the vent. "I go on the other side, then you move very slowly to the edge, and I lower you into Grim's arms."

She braced her hands and feet against the sides of the duct and crab-walked along the wall, right over the open vent.

Toby shuffled to the edge of the vent and looked down at Grim. "You're going to catch me, right?"

Grim held out his arms. "I've got you."

Nickie dug into the vent with her armored boots and grasped the belt as Toby gingerly put his legs over the edge. "You ready?"

Toby gulped and nodded. "Uh-huh."

Nickie grinned. "Brave kid. Grim, you ready?"

"Lower him," Grim called.

Nickie took Toby's weight and lowered him slowly until she felt Grim take over. "You got him?"

"Affirmative," Grim replied.

Nickie let go of the belt and waited for Grim to clear the space below before unhooking her feet from the duct wall and completing her exit the only way gravity would allow.

Already half out of the vent, she went with the inevitable fall. She had positioned herself to land in a forward roll and came to her feet in one fluid motion.

Grim had Toby cradled in his arms. "What are we going to do about the elevator shaft?"

Nickie took her belt back from Toby and fastened it around her waist again. "We'll work it out when we get there."

There may not be time, Sayomi interrupted. *I am detecting activity aboard the Ooken ship we destroyed. It would be foolish to discount the possibility of survivors making their way back here.*

Nickie replied over the comm to avoid scaring Toby again. *You think we're going to get company?*

I would count on it, Sayomi responded.

Nickie turned to Grim. "We need to find Toby a suit so he can get to the Pod."

"There's a locker room with EVA suits by the airlock," Toby volunteered.

Nickie nodded. "Then let's move. We have a hell of a climb to get there."

CHAPTER 19 NICKIE

Station Wreckage, Elevators

The company of three ground to a halt at the open elevator door.

Grim put Toby down gently with his back to the wall so the boy could rest. "What are you thinking we do about getting him up there?" he asked Nickie.

Nickie walked toward the nearest door along the corridor. "I'm going to find something better than my utility belt to strap him to my back with, then I'm going to climb the damn ladder."

What about the Ooken? Grim asked over the comm. *Do we have time to get back to the Pod before they work out we're here?*

I fucking hope so, Nickie replied, clearing the room before she entered. *We've got a kid to protect, which outweighs wanting a fight any day.* She saw what she wanted right away.

Grim ducked his head around the door when she snapped the body of the chair away from its legs. "Oh, I see. You need something to secure it with. I'll start looking."

Nickie smiled and moved past Grim to go sideways through the door, holding the chair body out to the side and got back to searching.

"What are you looking for?" Toby asked when Nickie put the chair down by the elevator.

"Something to tie the chair to my back," Nickie answered.

Grim called out from another room. "I've got something. He returned to the corridor draped in a curtain, the pole still attached to the end trailing behind him. "Will this do?"

"Perfect." Nickie took the curtain and discarded the pole. She tore the fabric into strips a few inches wide and passed them to Grim. "Give me a hand."

Grim lashed the thin plastic chair body to Nickie's back with the first four strips of fabric, then lifted Toby into the chair and harnessed him in with three more. "How does it feel?" he asked them both.

Nickie checked her balance, and that her climbing muscles weren't hampered by the hasty rig. "Yeah, I'm good. How about you, kid?"

Toby shifted a little, testing the viability of his perch. "I'm not going to fall out," he concluded. "I think we're good."

Grim clambered down into the depression at the bottom of the shaft. "I'll be right behind you, Toby. I'll catch you if you fall."

"Nobody is going to fall," Nickie told them. "Just keep still while I'm climbing, okay?" She smiled at Toby's rapid agreement and reached for the maintenance ladder, hyper-aware of every shift the rig made as she stepped onto the rung. "Now for the real test. Are you down there, Grim?"

"Ready and waiting," Grim confirmed. "But it's not necessary since I know my knots are sound."

Nickie rolled her eyes at his attempt to sound reassuring and started to climb.

Toby bounced around some, but his weight wasn't enough to pull Nickie off-balance. There was no reason for the boy's rising nervousness. "It's a good thing it's not Grim I'm hauling up here. Can you imagine how sore my ears would be?"

Toby chuckled despite himself. "He does complain a lot," he agreed.

"He's a very good friend," Nickie confided in a conspiratorial tone. "So I don't mind so much. But don't tell him I said that, or he might complain three times as much."

"I would never," Toby replied solemnly. "I swear."

Sayomi spoke again as they neared the top of the elevator shaft. *I have an update, and it's not good news.*

Is it the Ooken? Grim hazarded.

Better get it over with, Nickie told Sayomi, pulling herself up the final rungs to bring her and Toby level with the elevator doors. *How deep in the shit are we?*

Grim is correct, Sayomi confirmed. *An Ooken Pod just landed on the hull.*

Neck-deep, then. Nickie sidestepped onto the ledge and out of the elevator shaft. *Can't you just blast them?*

Not without killing you all, Sayomi told her regretfully. *I can only suggest you find somewhere to hide until the danger has passed.*

Nickie snorted. *I thought you were stone-cold. How many Ooken are in the Pod?*

Just one, Sayomi replied. *And it is not waiting for the airlock to admit it.*

Nickie focused her hearing and picked up the relentless beating on the outside of the wreck. *Shit. How long until we get some backup?*

We are actually closer to High Tortuga and the Federation than Devon, Sayomi informed her. *The wisest course of action would be to remain at a distance and cause the Ooken as much damage as you can without being caught by it. That should buy us time for help to arrive.*

Looks like it. Thanks, Sayomi. Nickie had already come to a conclusion along those lines.

She cut the link to Sayomi and turned back to Grim, gesturing to him to help her out of the rig. "Okay, folks, change of plan. Our exit is blocked, but there's help on the way. Toby, you're going to stay with Grim for a while. You two are going to go find a safe place to hide." She pulled at the knotted fabric to escape it. "Quickly, since we're short on time. The room at the end of the corridor has two exits. Go through there, and I'll come find you when I'm done."

"What's going on?" Toby asked, the tremor returning to his voice.

"Nothing to worry about," Grim assured him as he helped the boy down from the rig, taking extra care not to disturb his injured arm. "Nickie will handle it."

Nickie pulled the last piece of fabric from her body and drew her Jean Dukes Specials as Grim led Toby away. "Damn right, I will."

. . .

Station Wreckage, Airlock Corridor

Nickie waited halfway along the corridor, out of the Ooken's reach but within weapons range. Although, what *wasn't* in range when you were armed by her Grandma Jean?

She debated opening the airlock and cutting out the wait, her every fiber aching with impatience for the moment. However, she had grown beyond the need to act on her impulses.

Recalling the reckless brat who would have blown the door and be damned made her cringe.

The one who had broken her mother's heart without a thought for what she was doing. The one so unwilling to contain her impulses that she'd had the temerity to tell the Empress of the Etheric Empire to go fuck herself.

Bethany Anne had been right to exile her.

Nickie could look at herself now without looking away. If she was honest, that was the thing that mattered to her most. That she had found a path to honor despite the dark beginning she had created for herself. She was no longer that person, to chase a high because escaping from reality was simpler than facing the consequences of her choices.

What had she had to complain about back then? Sure, she had been lonely, but she could have done more to participate in her own life. To take the olive branch she had slapped back in her mom's face time and time again.

She could have funneled her anger into training with her grandfather, another lifeline she'd tried to reject. Thank fuck John had been tougher than her mom. If she ever saw him again, she was going to beg his forgiveness for being so stubborn all those years and pretending to hate every minute he put into shaping her when she grudgingly loved the challenges he threw her way.

Nickie tested the magnetic soles on her armor's boots again, still not understanding how her Grandma had come up with a way for them to move with her body with the zero-gee locks on.

The airlock shook from repeated impacts. It was going to give; that wasn't in question. At that moment, Nickie felt the peace of acceptance settle over her. She realized the failure she had been was an essential part of who she had become. Here she was, standing between a child and his horrific death.

If it meant she had to suffer that death instead, so be it.

The fight wouldn't be completely one-sided. She had a shit-ton of advantages, the first and foremost being her sharp mind. It was worth a little boredom to know the Ooken was tiring itself, and it had to be picking up injuries from using its body as a battering ram.

Let it take its sweet time breaking in. It just gave Grim more time to hide somewhere safe with Toby.

You're quiet, Mere.

You don't need me, Meredith replied. *Look at yourself, Meredith Nicole Grimes.*

What? Nickie joked. *Standing in the middle of a massacre waiting to die punching?*

If that happens, you'll die for the right reason, Meredith praised her.

I was just thinking along the same lines, Nickie admitted. *If I make it out of here, I'm going to visit my mom. My only regret in this situation is that I haven't apologized to her in person yet.*

You will get a chance, Meredith assured her. *You're going to fight smart, just like your grandfather taught you to.*

Nickie smirked, feeling the comforting weight on her utility belt as she shifted her hips to a more comfortable stance. *Aw, you think I'm going to follow the rules. I said I was reformed, Meredith. Not lobotomized.*

Meredith snickered. *It's a good thing. A fair fight isn't going to get you on the transport out of here.*

Nickie heard a crack as the airlock began to give. *Are you sure I'm not going to get sucked out into space?*

Definitely, Meredith assured her. *You won't be exposed for more than a couple of seconds. The emergency seal will activate as soon as the Ooken breaches the inner airlock and triggers the system. The gap will be filled with expanding permacrete foam almost immediately.*

Nickie nodded, feeling a little better about the hole the Ooken was beating into the only barrier between her and an icy end. She dipped her hand into the pouch on her belt that contained Tabitha's drones and released them. *Do your thing, Meredith.*

The drones hovered in place for a moment, then shot off down the corridor to circle above the airlock.

Nickie thumbed the button above the grips of her Jean Dukes Specials to switch the regular load for taser rounds. *If you say anything that contains the words "shockingly good welcome," I promise I'll take you to join CEREBRO myself,* she told Meredith.

Really? Meredith's tone was laced with snark. *And there I was, desperate to make a terrible joke.*

Here it comes, Nickie murmured, mostly to herself.

You've got this, Meredith replied.

Nickie braced herself, grabbing the guide rail as the airlock bulged inward under the pressure of the Ooken throwing itself against the door. The casement gave way, splitting with a grinding screech.

The Ooken pushed its tentacles in and pulled its body into the corridor. There was a rush as the atmosphere was sucked out through the hole it left in its wake.

Although Nickie's boots did their job and she remained stationary, she was tossed around until the vortex vanished just as suddenly as it had started when the emergency seals activated and the breaches were filled with the expanding permacrete foam.

Drones, Nickie ordered as she forced her knees to stop wobbling.

The drones zipped like pinballs around the Ooken, bouncing off its tough hide. Nickie lost one of the drone feeds when the Ooken flicked a tentacle and caught it in one of the hundreds of small mouths on the underside.

Nickie held her fire while the Ooken unfurled, looking for the weak spots where its rubbery flesh met its fur. *Draw them back,* Nickie told Meredith. She fired controlled bursts at the tentacles as they emerged, cutting off the Ooken's senses with shock after shock from her taser rounds.

The Ooken lurched toward Nickie by using four of its tentacles to hold its body off the floor, dislodging the thin layer of ice over its blue skin as all sixteen feet of it stretched up to brush the ceiling.

The damn thing towered over Nickie, the tentacles not supporting its body flailing for her with their tiny mouths salivating hungrily. She retreated slowly toward the elevators, firing into the gaps between the tentacles obscuring her mark.

She growled internally when yet another shot ricocheted off its skin. *Fuck my life, how do you kill these bastards?* She fired again, only this time Lady Luck must have breathed on her because the taser round found a new home in the Ooken's furry belly. *Score!*

The Ooken opened its beak and screeched as fifty thousand volts of electricity coursed through its body. It pitched forward, falling toward Nickie in a writhing mass of tentacles and teeth.

Nickie continued stepping slowly backward as the Ooken fought for control of its body.

It crawled toward her, snarling as it dragged itself along the corridor despite its inability to do more than throw itself an inch at a time in her direction.

It is one thing to read that these monsters are programmed to destroy even at the expense of their own lives, Meredith remarked.

Our Queen has a rather unique approach to dealing with that, Sayomi replied.

How about you two take your chit-chat somewhere I can't hear it? Nickie snarked. *I'm kind of in the middle of something here.* She fired a round each time the Ooken looked to be regaining enough control to get up from the floor, wondering how it was recovering so quickly from each shock. *How* does *Bethany Anne kill them?*

By the millions, Sayomi stated. *She finds it much more efficient that way.*

Nickie contemplated the single Ooken she had to contend with. *Shit.*

The Ooken was almost where Nickie wanted it. She laid off the taser rounds, switching back to regular kinetics, and stood her ground, giving it time to recover enough to move.

Her plan went sideways the second the Ooken regained control of its central nervous system and whipped her with its tail, grabbing her around her armor's collar with the prehensile end.

Nickie shot the tail off at the root, catching it as it fell harmlessly away from her neck. Her armor was scratched and dented but still good. "Nice try, asshole," she bitched, winding up to use the handy weapon she'd just made. "Let's see how you like a taste of your own tentacle, huh?"

The tentacle was slippery as fuck, but Nickie didn't give a shit. She beat the Ooken with its own tail, noting that the teeth on the underside caused damage to the rubbery blue flesh. *I'll be giving that bit of info to Grandma. Want to bet we get Ooken tooth rounds soon?*

Nickie whipped the Ooken's face with the tail, holstering her JD Special for the moment. She leapt for the Ooken's back and looped the tentacle around its neck like a halter.

The Ooken reared, shrieking with outrage as Nickie dug in her knees to pin the tentacles that protruded from its upper back and jerked hard with both hands.

Nickie had tried to ride a wild bistok once. It was nothing like riding an Ooken. She fought to steer it toward the open elevator shaft, taking blow after blow from the tentacles she had no control over.

Nickie, Meredith began.

Not now, Nickie growled.

Nickie held on as the Ooken bucked and fought, slipping in the blood pumping from its severed limb. She felt her armor give at the shoulder, then the pain of a plug of flesh being pulled from her body.

She tightened her grip on the tail until the Ooken was forced to concentrate on keeping its throat intact. It screeched, helpless to fight the barbs of its own teeth cutting into its throat.

Nickie jerked her ad-hoc reins and the Ooken staggered, one step at a time, closer and closer to the shaft. Her armor was almost shredded by this point. She ignored the pain, the bites, and the burning sensation they left behind and pulled hard on the tentacle, pushing off with her feet to propel the Ooken the final few inches into the elevator shaft.

The Ooken threw its tentacles out to the side, the friction as it slowed its plunge causing an earsplitting shriek to echo up the shaft. Nickie dropped to her knees at the edge of the shaft and pulled a small but deadly sphere from her belt.

She pushed the button to activate the grenade and dropped it into the elevator shaft before diving back and shuffling on her ass to get out of the way before the Etheric charge fried her as well as the Ooken.

A flash of light whited the corridors out for a second as the explosion went off, and a moment later, the shaft emitted a hot, rubbery belch.

Nickie's left shoulder tingled as her nanocytes patched her up. She crawled back to the elevator shaft and glanced down through the sight of her JD special.

She turned away from the gore-splattered shaft and

worked on getting to her feet. *Looks like Grandad John was wrong, Mere. Sometimes grenades are your friend.*

Meredith sniffed. *Then I hope you have a few more "friends," since Sayomi is busy taking care of another Ooken ship and there is a Pod landing outside the airlock.*

Nickie rolled her shoulder to work out the stiffness in her newly-healed muscles. *I'll deal. What's this stiff shoulder about?*

You were poisoned by the bites, Meredith explained. *And your armor has been breached in multiple places, so you need to be cautious.*

Nickie snorted with more confidence than she felt. *I haven't got the luxury of time to be cautious. The Ooken die just like everyone else. It just takes a bit more effort to make it happen.*

Station Wreckage, Airlock Corridor

Nickie held onto the guide rail to steady herself against the impending suction. Her heart was slow and strong, her breathing regular and deep.

There was a lull in the pounding and a drop in the corridor's air pressure, which signified that the Ooken had broken through the emergency seal on the exterior of the hull.

Nickie brought up her arm to shield her faceplate from a peppering of sharp permacrete flakes when the inner seal exploded outward in a spray of dust. The Ooken forced its way through the resulting gap.

Nickie's jaw dropped as another Ooken followed it. *Double fuck.* Her imperative was taking out the first Ooken before the second squeezed its freaky self through the hole. She dipped a hand to her belt in the knowledge that her only way out of this was going to fucking *hurt*.

Nickie activated the grenade and launched it at the space between the two Ooken, then dashed around the corner and pressed herself against the wall with her Jean Dukes Specials held ready in case of a fuck-up.

The resulting explosion granted Nickie's wish in the same way a waterfall would quench your thirst.

She thanked her Grandma Jean for the protection of her armor as the nearest Ooken was thrown into the elevator corridor. It bounced off the wall and landed in a messy heap on the floor.

Nickie's legs shook from the impact, although most of the force was absorbed by her armor. She took three steps to give herself a dual view of the unconscious Ooken and the airlock corridor, turning both her JD Specials on the unconscious Ooken when she saw that the entire airlock corridor was filled with solid permacrete.

Unless the second Ooken could breathe that shit, it wasn't coming after her any time soon.

The Ooken on the floor stirred, then flowed to loom over Nickie in that half-suspended position she was beginning to hate.

Nickie sprayed the Ooken with the remainder of her basic kinetic rounds, driving it backward. The half-moment she paused to think saved her from the attack that came.

It lashed at her with tentacle and claw, emitting a shriek that burst Nickie's eardrums.

Nickie ignored the pain, choosing to focus on the upside to temporary deafness. "Fucked yourself there," she yelled, blocking the tentacles as they came at her. "Now I can't hear you bitching. Win for *meeeee*."

The writhing nightmare didn't seem to understand her. It whipped two of its thinner tentacles at Nickie, trying to pull the same distraction technique the Ooken she'd wasted earlier had almost succeeded with.

Nickie ducked and whirled, stepped and fired.

A tentacle fell to the floor, but another managed to snake around her ankle and jerk her leg. Her boot locked to the floor, and Nickie raised the other to stamp on the tentacle around her ankle. "Grabby assholes," she bitched. "Doesn't matter where I go, there's always some fuckwit who wants to get his slimy hands on my body."

She shook the tentacle free and dived at the Ooken, past caring about anything except making sure it breathed its last—and soon—so she could get Grim and Toby out of here.

Nickie, NO! Meredith yelled in her ear.

Too late.

Nickie plowed into the Ooken, driving them both backward.

The Ooken resisted, using all of its tentacles to manipulate the space around them as they fell. Nickie found herself disoriented by the writhing tangle she was caught up in. She dropped her weapons, instinct driving her to tear her way free as the Ooken cocooned her in its deadly embrace.

Nickie's efforts to reverse the situation as they hit the floor only gave the Ooken more opportunity to tighten its tentacles around her. She growled, twisting and turning, doing anything she could to prevent the Ooken from getting a grip and crushing the life out of her. *Meredith!*

Just hold on, Meredith begged. *Help is almost here. Fight it, Nickie.* She cut the warnings shrieking throughout Nickie's armor, pointless since every plate of it was crumpled and cracked.

Nickie's mind went blank as her world was reduced to the life or death battle to draw breath. She bit, and kicked, and squirmed, to no effect. The harder she fought, the tighter the Ooken squeezed.

Nickie's vision swam, and every nerve of her body screamed in pain as the Ooken's tentacles bit into her with a hundred thousand tiny teeth.

Meredith. Where was Meredith? She didn't want to be alone at the end.

Her blurred vision was overlaid with dark spots as the smaller tentacle around her neck cut her air supply off completely.

Nickie had no regrets. Everything she had been through, every lesson she had learned along the way…

None of it mattered.

Her crew was safe.

That *mattered*.

The lack of oxygen was causing Nickie to hallucinate. She thought she smelled the combination of old leather, sandalwood, and gun oil as the final breaths left her body. That wasn't possible, though, since she was here alone.

The tentacles suddenly relaxed.

Her lungs dragged in burning gulps of air as the constriction was replaced by that familiar scent again.

Just as quickly it was gone, and her brain was too fragged for anything except keeping her broken body ticking over.

She heard a voice in her head, fearful and full of grief.

Breathe in.

Breathe out.

Fight, Nickie. Live.

Nickie. Was that her name? If she had a name, and someone to call it, then she had something to fight for.

She obeyed the voice, holding on to it while she fluttered in and out of consciousness, battling against being sucked into oblivion.

A shadow passed over her, unnoticed, and she was picked up. She let it happen, too weak to struggle even if she knew how to make herself move to defend herself.

The scent returned, calming her with its feeling of home.

Nickie's mind relaxed.

"Let's get you out of here," a deep voice murmured against her hair as she succumbed to the darkness.

When Nickie woke up, she found herself in a featureless landscape. She turned a half-circle, looking around for anything that would give her a clue as to where she was. Nothing but mist for as far as she could see. "Anyone here?"

Nothing.

She glanced at her hands, realizing she could sort of see through them if she moved a certain way.

Fuck it. I'm dead?

Grandma Jean would be so disappointed if she knew that the afterlife was pitchfork-free.

Funny sort of afterlife, huh? she remarked to Meredith.

She waited for Meredith's reply, her heart falling when none came. *Oh, yeah. Dead. No EI.*

"Turn around, Nickie," Bethany Anne instructed.

Nickie spun around and found Bethany Anne lounging in an armchair that seemed to be made from the mist.

"Where are we?" Nickie asked, narrowing her eyes. "Are you God? Bethany Anne would be thrilled to know you borrowed her image." *Not.*

Bethany Anne waved a hand and another chair appeared facing hers. "You're not dead, Nickie. This is the Etheric. Take a seat. You and I are long overdue a discussion."

Nickie hesitated before trusting the misty construction with her weight. "Can I start?"

Bethany Anne tapped her fingers on the chair arm. "As long as you don't intend to open your mouth and say something that gets you exiled for another seven years. That shit could become tiresome."

Nickie snorted, wishing she had a footrest. She lifted her feet in surprise when Bethany Anne flicked a finger and the mist beneath her feet rose up and coalesced into a solid cube. "Neat trick. I want to apologize. I owe you and everyone else for the way I acted. I can't take it back, but I *can* do better, and I have been for a long time now."

Bethany Anne smiled. "I know. Which is why we're having a pleasant conversation instead of the ass-whupping you got the last time we met. You get what you earn, Nickie."

Nickie sat back and put her feet up. "I get that now. Grim and the kid are okay, right?"

Bethany Anne nodded. "They are. John and Eric picked

them up just after they found you."

Nickie frowned as a snatch of memory whisked past before she could grasp it. "Fuck. Grandad was the one who rescued me? Am I gonna be okay? My body is in a Pod-doc, yeah?"

Bethany Anne made a see-saw motion with her hand. "You were pretty chewed up." She grinned at Nickie's scowl. "You deserved that. What were you thinking? You *died*, Nickie."

Nickie's eyes widened. "For real?"

Bethany Anne nodded. "Just as John got you to his ship. He's been sitting by your side, giving you blood."

Nickie blinked back tears. "Shit."

"Shit indeed," Bethany Anne agreed. "I have to admit, I had a very different vision of how this would play out when I sent you out there all those years ago."

"What did you expect?" Nickie asked.

Bethany Anne scrutinized her for a moment. "I don't know. Definitely not that you would die for someone else. You always had so much potential, and I guess I got sick of watching you fritter it away." She slid her eyes away for a moment, then pinned Nickie with her gaze. "What do you think you've gained from your experiences?"

Nickie considered the question carefully. "Can I be honest? I didn't learn anything you and the rest of the family hadn't already taught me." She paused. "Maybe...I learned to listen after a few years of bitching about how you all rejected me. I had to let people in and trust them to not hurt me." She wrinkled her nose. "That all sounded like touchy-feely bistok shit before."

Bethany Anne lifted a shoulder, her impassive face softening at Nickie's confession. "We all have to deal with the touchy-feely bistok shit every now and then. How does it sound to you now?"

Nickie dropped her head, shaking it slowly as the ridiculousness of her childish attitude fully hit home. "It was beyond stupid to tell myself I was okay on my own, or that I didn't have a responsibility to people in a worse position than me." She straightened in her chair, adjusting her feet. "But it happened, and I can't change what I was in the past. What I *can* do is work every minute of the rest of my life to make up for the damage I caused."

Bethany Anne's black eyes pierced Nickie's soul. She got to her feet and held out her hands, smiling at Nickie. "You already have."

Nickie stood, completely confused. "I don't get it."

Bethany Anne walked the two steps to Nickie and enveloped her in a warm embrace. "You came home to us."

Bethany Anne disappeared as the mist dissolved around Nickie.

"Here we go again," she grumbled as her vision faded to black.

Nickie forced her eyelids apart, the gargantuan effort almost enough to make her go back to sleep.

A blurry face peered through the viewing window, then the Pod-doc lid clicked open.

Nickie drifted off again as she was scooped up in strong arms her body remembered as the most secure location in existence.

. . .

Devon, First City, The Hexagon, Penthouse Apartment

John paced the living area, his unusual action the only testament to the depth of his emotions as he waited for Nickie to wake up.

Tabitha came out of the hallway leading to the bedrooms. "She's still asleep. Meredith says she's fine, just weak."

John frowned, pausing by the window to stare out at nothing. "She'd be less weak if she woke up and ate the steak Grim brought her."

Tabitha pressed her lips together, patting John's back as she passed. "I'm not arguing. Emergency enhancement is a shot in the dark. She's lucky you were there to be the donor."

"Yeah. Can you imagine if it had been you, and I got your ass as well as your nanos?"

John and Tabitha whirled.

Nickie let go of the wall and staggered toward them. "Don't look so shocked. It looks like you didn't know I was here."

John was by her side in an instant. "What are you doing out of bed?" he demanded softly, wrapping his arm around her for support.

"Over here," Tabitha ordered, pulling out two huge pillows and an overstuffed duvet from the ottoman between the couch and the coffee table.

Nickie slung an arm around John's waist and allowed him to guide her to the makeshift bed. "It's good to see you both."

ELL LEIGH CLARKE & MICHAEL ANDERLE

Tabitha tucked her in while John hovered nearby. "We'll talk later, *chica*. Sleep." She leaned over and kissed Nickie's forehead. "Heal. I'll be home in the morning, and I expect you to still be sleeping when I get back." She raised an eyebrow at John. "Don't keep her awake, you hear?"

John held up a hand. "No intention of it. Bitches' honor."

Tabitha jerked her chin at him, waving a finger in a circle as she turned to leave. "I have eyes all over this place, so I'll know if you lied."

John sat on the edge of the ottoman after Tabitha swept out of the apartment. "We're all going to be a hell of a lot happier once Tabitha has the uh, 'diplomatics' in hand."

Nickie snickered, settling back into the pillows with her eyes closed. "She still working on the thing with the royal aliens, or whatever?"

John nodded, a sliver of a smile cracking his serious exterior. "Yeah." He chuckled dryly. "More than seven years, and the first thing we do is avoid having a real conversation. Your Grandma is right, we're too alike. I just decided."

"Shit, don't tell her. You'll never hear the end of it." Nickie peeked out of one eye when he didn't laugh at her joke. "I'm so sorry, Grandad. For everything."

John nodded, his chest tight with relief. "I know, sweetheart. It's in the past now, where it belongs. I wanted to tell you how much it means to have you home. You pulled yourself out of the shit you got yourself into without any of us around to wipe your ass, like a true fucking Grimes. I couldn't be prouder, Nickie."

"You know, that might be the most words you have ever

said to me in one go," Nickie teased through her tears, unable to resist. She sat up to wipe her face. "Thank you for still being here," she managed through the lump in her throat. "I couldn't have survived half the disasters I ended up getting into without your training."

"Or my ship," John told her, smirking. "You made quite an impression on Sayomi."

Nickie glared at him. "I *knew* that AI wasn't nearly psycho enough. What did you do to her, put a child lock on her destructive tendencies?"

John shook his head. "Nope. She just took a shine to you. Truth be told, I'm a little annoyed. She does nothing but give me shit the whole time I'm aboard. Thank fuck I don't have to carry her around in my head, right?"

Nickie's eyes widened. "Meredith." She scrambled to her feet, searching her mind for her EI's presence.

I'm here, Meredith assured her.

The crew was Nickie's next thought.

The crew is fine. They're here on Devon. Sleep. You need to rest your brain.

The flash of panic faded. *Okay. I'm too tired to argue with you.* Nickie yawned, lying back down as exhaustion washed over her again.

John got to his feet to tuck her back in, then pressed a hand to her hair, rubbing her forehead with his thumb. "I guess there are uses for an onboard EI. Sleep. There will be plenty of time to talk when you're rested."

Nickie looked up at John, her eyes closing despite her effort to keep them open a moment longer. "Will you stay with me until Tabitha gets back?"

John dropped to the floor beside her and sat with his

back against the couch. "I'll be right here for as long as you need me."

The next day

Nickie woke to a small, curious face just inches from hers. She smiled at the messy-haired boy who had her aunt's eyes as she slowly sat up to stretch. "Hey, you must be Todd. I'm Nickie."

The boy tilted his head. "How do you know my name? You look like Aunt Lillian, but not so grumpy." He narrowed his eyes at her and took a step back. "Are you going to kiss me?"

Nickie looked at him in confusion. "Um, no?"

"This is your Aunt Nickie, Trouble." Tabitha chuckled and scooped her son out of Nickie's space. "Your mom doesn't think anything of trying to smother my boy's adorable face in lipstick every time she sees him," she explained. "How did you sleep?"

Nickie blinked as her brain clicked into place. "Yeah, good. Are you going to let me get off this couch today?"

Tabitha rolled her eyes, releasing a squirming Todd to play. "That depends. Are you gonna collapse and ruin my good rug?"

Nickie smirked, throwing off the duvet. "You have no idea how much I've missed you."

"About as much as I've missed having my partner in crime around? I almost missed you *forever*, Nickie." Tabitha wiped her eyes and held out her hands to pull Nickie to her feet. She didn't hesitate to throw her arms around her niece. "All the time I spent worrying about you dying somewhere we couldn't get to you, and you decide to make a statement right on our doorstep."

Nickie sank into Tabitha's hug. "You know how I love to make a statement."

The only sounds in the apartment for the next few minutes were Todd's pew-pew noises. He ignored the adults hugging in the middle of the room and continued to run around with his toy spaceship.

Tabitha released Nickie eventually. She headed to the kitchen, waving a hand over her shoulder at Nickie. "I hate to be the one to tell you, but Grim got it into his head he had to throw you a 'congratulations for not dying horribly' party. I can make him cancel if you don't want to go."

Nickie followed Tabitha into the kitchen and leaned on the counter as her aunt chatted about what everyone had been doing while she was out cold. She didn't recognize many of the names, but a couple sounded familiar.

It shook Nickie to realize how normal it felt to be there in the thick of her family again. How much she'd missed just…belonging. She might belong out there on the edge, but she had regained the right to call her family her anchor.

Tabitha snapped her fingers in front of Nickie's face, disrupting her wandering thoughts. "The party. Should I tell Grim to cancel?"

Nickie shook her head. "Um, no. He'll only get butt-hurt and throw an even bigger one as payback."

Nickie smiled as Tabitha nodded and continued giving her a rundown of the city's gossip as she turned away to open a cupboard.

She was home.

EPILOGUE

Devon, The Hexagon, Private Hangar, Aboard the *Penitent Granddaughter*

Nickie picked up her purse and took one last glance in the mirror before going to answer the insistent buzzing at her door. "All right, all right. I'm coming already!"

Adelaide's mouth fell open when Nickie opened the door, her impatience forgotten. "Wow. Nickie, you look...amazing!"

Nickie smirked, brushing her fingers over the red velvet dress she'd spent far too much on after her last argument with Barnabas. "You like?"

Adelaide gazed longingly at the detail on Nickie's sandals. "Honey, everyone is going to like. I wish I could wear heels like those without tearing my feet to shreds."

Nickie snorted, closing the door behind her. "You look perfect, Addie. Besides, I wouldn't wear them either if I couldn't heal the damage instantly." She threaded her arm through Adelaide's and ushered her along the corridor to the elevator. "The only downside is, I'm so out of practice we're gonna have to keep moving, or I'm going ass over tits."

Adelaide giggled. "We'd better make sure that doesn't happen."

They met Keen and Grim by the exit ramp, both of them dressed to the nines.

Nickie smiled fondly at Keen, looking handsome in his pressed dress uniform. "Looking good there, Marine."

Keen sucked in his stomach another inch and grinned back. "Got to look my best. It's not every day we get invited to party with the royal family.

Nickie narrowed her eyes. "Don't tell me you're a closet royalist?"

Keen tapped the side of his nose. "Wouldn't you like to know?" He offered his arm to Adelaide. "Shall we?"

Adelaide curtseyed and took Keen's arm. "Don't mind if I do. Meet you down there," she told Nickie.

"We'll be along as soon as Durq and Missy are ready," Nickie replied, wondering where the Skaine contingent of her crew was. "You should head down with them, Grim. This might take a while if Durq is feeling anxious."

"Good luck with him," Grim told her. He waved as he hurried out the hatch before Adelaide and Keen left without him.

Nickie opened the ship's comm system. "Durq, Missy, we're going to be late."

They appeared at the head of the corridor a few moments later, panting slightly.

"Sorry," Durq gasped. "I couldn't work out the human neck restraint." He pointed to his loose tie when Nickie frowned in confusion. "I cannot see the reason for this garment."

"I thought they were used to lead human males around," Missy admitted with some embarrassment. "Like a leash?"

Nickie snorted, bending at the knee to fix Durq's tie. "That's...no. They're just an accessory."

Missy tilted her head. "Well, you learn something new all the time."

They left the ship and made their way through the Hexagon to the outdoor arena.

"This place is fancy," Missy remarked as they passed through the atrium. "How come you know where we're going?"

Nickie indicated the signage posted on the walls. "You can access all that through your neural chip. The building's EI, Winstanley, is giving me directions while we walk." She paused in her explanation when she felt a presence at her back.

She drove her elbow back into a hard stomach, then turned to drop the person sneaking up on her.

Rickie groaned as the air was driven from his body. "Dammit, Nickie! Can't you just say hi like a normal person?"

Nickie glared at him with her hands on her hips. "Serves you right, Rickie. What were you thinking, sneaking up on me like that?"

Durq stepped carefully around them, leading Missy by the hand. "We'll see you inside."

Nickie nodded, distracted by Rickie's unexpected appearance. "Sure. Tell everyone I'll be in in a minute." She turned back to Rickie, lost for words for once. "You, um, look good."

Rickie folded his arms, distracting her further with the play of muscle in his forearms. He said nothing for a moment, just looked at her oddly. "Hey, Nickie. I didn't think you were ever gonna make it to Devon."

Nickie suddenly felt acutely aware of everyone around them, making their way in through the huge steel doors. "Yeah, it only took almost dying to get me here." She indicated the arena with a nod. "You want to go and find something to drink?"

Rickie smiled. "You're not gonna get an argument from me."

Nickie tilted her head to look up at him, noting the fine lines etched around the corners of his eyes. "Tough day?"

"Tough life," Rickie shot back, looking around for a bar. "But who has it easy? No one I know."

Nickie shrugged. "Can't disagree. I see the bar."

Rickie held up two fingers to the bartender and received two disposable cups of something his nose told him had enough alcohol to be acceptable. He handed one to Nickie, still trying to process the difference in her. "You grew up," he mumbled.

Nickie narrowed her eyes at him. "I don't get where you're going with that, but sure. I've been an adult for a while now."

Rickie's face reddened. "Yeah, I've been thinking about that since we bumped into each other."

Nickie scrutinized Rickie's face for any clue as to what he was talking about. "Nope, you lost me. What are you thinking about?"

Rickie shook his head, waving her off. "It's nothing."

Nickie's heart skipped a beat at the possibility that Rickie might be seeing her as a woman for the first time ever. "Are you trying to ask me out?"

"Um…" Rickie met Nickie's eyes and grinned at the interest he saw there. "Shit, I think I am. What do you say? Wanna give an old dog a chance?"

Nickie considered persuading Rickie that this moment was the perfect time for his "chance." However, this party was being held partly in her honor, so skipping out wasn't an option. "I'm in no rush to leave Devon."

Rickie nodded. "We could— Oh, I see your mom."

Nickie glanced over her shoulder to see Lillian waiting patiently for her to finish her conversation with Rickie. She placed a hand on Rickie's chest. "We'll talk tomorrow."

"Wouldn't miss it." Rickie squeezed her hand and turned to leave.

Nickie watched him go, then turned to face her mother.

Lillian held out her arms, and Nickie found herself breaking into a half-run to throw herself into them. Everything that had passed between them previously was insignificant compared to her desire to be held. "I'm sorry," she choked out through the lump in her throat. "I'm so glad to see you, Mom. I was such an asshole."

Lillian released Nickie and wiped the tears from her eyes. "You're home now," she murmured, pulling Nickie in for another hug. "That's all that matters."

They broke apart when Tabitha arrived with Peter and Todd.

"How's my favorite little man?" Lillian cooed to Todd.

Todd squirmed to get free of Peter's hand and dashed off.

"What did I say?" Lillian asked.

Nickie snickered. "You're the kissy aunt," she teased. "The kid's right to escape." She spotted Adelaide and Keen looking a little out of place around one of the seating areas. "Excuse me? My crew doesn't look happy. I should take care of them."

She left Lillian and Tabitha to continue chatting and made her way over to the seating area, snagging Durq and Missy as she went, as well as a bucket of beers.

Grim came over to join them, bringing a huge tray he'd loaded with a little bit of everything from the buffet.

Nickie sipped her beer, listening to Grim and Keen bitch good-naturedly about what did and did not constitute barbeque with her mind mostly elsewhere.

Home had been wherever she made it ever since her exile, but nowhere had she felt the depth of belonging she did here. Even the furry aliens dotted among the crowd seemed to sense it.

The music went up in volume, and Nickie suddenly felt like she had to move. She put her drink down and grabbed Durq's hands, pulling him to his feet despite his protests.

Durq turned a peculiar shade of green when she began to spin them both in time to the music. "What are you doing?" he pleaded.

Nickie threw her head back and laughed. "We're dancing, Durq."

AUTHOR NOTES - ELL LEIGH CLARKE

JUNE 4, 2019

Thank yous

Lots of people go into making a series such as this. I'd like to say a massive thank you to the team of folks who make this series possible.

JITers

Massive, uber thanks also go out to our JIT team headed up by Steve for all their hard work. They ensure that the words reach you well-proofed, read and re-read, with all inconsistencies corrected. Thank you so much for all the care and attention you put into the process.

We couldn't do this without you.

Reviewers

Mega thanks also goes out to our Amazon reviewers. It's because of you that we get to do this full time. Without your five-star reviews and thoughtful words on Amazon we simply wouldn't have enough folks reading these space shenanigans to be able to write full time.

You are the reason these stories exist and you have no idea how frikkin' grateful I am to you.

Truly, thank you.

Readers and FB page supporters

I'd like to also thank *YOU* for reading. Your enthusiasm and support are what keep us working hard to bring the next episode to you.

Thank you for being here, for the banter, for reading, and reviewing. You rock, and without you, there really would be no reason to write these stories.

Thank You to Our Growing Patreon Family

Last and by no means least I'd like to say a huge thank you to our growing Patreon family.

Allan MacBain, Andrew Volz, Anne Henderson, Brian Roberts, Cynthia MacLeod, Darrell Heckler, David Pollard, Don Gannon, James Burrett, Jolie Brackett, Judith Wiseman, Kelvin Saggers, Kendra Gilmore, Lester Nye, Maps Cat, Mary Morris, Nat Thongchai, Paula Fletcher, Russell Peake, Sandra Chapman, and Suellen Wiseman.

You may also occasionally notice that a "human" name is used for characters here and there. That is because this is one of the ways we honor our Patreon members – we name characters after them!

Unfortunately, sometimes these characters die... but that doesn't seem to bother some folks ;) They tell me it's still a thrill to see their name in print.

I'll look forward to hanging out with you over there – either through the Author Shenanigan videos, or on one of our live streams.

If you'd like to get a character named after you, and to continue the back stage shenanigans, feel free to join us over at:

www.Patreon.com/ellleighclarke.

What's Next?

Wrapping up Deuces Wild – Nicky found her way back to the fold. I'm sure she'll have many more adventures, but book 5 marks the close of this tumultuous part of her life, and the series. I'm so grateful that you join us for the ride.

So what is next? I hear you cry…

<Michael Edit: MORE NICKIE! <not really, just wanted to see Ellie's eyes bug out.>

<<Ellie Edit: Ha! You're hilarious!>>

Bentley

Well, as of writing the Bentley series, aka "The Sword Mage Chronicles" is live. If you haven't checked it out, just search for Ell Leigh Clarke or the Sword-Mage Chronicles and you'll find it. There are currently seven books in the series and an eighth book plotted.

Jayne

As for MA and I, we continue to spawn more concepts and characters for your reading pleasure….

Our most recent one to hit the 'Zon was *Spy for Hire*, (internally known as the Jayne series.)

Jayne Austin is a spy, kicked out of the spy academy - just ahead of graduation - for political reasons. Sure, she's a loose cannon, with a healthy disrespect for authority, but this would be the kind of highly trained agent you'd want to keep close.

If you knew what was good for you.

Well, anyway, the dean of the school has other ideas of what is good for him (and his career), and Jayne is left to fend for herself, or head home to mom. Of course, heading home is admitting defeat, so instead she decides to use her training to make a living… err, I mean, for the forces of good.

Within hours she's got herself into some major-league trouble, found some friends to help mitigate said trouble, and so begins the swashbuckling adventure you'd expect from a story with a cover of a girl with a gun, explosions in the background and a series title, "Spy for Hire".

All that is great, but my favorite part about this series is the Hannibal-Clarice mentoring relationship that develops… minus the eating of humans, mind you. Now, this is three books in one, so you'll have a few adventures before you get to my favorite bits…

<Michael Edit: A real Hannibal the cannibal type character would be a new one for us.>

<<Ellie Edit: yeah and perhaps a little off genre!>>

And we've got Jayne 02 (which in normal book lengths would have actually been Jayne 04) coming in the next few weeks. If you're not already up to date, I'd get cracking on this one asap, so that when Jayne 04 hits you're all caught up.

Maths, Maths, Maths

Back in November I picked up a copy of Chris Isham's *Lectures on Group Theory and Vector Spaces*. These are essentially his lecture notes from Imperial back when he taught the course of the same title. I may have mentioned to you before about how in awe I was of this professor. I only ever had him for a substitute lecture once when one of our regular course lecturers was away, and Professor Isham filled in.

But this dude... He blew my frikkin' mind when he talked about how maths are just windows onto the world. It took me the next twenty years to really understand what that meant, and as I'm studying group theory applied to physical systems now, it's making more and more sense.

That's one of the things I envy most about smart people – their ability to cut through the details and nuances and see what is really going on, with a sophistication but simplicity that eludes everyone else.

<Michael Edit: This ^^^ is Exactly how I explain Ellie to others. "I give her three to four large paragraphs of information and she gives me back 1...maybe 2 sentences distilled down. Freaking smart.>

My whole life I've been acutely aware of how little clarity I have, and when I do achieve moments of clarity, it's like a Tetris block clicking into place, which then disappears into my own personal schema of the world, never to be truly recognized again. These moments leave me longing for another moment of clarity in amongst the wash of near-constant confusion, very much like Teresa d-Avila talks about how a moment of enlightenments leaves you longing for more for the rest of your life.

I guess this is what drove me to seek out his book. Technically my degree would have covered everything in that text, but somehow I managed to struggle through the entire process of exams and thesis without truly getting it all.

I actually recall quite vividly a moment when I was chatting with one of my Quantum Information professors standing on the walkway outside the common room, and I said something DUMB about classical mechanics. Instead of correcting me, he just said I'd probably need another degree to get it all.

I don't think he was being rude... I think he was right.

Anyway, since knuckling down with Isham's book all those months ago, I've slowly been getting a grip on the nomenclature, the abstract ideas, and gradually making progress in the subject. My strategy was to nail down the basics and really get to grips with it, so that everything else that I studied later would make more sense, kinda like learning the alphabet and a few basic verb conjugations in order to learn a new language.

I feel like I need to get a proper grip on the Quantum Field Theories and explore the other string theories that I didn't use in my thesis so that I can see the bigger picture. Already, I'm starting to glimpse how the abstract group theory, Lie algebras, and the like, fit in with Hilbert spaces and how it is going to help me understand much better where the undergraduate quantum mechanics was going. I wish I'd had more time to read, think and digest what we were meant to be learning at university – but I guess that's what free-time is for when you're a grown up, and no longer have exams to pass!

Anyway, my plan is to master the group theory applications, refresh QFT (QCD and QED) and then move onto the gravitational theories later this year. I also want to dip back into Quantum Information, because not only is it super relevant to technology like quantum computing and cryptography, but it's also lends itself to a more abstract and encompassing view of the world. Like the professor mentioned above says: *Everything is Information*. (And he meant physically too – on an atomic level. #Mind-blowing. I'll update you on that another time later in the year when I've got more of a handle on the implications!).

A few weeks ago I was just finishing a call with MA and I mentioned that I was going to take a nap and then do some maths.

He thought it was hilarious. So much so, he felt we should put it into a character.

And so we designed a news series…

<Mike edit: C'mon! Who goes to take a nap THEN plans on doing maths? You are a walking 'Big Bang Theory' character … Except *in real life*.>

<<Ellie edit: ermm… thanks? (I'm hoping he doesn't mean Sheldon!)>>

He made the main character, into a vampire. A vampire that runs a detective agency but in her spare time does "maths and science and shit", as he puts it. "Like the English aristocracy used to."

We've also got an Archer-like character, playboy turned responsible apprentice type, who is going to help run the agency during the daylight hours. It's turning into an absolute blast.

The series is still in its early stages, but stay tuned to the email lists and we'll let you know when it is released onto the 'Zon.

Speaking of, here's the link if you're not already hooked up:

www.ellleighclarke.com

My Book Report

For those who have been following my Author Notes in the Bentley series, you may recall that I'm planning to read fifty books this year.

So far I'm around number 25 and we're just heading into June, so I'm *just* ahead of schedule. I'm planning on counting a bunch of the textbooks I've been reading too, once I've completed them... but they're a much longer read for obvious reasons.

Why am I doing this? Well, if you recall, my friend Claire reads 100 books a year, and told me that Bush (as in Junior, yep, you read that right) used to read 100 books every year, even when he was in office. I realized I really have no excuse – plus it's really helping me fill in all the data points I'm missing to understand a ton of stuff I want to be versed in. It's helping me get my learning mojo back too. The problem is, the more I learn, the more I want to learn.

The secondary problem is forgetting. The more I learn, the more I forget, and I'm guessing I'm retaining less than 10% of what I take in over time... despite the memory and speed reading course I've been plugging through.

I'm having to resign myself to the idea that at least it's helping me fill in the blanks and build up a landscape of what I want to understand, even if I don't have all the details at my fingertips.

Incidentally, I'm noticing that my brain is recovering as I crawl back from the adrenal fatigue. Yay! I'm able to concentrate for longer and longer periods each day, as if the fog lifts for a few hours before descending again. The only frustration with this is that I have extended periods of time at the end of the working day when I am SERIOUSLY motived to learn and understand things, and get stuff done, but my cortex kinda gives out and can't keep up and the fog descends again. I find myself forgetting thoughts on a moment to moment basis.

Sometimes I worry I'm getting old.

Or worse... becoming my mother. ;-D

<Mike edit: Oh, I'm using this against you in our future conversations...Just Saying.>

But I think if I put my anxieties of mortality aside, it's likely just a hangover from the adrenal fatigue and eventually I'll be back at full capacity, a little older, and much, much wiser.

And on that note, for those who push themselves and stay in high stress situations, let this be the cautionary tale. This is now nearly two years later and I'm still recovering.

Slack Shenanigans

It's been a while since we last updated you with the ongoing banter and shenanigans that go on when we're not writing Author Notes or recording episodes of our Author Shenanigans videocast.

It probably doesn't come as surprise to you that incidents that you witness are going on behind the scenes All. The. Time!

Here's a sample of the most recent ones. All I did was search the hashtag #AuthorNotes in my slack channel with MA.

<Mike Edit: Thank God you can't see the video comments...>

March sometime...

michael [10:25 PM]

Ok, got to run, but here is something I'm excited about - no comments from ... well, no comments, let me have my 12 hours of jubilation before we critique it ;-)

ellleighclarke [10:26 PM]

oh you're posting smthg?

>> Ellie edit: Nothing was happening... then I realized he was uploading something and that was what was causing the delay. <<

michael [10:26 PM]

(Upload appears – it's an image of some busty girl, touting a weapon, smiling seductively at the camera. It appears to be a new book cover. I'm very confused, trying to figure out which project this is for.)

ellleighclarke [10:26 PM]

and I've not to give you my (honest) opinion

till tmw?

michael [10:26 PM]

right

;-)

ellleighclarke [10:26 PM]

is this tabitha?

michael [10:26 PM]

No, Katie - New Character for Torn Asunder - My pet name project

<Mike edit: NOTE: This was over a year ago... We have been a little tardy on these.>

<<Ellie edit: was not...>>

(seems to be the cover for Katie – the demon possessed heroine of his new series... that I wasn't involved in, hence my confusion.)

Tweaked 3d

ellleighclarke [10:26 PM]

ohh

she had biiiiig boobs!

michael [10:27 PM]

Sex sells...I'm willing to figure out how well.

ellleighclarke [10:27 PM]

yeah, she looks hot.

(well, what else am I suppose to say??)

michael [10:27 PM]

Actually, "Are those big boobs, or do you have a demon inside of you?"

ellleighclarke [10:27 PM]

does she have a demon inside her?

(this is fast becoming pornographic, I'm thinking to myself, not quite knowing how to respond appropriately!)

michael [10:27 PM]

'Oh...Demon... Uhhhhh, I'm gay

yes

ellleighclarke [10:28 PM]

I hear they can mess with your figure...

huh? gay?

who's gay?

katie?

michael [10:28 PM]

No... character example

<Mike edit: In my defense, I hear characters talking in my head all of the time. The Protected by the Damned series is complete (24 books) and I wanted to be able to say something not exactly PC and blame it on the demon... inside the character ;-) >

ellleighclarke [10:28 PM]

you've got a gay protagonist?

(see what I have to deal with? When I say I only understand about 80% of what he writes me, I'm not exaggerating!)

michael [10:28 PM]

Joke missed.

(And somehow it's my fault!)

ellleighclarke [10:28 PM]

oh

michael [10:28 PM]

;-)

ellleighclarke [10:28 PM]

you're trying to do this over slack. in words.

I only understand about 85% of what you write to me.

michael [10:28 PM]

jumping out, yeah-

(this means he's leaving... to go eat or something... so he won't be responding to my messages...)

ellleighclarke [10:29 PM]

of what you write. lol

michael [10:29 PM]

I tried!

So...(#authornotes)

;-)

ellleighclarke [10:29 PM]

ok cool. ttyl

michael [10:29 PM]

laterz

(Laterz?! FYI this is a 50 Shades word, so no matter what he says about not reading romance, I think he's let a clue slip!)

ellleighclarke [10:29 PM]

zzzz

michael [10:29 PM]

ROFL

++

A few weeks later(z)...

michael [1:26 PM]

I hope you are feeling better!

NOTE: Please remind me if I forget - we need to do the author notes for the next book tomorrow as well.

(he's talking about recording them on audio...)

ellleighclarke [1:53 PM]

Ok. I'm out sick at the moment. Haven't managed to get out of bed and told poker guys I'm not playing tonight. See... It's serious if I'm missing poker!

michael [2:24 PM]

That is true! As they say, drink lots of clear fluids (no, not gin or tequila) and rest rest rest!

ellleighclarke [2:31 PM]

Hahahaha. I've found that tumeric and honey act as an antibiotic. I wonder if it's possible to OD on tumeric...

michael [2:39 PM]

Uhhhh... Trust you to find out :-)

#Authornotes

+++

AUTHOR NOTES - ELL LEIGH CLARKE

Then it was his turn to be sick...

michael [10:24 AM]

good morning, but best I can offer (headache) is :face_with_head_bandage:

ellleighclarke [10:32 AM]

oh no - how come?

michael [10:58 AM]

weather (I think) here in LA. I'm driving back this morning, so it should go away.

>Mike edit: I seem to remember it doing better leaving LA – but not sure.<

ellleighclarke [11:04 AM]

oh heck. That's a pain if you spend any time in LA. Normally that kind of thing is high pressure no?

anyway, happy driving. feel better

michael [11:04 AM]

Thanks and I agree, I think it is high pressure :-)

ellleighclarke [11:05 AM]

if i'm right, i don't think that happens in the desert ;-)

(I have no idea if this is accurate. I'm planning to study the geography of weather in my mum's Flight Briefing for Pilots books which I brought back from the UK a few months ago. My fascination for group theory in physics has kept me distracted though. But still, I think there is something to my point. It convinced MA at any rate!)

<<Ellie edit: Just had a note from Brittany, saying... Fun fact: High pressure is a characteristic of desert climates, and actually plays a key part in their formation. That saves me having to look it up and get lost in a swirl of research.>>

michael [11:06 AM]

Oh... good point.

ellleighclarke [9:37 PM]

#authornotes

michael [10:08 PM]

It helped.... thank you #authornotes - I wasn't in the desert.

ellleighclarke [10:44 PM]

But Vegas is...

(Plus, I'm pretty sure relatively speaking LA has a number of desert-like characteristics...)

Finally, we're getting close to publishing the Jayne series...

michael [7:40 PM]

Do we have titles for the Jayne books???

ellleighclarke [8:03 PM]

yeah, the ones she's (the designer) been putting on the covers ;-)

michael [8:43 PM]

damn!

>>Mike edit: Yeah, this was a facepalm sort of moment. <<

<<Ellie edit: anyone else noticed how he not only reversed the arrows on the previous interjected comment, but now he's doubling them? ;) No consistency... *This* is what I have to work with! >>

ellleighclarke [8:58 PM]

#authornotes

michael [9:06 PM]

...damn....

:confused:

Ok, I'm right up the 3000 word limit of what we can

use in the back matter. I hope MA doesn't have tons he's planning to say to you, else I'll be in the dog-house.

Looking forward to chatting over on Facebook and Patreon. Thank you again for reading... and I hope to see you in the next Author Notes on one of the other series!

Ellie x

THANK YOU for not only reading this story but these *Author Notes* as well.

(I think I've been good with always opening with "thank you." If not, I need to edit the other *Author Notes*!)

RANDOM (*sometimes*) THOUGHTS?

I'm presently driving (well, not me) to Dallas/Fort Worth to pack up the house I was living in when I wrote *Death Becomes Her* and set off what became The Kurtherian Gambit Universe.

Without that book, I would never have been introduced to some fantastic people, including my 'maths' partner Ell Leigh Clarke. Without her, I would not think to create a vampire who is a bit of an elitest.

<<Ellie edit: I'm not elitist! I have loads of stupid friends... Michael. >>

And yet, you absolutely would not want to get on her bad side.

Then, add into the mix *Moonlighting* (which I've never

seen but understand the concept of, I think), and we have a new series.

One where we grow up a young man with a new reality – one where the paranormal is real.

I'm looking forward to working this series with Ellie because who wouldn't want to read about a female vampire who might be just as dark as the rumors suggest and yet is willing to help out a prodigal son at the same time?

AROUND THE WORLD IN 80 DAYS

One of the interesting (at least to me) aspects of my life is the ability to work from anywhere and at any time. In the future, I hope to re-read my own *Author Notes* and remember my life as a diary entry.

Traveling near Armarillo, TX heading to Trophy Club, TX

We are up in the panhandle of Texas, where the HUGE windmills creating power tower up from the flat plains.

They are majestic, their arms turning lazily in the wind as their insides create electricity to run little plugs that power Kindles...or smartphones / iPads.

Anything that can power the Kindle software to read our books makes me happy.

Now, I'm back in Texas and I need some Tex-Mex.

CORN

So, the other day I'm talking with Ellie and I mention that I'll enjoy a little food when I get back to Texas.

She mentions she LOOOVVEES the Mexican food there in Austin now. (Remember, she is from England.)

She's all, "Oh! I love the corn in my…" <??? – I got stuck when she said corn inside something.>

I have to (because…Born Texan) remind her that she is probably talking about Tex-Mex, not Mexican food.

She didn't even argue with me.

I was shocked. She must really love the food not to argue with me that it was a Texas type Mexican food.

For the record (for those who have followed us from *The Ascension Myth*) she is also loving the pizza she eats.

I don't think she does pepperoni yet.

FAN PRICING

$0.99 Saturdays (new LMBPN stuff) and $0.99 Wednesday (both LMBPN books and friends of LMBPN books.) Get great stuff from us and others at tantalizing prices.

Go ahead. I bet you can't read just one.

Sign up here: http://lmbpn.com/email/.

HOW TO MARKET FOR BOOKS YOU LOVE

Review them so others have your thoughts, and tell friends and the dogs of your enemies (because who wants to talk to enemies?)… *Enough said ;-)*

Ad Aeternitatem,
Michael Anderle

with Michael Anderle

Darkest Before The Dawn (3)

Dawn Arrives (4)

Interplanetary Spy For Hire
with Michael Anderle

Expelled

Deuces Wild
with Michael Anderle

Beyond The Frontiers (1)

Rampage (2)

Labyrinth (3)

Birthright (4)

The Sword-Mage Chronicles

Awakening

Taken

Heist

Resistance

Legba

Storm

www.ingramcontent.com/pod-product-compliance
Lightning Source LLC
Chambersburg PA
CBHW020359110726
47899CB00006B/1780